Chalice and Master

"I was prepared for something like this; I thought I was prepared. But I believed that we would reconnect in the land—I would not have come otherwise—and that has not happened. I have begun to fear that perhaps I do not hear the land any more either."

"Do you?" she said. She did not think that this speaking out of turn was much worse than her last, although to ask a Master if he could feel his own land was beyond any conceivable breach of etiquette, of law; if she had thought of it, she would have expected lightning—the Fire of the sky—to strike her dead before she finished saying *you*. But she did not think of it. She thought of her land—their land—which so badly needed its Master, and what she heard in Willowlands' Master's voice was despair. She knew despair, and she would draw him away from it, if she could. . . .

FIREBIRD
WHERE FANTASY TAKES FLIGHT™

CHALICE

ROBIN McKINLEY

FIREBIRD
AN IMPRINT OF PENGUIN GROUP (USA) INC.

FIREBIRD
Published by the Penguin Group
Penguin Group USA Inc., 345 Hudson Street, New York, New York 10014, U.S.A.
Penguin Group (Canada), 90 Eglinton Avenue East, Suite 700, Toronto, Ontario, Canada M4P 2Y3
(a division of Pearson Penguin Canada Inc.)
Penguin Books Ltd, 80 Strand, London WC2R 0RL, England
Penguin Ireland, 25 St Stephen's Green, Dublin 2, Ireland (a division of Penguin Books Ltd)
Penguin Group (Australia), 250 Camberwell Road, Camberwell, Victoria 3124, Australia
(a division of Pearson Australia Group Pty Ltd)
Penguin Books India Pvt Ltd, 11 Community Centre, Panchsheel Park, New Delhi - 110 017, India
Penguin Group (NZ), 67 Apollo Drive, Rosedale, North Shore 0632, New Zealand
(a division of Pearson New Zealand Ltd.)
Penguin Books (South Africa) (Pty) Ltd, 24 Sturdee Avenue,
Rosebank, Johannesburg 2196, South Africa

Registered Offices: Penguin Books Ltd, 80 Strand, London WC2R 0RL, England

First published in the United States of America by G. P. Putnam's Sons,
a division of Penguin Young Readers Group, 2008
Published by Firebird, an imprint of Penguin Group (USA) Inc., 2010

1 3 5 7 9 10 8 6 4 2

THE LIBRARY OF CONGRESS HAS CATALOGED THE G. P. PUTNAM'S SONS EDITION AS FOLLOWS:
McKinley, Robin.
Chalice / Robin McKinley.
p. cm.
Summary: A beekeeper by trade, Mirasol's life changes completely when she is named the new Chalice,
the most important advisor to the new Master, a former priest of Fire.
ISBN 978-0-399-24676-0 (hc)
[1. Fantasy. 2. Bees—Fiction.] I. Title.
PZ7.M1988Ch 2008 [Fic]—dc22 2008000704

ISBN 978-0-14-241720-1

Printed in the United States of America

Designed by Katrina Damkoehler
Text set in Columbus MT.

To Molly, Gard, Chiron and Guenevere

CHALICE

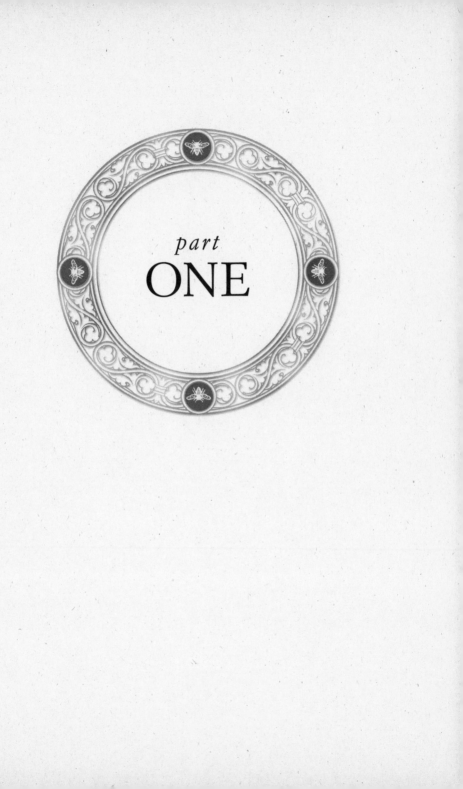

part
ONE

Because she was Chalice she stood at the front door with the Grand Seneschal, the Overlord's agent and the Prelate, all of whom were carefully ignoring her. But she was Chalice, and it was from her hand the Master would take the welcome cup.

From the front door of the House, at the top of the magnificent curling sweep of stair, she could see over the heads of the crowd. The rest of the Circle stood stiffly and formally at the foot of the stair with the first Houseman and the head gardener, but nearly the entire citizenry of the demesne seemed to have found an excuse to be somewhere in or near the House or lining the long drive from the gates today.

Their new Master was coming home: the Master thought lost or irrecoverable. The Master who, as younger brother of the previous Master, had been sent off to the priests of Fire, to get rid of him. Third and fourth brothers of Masters were often similarly disposed of, but the solitary brother of an unmarried Master without other Heir should not have been dealt with so summarily. So the Master had been told. But the two brothers hated each other, and the younger one was given to the priests of Fire. That had been seven years ago.

A little over six years later the Master died, still without other Heir. The Grand Seneschal had sent immediately to the priests of Fire to say that there was urgent need of the younger brother of the Master of Willowlands, for the Master had died without having produced a son. Such a request—a plea—had never been made before. Once someone has gone to the Elemental priests, they do not return.

But a demesne must have its Master. And a change of family, of bloodline, in any demesne, upsets all, often for generations, till the new family has settled into its charge. The nearest other living relative of the old Master of Willowlands was a fourth cousin who had already married someone unsuitable and had three children by her. The priests of Fire said they would see what they could do, but they promised nothing. The younger brother of the old Master had just crossed into the third level, and by the third level Elemental priests can no longer live among ordinary humans.

But six weeks ago the Grand Seneschal had received another message from the priests of Fire: that the Master of Willowlands was coming home. It would not be an easy Mastership, and the priests were not sure it was even possible, but the Master himself felt the responsibility to his demesne, and he was determined to try.

Mirasol—straining her eyes toward the gate, partly as a way to ignore the three men who were ignoring her—remembered the younger brother: his strength of purpose, his feeling of obligation to the demesne, his feeling for the demesne. It was what the brothers had quarrelled about. The elder brother had loved the power of the Mastership, not its duties, and he was not the least willing to bear lectures on his behaviour from his younger brother. She wasn't surprised the younger brother was coming home, even from the third level of the priesthood of Fire.

She had dreamed of the message to the Grand Seneschal the night before it arrived: she had felt the fire and smelt the burning. She knew the Master would come. She knew too that the smell of burning was a warning, but she did not know of what. Might the demesne itself burn, or its new Master?

She could see only a little way down the drive as it curved toward the gates half a league distant. But she could see when people better placed than she for first sight of the arrival stiffened and stared. The three men standing with her drew themselves to attention.

She could hear carriage wheels now.

It will be all right, she told herself. It must be all right. She settled her shoulders with a tiny, invisible shake, and fractionally raised her chin.

Six horses drew the coach: four of them coal-black, clinker-black, two of them ashy grey. The coach itself was also black, but black was always fashionable among the great and grand and would draw no comment. But the curtains at these windows were drawn closed, and they too were black. A light flickered behind them, red and wavering, like firelight.

Again she smelt burning, but she did not know if she imagined it.

The welcoming of a new Master was a time of rejoicing. The ceremony of investiture was the official occasion, and after the rites were done there was an enormous banquet with musicians and dancing for everyone who belonged to the demesne—and for anyone else from any other demesne who wished to join in the festivities at the price of some enthusiastic contribution to toasts and cheers and acclamations. But the informal arrival of a Master should still be a happy moment. And she knew she was not the only person present who felt that the brothers had been born in the wrong order: it was the younger who would have made the better Master from the beginning.

But no one clapped or called. No one smiled. It was as if everyone was holding their breath.

The coach stopped in front of the House, where the gravel had been raked in a perfect circle, a symbol of good luck. Any coach wheels and any horses' hooves would have broken the circle, splintered the careful spiral; that it should be so broken was a part of the welcome, like opening and pouring out the contents of a bottle of wine. There was no reason for her to feel uneasy, watching the horses dance as they halted, kicking pebbles every way, to feel that something fragile and vital was being destroyed.

The body of the coach rocked on its wheels, and little spurts of gravel pattered out from under them.

Then the door opened.

Perhaps she imagined the cloud of darkness like smoke that billowed out; no one else reacted, and she bit down on her own gulp of astonishment. And of sudden fear. She remembered the younger brother. She had not known him—it was not for such a one as she had been to know the Master's family—but she had known a good deal of him. She had known more of him than of the Master, before the Master sent him away, because he was the one who rode or walked round the demesne, seeing that the fields and woods grew and throve, and the temples and places of power were serene and well tended. He was not tall and handsome and flashing-eyed like his older brother, but there was kindness and grace in him, and intelligence in his unremarkable brown eyes.

She knew little of the Elemental priests, nothing of their initiations, and only folk-tales of what the priesthoods did and were capable of. She knew that Fire frightened her worst, more than Earth or Air. And the Fire priests themselves had said that Willowlands' new Master could no longer live among ordinary humans.

As the coach door swung back, one of the House servants jumped forward as if suddenly recalling himself, and lowered the steps. Two figures climbed carefully down. They both wore black capes with hoods that hid their faces, but they carried themselves and moved and looked around as anyone might. As any ordinary human might.

There was a collective letting-out of breath. Talisman, the tallest of the minor Circle, seemed suddenly shorter; Sunbrightener, who was the fattest, seemed fatter.

That was until the third figure climbed down from the coach.

He too wore a black cape with a hood, but the cape bulged and seethed weirdly around him, and he let himself carefully down the steps as if he did not know or could not remember how to use his feet for such an activity. The two figures who had climbed down first reached their hands to help him, holding him at the elbows and under the arms, but she felt, looking on, that their hands did not grasp quite where elbows and armpits should be.

He half limped, half rolled up the steps toward the House's front door with his helpers still on his either side. She seemed to hear a distant roar, like a fire caught in a sudden updraft. She wanted to glance at the faces of the other people, the people who had come here this morning to catch a first glimpse of their new Master, wanted to see if they looked frightened or appalled. But she couldn't drag her own gaze away from the great roiling black loom of the third figure coming toward her.

She felt the three men standing beside her struggling not to step back and away as she stepped forward. She had been clutching the welcome cup against her body so tightly that her stomach ached where the extravagantly ornamented brim had bitten into her. The roughness of the intricate overlay on the cup's bowl gave her suddenly cold stiff fingers better purchase as she moved her hands to their proper places on its stem.

She was Chalice, and hers the first greeting.

The top step was a wide smooth half-moon of white stone before the door. There was plenty of space for her and him and his two aides, as well as the three men behind her, and the door-keepers back farther yet, flanking the doorposts. She raised her cup, grateful that the weight of it prevented her hands from shaking, and looked down. Three faces turned up toward her, two of them brown and ordinary and worried-looking.

The third face was black, as black as the coal-coloured horses that drew the black coach, and its—his—eyes were red, flickering like fire around the black pupils. She recognised nothing in that face from her memories of the younger brother of the dead Master. She looked at him steadily, willing herself to see something—anything—that she could welcome as Master, and in the final seconds it took him to climb the last step, she saw what she needed to see: comprehension. He knew her for Chalice and knew she was there to welcome him, because he came as Master.

When he stood with her on the top step he gave a little shudder, or ripple, and his two aides dropped their hands and stepped back. As they let go of him she saw that they wore gloves. Her mouth was dry, as dry as if she had been eating ash, and she was slow to say the two important words: "Welcome, Master."

She was slow, but he was slower. He should reach immediately to take the cup from her, hold it briefly over his head for everyone to see that he accepted it, taste its contents and hand it back to her. It was possible that he would thank her, but it was not necessary.

But he only stood, looking at her. The hood shadowed his shadow-dark face; she thought she was glad of it. He twitched, a tiny spasm, once, twice. Perhaps he was trying to raise his hands. The third time he succeeded, the sleeves of the cape juddering back as if blown by a wind, and she saw that he too wore gloves, long heavy ones, laced snugly to the elbows.

She could not give any Chalice cup to gloved hands. She looked back into his face—into the shadows where his face was. She did not know what to do. She thought she must have imagined the comprehension she had seen there a moment earlier; she could read no expression on that black face now.

Clumsily he raised his left hand and drew the fingers through the laces of the glove on his right. The cords fell away in uneven shards, as if charred. Slowly he peeled the glove away from his arm—and the heat of his flesh raged out at her. The air between them was almost too hot to breathe. Even more clumsily he raised his naked right hand, the fingertips glowing like embers, to touch the cup. She held her ground while the fingers of that fiery hand curled round the bowl of the cup inches from her face. The enamelled metal of the goblet grew uncomfortably warm against her skin and steam rose from the liquid within it.

The weight of the cup did not change and she supported it as he stood with his hand around it. He looked at it and back at her.

"What . . . do you give . . . me to drink?" His voice was as eerie as his appearance, but perfectly intelligible.

Her answer to this question had been in no record she had consulted about the rite of welcome; but then no one had ever welcomed a third-level Elemental priest as Master either. She had held her own against the preferences of the Prelate and the Grand Seneschal only because she was, in the end, Chalice, and they could not order her to give him the earthed wine customary for a welcome cup. But she had not expected to have to announce publicly her departure from tradition: only the Master himself would taste the contents of his welcome cup. She felt as if she were being wayward, unreasonable and oblivious all over again when she had to reply, "Water—plain water from the Ladywell—and a spoonful of honey, Master."

She was sure—she was almost sure—she did not imagine it that he smiled. And it was only after her answer that she felt him begin to draw the cup toward himself. Still he did not—or could not—bear its weight, and so she carried it for him. Together they made only a faint gesture of holding it above his head, for the audience to see; and then she tipped it gently against his mouth, and saw him drink; and also saw a tiny rivulet run down by the side of his mouth and hiss off his chin, briefly leaving a fire-red tracing thread behind it.

He let her draw the cup back toward her again with his hand still around it. She looked again into his face and saw, though she could not have explained how she saw, that he was tired, tired almost to death; and so she knew that it was only weariness that made him clumsier still, that when he lifted his hand away from the cup, he was not able to do it cleanly, and his hand dropped a little, and glanced—only barely, fleetingly glanced—off the back of her hand, where it seared the thin flesh to the bone.

At the time it almost didn't matter. She found that she had been half expecting something like it to happen, and did not flinch when it did. She lowered the goblet only a little bit hastily, and tucked the weight of it against her body again so that she could drop her wounded hand to her side and let the long sleeve of her robe cover the burn. This made it throb worse than if she could have held it up, but that couldn't be helped. No one farther away than the three men behind her awaiting their turn—and possibly the Master's two aides—would have seen anything, and she wished to keep it that way.

But the three men waiting just behind her would have seen. The Grand Seneschal might have kept his mouth shut for his own good—it was he who had negotiated with the priests of Fire in the first place, and he who had received the news that the priests did not believe what he was asking could be done. She didn't know the Prelate well enough to guess after his motives, beyond a growing suspicion he had few of his own and preferred to borrow them from some stronger character. But the Overlord's agent would have every reason to tell the tale—and doubtless had. While it would upset the balance of the entire country if one of the demesnes were realloted, the process of the reallotment would hugely increase this Overlord's power, and bind the new Master to the Overlord with a political gratitude it would take generations of Masters and Overlords to bring into equilibrium again. And their current Overlord was a little too fond of political power— she among others believed—without such temptations as a Master who might burn his subjects by the touch of his hand.

By the end of the first day of the new Master's return, the people she met were looking first at her right hand. Gossip travels as fast as fire. By then she had dressed and bandaged it, so there was nothing to see but the bandage; but that was enough. And there was no way to shrug off what had happened as an accident. Of course it had been an accident: no Master could remain Master who deliberately harmed any of his people. What had happened to her should be viewed as no worse or more significant than if one of his coach horses had shied and trodden on one of the onlookers: an unfortunate mishap. That's all. But of course it was not, for it was not an accident that should have been able to happen. If the new Master were not a priest of Fire. If the new Master were still human.

"It is nothing," she said to the people she caught looking at her hand. "It is nothing." Sometimes she tried to smile. She'd smiled at Sama, when she'd asked for lint and salve; Sama was a House-woman with a round, happy face and three children, and she and her children were excellent customers for Mirasol's honey. "I was clumsy. It is no more than if I brushed my hand against a dish just out of the oven."

"It don't look like nothing," said Sama, whose round face was not happy today. "And oven burns hurt."

"Of course they hurt," Mirasol said briskly, trying to be competent with one hand and failing. "But we bear them because we are clumsy—and because we still like our food cooked."

Sama's face closed a little more, but she did reach out to help Mirasol with her bandage.

"It is not as though we had had a chance to practise our roles," Mirasol said, trying to make a joke, but she realised as soon as the words were out of her mouth they were a mistake. Usually a new Master was well known to the demesne; usually the Chalice's welcome cup to the Master entering his House as Master for the first time was a formality only.

Usually a new Master was human.

"But—" Sama began.

"He is our Master," said Mirasol firmly.

There was an uncomfortable pause while Sama finished tying up the bandage. When she was done she raised her eyes to Mirasol's and said, "As Chalice wills."

Mirasol almost blurted out, It's not what I *will!* It is what has happened!

A few months ago she would have spoken so, spoken before she thought, a few months ago when her Chalicehood was still so new that every reminder of it was like a burn. But she was Chalice now, and all things had changed, herself most of all. Before the Chalice had chosen her, Sama would have argued with her; would have held her own opinion against Mirasol's. She would not argue with her Chalice; it was her duty to accept the Chalice's ruling.

Mirasol hoped she was right.

She told herself it would have been worse if it had been an ordinary accident like a coach horse blundering into the audience, because that would so clearly have been a bad omen. The new Master *was* a priest of Fire, and adjustments had to be made. That's all. That's all. She could not help the bandage on her hand, but once she realised there was no point in trying to hide it, she used that hand freely, as if it did not hurt her. She had to hope that the fixed expression on her face that this usage provoked—because it did hurt a great deal—only looked like the Chalice's professional mask.

But if their new Master believed he could be Master, then she wanted him to have his chance. In the first place this was only her duty: the Master was the Master, but no Master could maintain his land without his Chalice. But in the second place she wanted this Master to grasp and hold because these first six months of her abrupt and lonely Chalicehood had been almost beyond her strength. She did not think she would be able to bear—to contain—the tumult if Willowlands were given a new, outblood Master; and she did not think this or any demesne could survive an outblood Master and a second disastrously new, inexperienced and untrained Chalice together.

It was bad enough as it was. Willowlands was restless, hurt and unhappy: half mad with it, she sometimes thought, delirious as a child with a bad fever. Whether this was a result of being Masterless for seven months or from the seven years preceding the previous Master's death it was impossible for her to say. But she knew it was also because she, the new Chalice, was herself rough and raw from having had no teaching. She thought of her Chalicehood in wild metaphors: like a blind woman asked to paint a portrait; like a scullery-maid dragged out of her kitchen, given a plough with no horse and told to raise six hectares of barley by sundown. And yet if she lost her fragile balance as a result of an outblood Master and the Chalice passed to someone else, there was no vanity in her bleak awareness that this would be a catastrophe.

She had learnt enough to begin piecing together ways to calm a little of the appalling strain and distress the deaths of the last Master and Chalice had caused. But she had learnt by precarious methods: feverishly reading the old books, following her nose through the footnotes and annotations, leaning hardest on the advice of the oftenest-cited manuscripts, when she could find them, when the House library or the old Chalice's rooms contained copies of them, guessing miserably from scraps and fragments when she could not find what she needed. The changeover from Master to Master and Chalice to Chalice should never happen—had never happened—as it had just happened here; most of the information and guidance she needed simply didn't exist.

And she had only barely begun. She still had far more questions than answers, far more unknowing than knowing, about everything to do with Chalice work. And yet she was all there was. The people rarely came to her with their individual problems and disturbances, but while this meant she was not yet well accepted as Chalice, which was in itself unsettling to the land and its people, she had as much and more than she could do merely responding to the most savage ruptures in the fabric of the demesne. And she felt as if she were using embroidery silks to mend plaster and lath. No, she thought, that's not it. It's more like putting out fires: like harvesttime after a dry summer. And they were in a drought that might destroy all.

Sometimes the demesne's disquiet manifested as literal tremors of the ground, when the trees shook as if in a high wind, plates flew off shelves, and fences didn't merely fall down but burst apart. Usually she could hear these in her mind if they were too far away for her feet to feel them. Sometimes the Grand Seneschal sent her a message. (She tried to tell herself this was an indication of some measure of approval, but she feared it was only that as Seneschal he knew what she, who was Second of the entire Circle, second to the Master himself, ought to be capable of. The Grand Seneschal was only Third: but she never remembered this when he was glaring at her, or when another of his brusquely worded messages arrived.) The rest of the Circle were little use. The violence of the deaths seven months ago had damaged and disrupted all their abilities as it had damaged and disrupted everything to do with the demesne; only the Grand Seneschal had pulled himself together again to take the full weight of his place in the demesne framework.

Once, only a few days before the homecoming of the new Master, a farmer, Faine, had come thundering up to her cottage on the back of one of his work-horses, still wearing its ordinary harness and looking as wretched and confused as its master. She'd heard the commotion and come outdoors—even her bees had scattered out of the way of these tumultuous visitors. She knew Faine; he was almost a neighbour. Possibly he had come to her because she was Chalice; much likelier he had come to her because of all the Circle she was nearest.

"Can you come *now*?" he said breathlessly.

She thought his eyes weren't focusing on her face: perhaps seeing the thing that he had left behind him. "There's a great cut opening in one of my fields," he said. "I've left my brothers getting the beasts away—it's big enough for one to fall in. And it's growing." He was speaking as if past her, as if looking at someone standing behind her. He was old enough, she thought, to remember the Chalice before the last one—she who had been Chalice to the father of the new Master and his brother. That Chalice had been much loved; Mirasol's father had consulted her once about a stand of trees that did not thrive as they should. "There was something wrong about the air around them," he'd said. "You could smell it as soon as you stood among 'em. I tried Oakstaff first, but he hadn't the time for the likes of me—but Chalice herself came." Mirasol knew of her own experience that these trees were now among the finest in what had been her father's woodright.

That Chalice would have known what to do. But that Chalice had never had to grapple with her demesne in the conditions Mirasol faced.

"A moment," she said, and flew back indoors. A tremor so ferocious it had ripped the mundane ground apart? She had no idea what she should do, but she had to try to do something. She snatched up the cup of balance, three of the Chalice stones that worked well with it, a handful of herbs, and thrust two pots of honey in the pockets of her cloak. She hesitated over her book of basic incantations; but basic incantations did not include crevasses opening in fields, and watching her fumble uselessly through a book would be good for neither Faine and his brothers nor herself. Her best hope was that the earthlines might tell her something she could use.

The journey to Faine's farm was so uncomfortable, holding on to the hip strap till her fingers were sore to keep herself from being jolted off by the big horse's bone-breaking trot, that she managed to avoid thinking about what she could do when they arrived. She didn't know what she could do. She might as well think about her sore fingers and bruised seatbones,

It was worse than she imagined and, she thought, glancing at Faine's face, worse than it had been when he had left to fetch help. A great ragged cleft had torn its way through the flat grassy pastureland; the red-brown gash looked eerily like a wound in flesh. Part of the awfulness of it was that the rest of the scene seemed so normal: the sun shone, the birds sang in the trees. The end near them was perhaps only two hands'-breadth across, but Mirasol could see it widened swiftly farther down the field. As she slid stiffly off the horse and her feet touched the ground, the ground shivered, like a horse's skin shedding flies; the tuft of grass at the end of the trench rocked wildly and then parted with a sound like tearing cloth, and the trench was suddenly a hand's-breadth longer. The birdsong faltered, and then took up again. Mirasol barely noticed; she was listening to the earthlines. Two passed through Faine's field, and they were weeping like children.

She looked around, and broke a small twig off an oak tree, thanking the tree for its help. She always preferred to find something she could use at the location itself, and she liked oak for Chalice work. She brushed her fingers over its leaves and murmured a few words of dedication. The now-familiar ritual was a little soothing—but what next?

Two men and a woman had seen them coming, and met them at the edge of the injured field, but the keening of the earthlines in Mirasol's ears was so loud it was almost impossible to hear human speech.

". . . the rest of them out," one man was saying.

". . . Daisy's calf ran in the wrong direction, and Daisy followed," said the other man. "They're . . ."

And then, as if the moaning of the earthlines was a curtain and they had parted it for her, Mirasol could hear the frightened bellowing of the trapped cow.

"Get a rope," Mirasol heard her own voice saying. "Two ropes.

You may have to drag them out. Your horse has a yokemate, I assume? Fetch him. How has this—rift—opened? Does it stretch from one end, or out from the middle?"

"The far end," quavered the woman. "It began there. Where Daisy is."

"Good," said Mirasol's voice again. "That makes it easier." It does? thought Mirasol. The earthlines whimpered. "Where is your spring?" Every farm in Willowlands had a spring; she hoped this one would be a strong one, and near at hand. "Bring me a flask of the water—freshly drawn—as quick as you can."

The woman turned and ran.

Mirasol walked to the edge of the field, took a deep breath, and climbed the fence. She was immediately deafened by the lament of the earthlines. It was not only the two in the field who spoke; the earthlines in the entire quadrant echoed their distress. She walked slowly along the length of the cleft; would she notice in time, she thought, if it decided to widen suddenly? She fished the cup of balance out of her pocket and rubbed her fingers over it; it was very difficult keeping her own balance between the strange space where the earthlines moved and spoke and the fact that if the crack opened under her feet in the mundane world, she'd fall into it. She tried to listen through the earthlines' misery for any sign or guide: What was the cut doing here? Why was it here in this field rather than in some other field? Why was it here at all?

Broken, wept the earthlines. *Broken, broken.*

Some of the groaning, she thought, was the ground itself, splitting, tearing itself from itself.

She was staring into the far end, where it was deepest—probably the height of two tall men, she guessed, easily enough to imprison a cow and her calf—when the woman came with a flask of icy spring water, and shortly after her one of Faine's brothers with a pair of horses.

Mirasol mixed her cup: water, the spring water this field would know, herbs for distress of mind and body and one for deep dangerous wounds that they will not fester; some of this year's spring honey, because spring was the season of joy for the future, and some honey tasting strongly of handflowers. Handflowers were lavender-pink, and inside they were striped red in such a way that they resembled the fingers and thumbs of two hands held cupped together. It was considered lucky to drink rainwater from the cups of handflowers—and anyone who regularly did then saw all things so clearly that they could not be deceived. I will not deceive you, said Mirasol silently to the earthlines. I don't know what I'm doing, but I'm here and I'm listening; and there is still joy in this world. She stirred the mixture with the oak twig. Last she dropped in the three small stones, which were for light in darkness, for compassion and for love.

"Someone will have to climb down there with them, you know, to put the ropes around them," she said.

The man nodded. "I know. I'll go." His face was pinched with worry and fear; he met her eyes, briefly, as if forgetting himself, and immediately looked away.

"Drink this first," Mirasol said, and offered him her cup. "Just a sip—you only need a sip." The Chalice stones clinked faintly against the side of the cup as he drank.

She turned away without waiting to see if her mixture had had any effect; she didn't have a second choice if it didn't. She knelt, and then lay down flat, just above where the unhappy cow bawled and thrashed. It was not a graceful procedure—what might the Chalice who had cured her father's trees have done about a trapped cow? Cows and sheep did get caught in natural cuts and hollows sometimes—but there was nothing natural about this one. She spilled several drops from her cup on the bits of cow that happened to be under them when they fell. At least once the sweet water landed on her nose—which was where she was aiming—and Mirasol saw the vast pink tongue reach up to lick it off. The calf, being smaller, and trying to hide under its mother, was harder, but she splashed it a few times.

And then she stood up, as if what she wanted and hoped would happen was going to happen.

The cow stopped bellowing.

"Go down now," she said. "Get ready. I'll start at the far end: that'll give you a few minutes." She didn't add, I have no idea how long the effect will last. I have no idea why it worked. If it worked. Maybe the cow just likes the taste of honey.

I have no idea if anything else will work.

She turned away, and began again the long walk—it felt twice as long this second time—to the far end of the grotesque crack in the ground. The high dreadful keening of the earthlines had diminished to a woebegone rumble; a rumble that seemed to be turning toward her—looking for her—looking for help, as Faine had done. She knew the usual conjurations to quiet an earth tremor—often a mere murmur of *silence and peace, quiet and calm*

22

was enough, like singing a lullaby to a fretful child—but these seemed hardly appropriate for an earthquake that had torn a hole in the landscape. But she found herself humming an old lullaby her mother had sung to her: *Sleep, my little love, sleep, my little one. Sleep is sweet and love is sweeter, but honey is sweetest of all.*

There were several ritual ways a Chalice could hold her cup; she chose the one—only practical on the slender, stemmed Chalice vessels—that allowed her to weave the fingers of her two hands together around it while her crossed thumbs held the other side: *connection, joining, linkage.* She tried several phrases from the incantation book she had left behind, but none of them suited her; none of them felt right, none of them settled to the work before her. She felt the earthlines listening—listening but waiting. Waiting to hear the thing that would reassure them, that would knit them together, that would call them home.

She reached the end of the crack and paused. It had, she noticed with some small relief, stopped growing. But when she turned and looked back along the length of it, it seemed leagues long; the two big work-horses as small as mice in the distance; the heavy ropes hanging off their harness and disappearing into the crack were barely visible threads.

"Please," she said clearly, aloud, as if she spoke to a person. "Please be as you were. I will try to help you." She hesitated, and pulled out the handflower honey and added a little more to the mixture in her cup. The water was faintly gold against the silver cup; the small stones in the bottom shone like gems. She did not want gold and silver and gems; she wanted ordinary things, commonplace things. Trees and birdsong and sunlight, and unfractured earth. "Let the earth knit together again, like—like darning a sock. Here are the threads to mend you with." And she threw a few drops from her cup into the trench. She saw them twinkle in the air as if they were tiny filaments; the pit was quite shallow here, and she could see tiny spots of darkness where they landed. Her fingers were sticky with honey. Absentmindedly she put one in her mouth; the taste of the herbs was clear and sharp, but the honey's complex sweetness seemed to carry mysteries.

There was a sudden sharp new tremor under her feet. Her heart leaped into her throat and she froze. The jolt loosened the dirt on the sides of the trench, and it pattered down. Quite a lot of it pattered down, till the trench was barely a trench at all, little more than a slight hollow.

"Here are the threads to mend you with," she said again, having no better spell or command to offer, and she tossed more drops from her cup into the wound in the earth.

The trench began to fill up.

She walked slowly back toward the deep end, murmuring to the earth and the earthlines, tossing sweet mysterious drops into the shadows of the ravine. The earth under her feet still shook, but the shaking now seemed more like that of something shaking itself back together again after a shock or an unbalancing blow: like the turning sock in the hands of the darner.

The crevasse was disappearing.

There was a shout ahead of her, and she saw the horses take the strain; and then they sank into their harness and began to pull. The ropes went taut—tauter; the horses began to move.

"And would you please let Daisy and her calf, and the man in there with them, climb out safely," said Mirasol, and flung more water and herbs and honey. The stones rattled; there was not much of her mixture left.

She saw the head of the cow emerge from the darkness; then her muddy body and finally her lashing tail. She staggered and stood, head low and feet braced. The horses halted, and someone moved to release her. The horses stepped forward again, but the second rope came easily, and a tiny, equally muddy version of Daisy popped out, like a terrier from a hole; and then someone— Faine—was lying by the crack, and reaching his arms into it, and there came the man who had gone into the trench to tie the ropes around Daisy and her calf, and he was the muddiest of all.

"Thank you," said Mirasol. "You can finish now, please," and she emptied the last dregs of her cup into the closing crack, catching the stones in her other hand. Perhaps she should not have run forward so quickly and eagerly; when the last of it closed, it closed with a tremor so violent that one of the horses stumbled and whinnied, and the man at their heads fell down.

But it closed. The field was a field again, with nothing to show for what had happened but a slender ragged ridge where the ravine had been, where the grass now grew at peculiar angles. Daisy turned abruptly, and began vigorously to lick her calf. Faine still had an arm around his muddy brother, and Mirasol realised he was laughing.

The words then came to Mirasol; perhaps she had read them somewhere, or perhaps the earthlines had whispered them to her after all. She said them softly, but Faine and his family turned and stood motionless, listening with the earthlines: *Lie thou there, thou earth. Stiller than starlight, stiller than silence, stiller than darkness, stiller than death.*

She thought of that day as she plucked at the fraying, grubby margins of the bandage on her hand. She changed the dressing every day, but wrapped it up again in the same cloth (which she had finally learnt to do one-handed). She should change it; a grimy bandage did not reflect well on the dignity of the Chalice. She sighed. A grimy bandage on the hand of a beekeeper would make no difference.

She wondered what Faine had said of the occasion. And she thought: nothing. He will have said nothing. It should not have happened; in a demesne not teetering on the edge of disintegration it would not have happened. It was less important to acknowledge that the Chalice had dragged them all back fractionally from that edge than it was to pretend that they were not that close to it in the first place. But this was, she thought sadly, extremely hard on the Chalice.

She recognised that she wanted this Master to succeed for reasons that were also to do with herself, Mirasol, within the Chalice, whose only apprenticeships had concerned bees and woodscraft. She wanted him to succeed because she knew how difficult accepting the Chalice had been for her—and how difficult it was for her now to put out fires and drag back from edges and be ignored. She wanted her Master's help—help because she was Chalice but also because she was Mirasol. Help to put their demesne back together so that the earthlines would never again cry, *Broken, broken.* Help to lead Willowlands home. But she recognised the exhaustion in the Master's strange eyes because she knew it in herself. And as the weeks passed after the new Master's arrival, she recognised something else in his eyes, though she had a harder time putting a name to it.

When she had been a woodskeeper, things like Chalice and Master—and Grand Seneschal, Prelate, and Overlord's agent—were impossibly beyond her. Even when everyone in the demesne knew that their former Master was out of control and his Chalice pulled in his cataclysmic wake, the ordinary folk, herself included, felt only anxiety and fear. There was no task or duty a beekeeper or woodskeeper could take on that would change the situation. The isolation of the Chalice was certainly on account of all the Chalice needed to know that no one else knew, all the tasks the Chalice needed to perform that no one else could perform; but she had never minded hard work, and her father's woodright and her mother's beehives had always been attentively kept because she would rather be doing something than not. It wasn't the work of the Chalice she minded. It was the vast unfathomable burden of its responsibility. She still felt the Chalice was incomprehensibly beyond her—even wished that it were incomprehensibly beyond her, so she could give up. In despair, perhaps, but because she had no choice. She felt that something of this same despair was in the Master's eyes now, and perhaps only she could read it there.

And perhaps it was her duty to report it to the Grand Seneschal, or the Overlord's agent. Because even above the Chalice's duty to the Master was the Chalice's duty to the demesne. But she would not report it, any more than she would report herself. She was not a good Chalice, but she was all they had. The Chalice had come to her, and it remained with her: and as Chalice, her judgement was for the new Master. She clung to this thought sometimes, when her mind blundered like a shying horse among all the shadowy, threatening-looking things she didn't understand, or like a bee caught indoors, bumping into walls and windows, looking blindly for a way out of this bewildering and inexplicable new landscape. Despair was a private weakness she could not afford to indulge.

But when she remembered that day at Faine's farm—or those many, many other days that she'd put out a fire or darned a sock or propped up a fallen fence—she didn't remember that she had succeeded. She remembered that she had had no idea what she was doing, and no idea why it worked. It did not feel to her, remembering, like an indication that she was learning her job, evidence that she was, after all, fit to be Chalice. It felt like something she had got away with, that she might not get away with again.

But there was something more that troubled her, something that troubled her most of all about the accident on the day of the Master's return—the accident that everyone believed was a sinister portent to begin the new Master's reign. She wondered if anyone but herself knew, or would remember, that it was a capital offence to injure a Chalice, even for a Master. She especially wondered if the Overlord's agent knew of this old law. In the early, barbaric days of the demesnes, at least one Master had been put to death for it.

She'd read about the execution in one of the oldest records available to her. Some of the Willowlands Chalice records were unique, she just didn't know which ones; and this one was obviously a copy, although there was no telling if any other copies still existed. Perhaps no one else knew that the law had ever been enforced. Most of the cruellest laws were no longer put into practise, but there were unpleasant traces of those old ways still. And the presumption remained that a law that had once been used, however rarely or long ago, was stronger than even a recent law which had never been anything but words in someone's mouth or written on a page. Much worse was the lingering belief that a law with blood on it was somehow *live*. Forever.

She was reasonably sure that no one could move against a Master for harming a Chalice unless the Chalice agreed to bear witness. But that would only place her in the trouble she wished to keep him out of, because perjury about a capital crime was also a capital offence, and the Overlord's agent had seen what happened.

There was so much she didn't know.

And then the wound refused to heal. This didn't surprise her; it was in a bad place, and she could not keep the hand still when she was in public, and so she forgot to keep it still when she was alone. It was also difficult to do even the most ordinary tasks with only one hand, especially when your mind was elsewhere—and, Mirasol thought grimly, my mind is always elsewhere.

Since the new Master had come, she had spent additional hours nearly every day at the House or one of the points of the Circle, holding a cup for this or that meeting or conference or rite. Since no one had ever tried to reclaim an Elemental priest for Master, there were no records of how that should be done either, and it was not surprising there were many discussions about it, and attempts to adapt the traditional bonds between Master and demesne, and repeated official visits to various important bloodright sites to reinforce, or recover, those bonds—to recover the demesne itself. Some of this was also the natural result of a new Master and his Circle learning to work together; some of it, Mirasol hoped, was that the other Circle members were taking up their tasks again. But she began to suspect that there were more of these meetings and visits, and her presence was more often required for the most minor of them, than would have been the case if her hand had not been burnt offering the cup of welcome in the first moments of the Master's coming.

And she became increasingly aware that the Circle, as it was now constituted, was not learning to work together. And that Willowlands remained still far from whole.

Every day her mind swam and struggled while her face and body demonstrated serenity and control. She went home exhausted every night, with the Master's exhaustion haunting her. What a pair, she thought sadly. Poor Willowlands. Furthermore she had even less time to pursue her studies—and she urgently needed to continue her studies. She had grown accustomed to sleeping badly as a result of not being able to turn her thoughts off; now she slept worse on account of the pain in her hand. She lay awake in the dark, thinking about what she could be learning if she sat up and lit a candle, and too bone-weary to fumble for her tinder-box.

But since the Master came, she thought, am I not putting out fewer fires?

Perhaps that is only because I am spending too much time bearing Chalice to a Circle who will not let me bind them together?

Is that my failure or theirs?

She should be asleep now. But you could pick at a dingy bandage in the dark and put off making even the tiny additional decision of lighting a candle.

Why had the previous Chalice taken no apprentice? Had her Master stolen even this from her? And had the rest of the Circle made no protest? Was there any protest they could have made, if he would not listen?

Eleven Circle members had apprentices (and the Master had his blood Heir). The Circle met to choose a new Circle member on the death of the previous one, but they were supposed to know which way the finding rods would fall before they cast them, because the rods had confirmed the choice of apprentice when it was made. There was a story that this Circle had had no idea if there were some other procedure involved in finding an unknown Chalice than a known one—and had cast the rods over and over, refusing to believe what the rods persisted in telling them—wanting to believe poor Clearseer, who had taken over from his master when the previous Clearseer had died with the Master and Chalice, was somehow undoing the unity of the Circle by his inexperience. She believed this story. It was one more item in the litany of confusion and chaos the previous Master had created.

Her own lack of apprentice was another. One of the first tasks of a new Circle member was to choose an apprentice: but a new Circle member should have spent years as an apprentice, and been ready to pick up both insignia and duties . . . including the training of an apprentice. And the demesne should be stable enough to disregard the small muddles a beginning apprentice had to make, to learn what she needed to. An apprentice relied on the Circle member who trained her to protect both her and the demesne from the things she did wrong, till she learnt better. Mirasol could not do this for herself, let alone for another, even more ignorant, even more inexperienced person; and Willowlands was not stable.

She had spent her first weeks trying to learn the very simplest of the rites that had been neglected in the weeks since the last Chalice died, complicated by the unbelieving daze of finding herself in the position to need to do so. She had had her own struggle to believe what the Circle had come to tell her. What had finally convinced her that the Circle hadn't somehow made a mistake was their own resistance—ranging from dismay to fury— to the idea that she was the chosen. That the terrifying things that had been happening to her in the wake of the old Chalice's death were something more specific than merely the general shambles that death had left. She had spent some time too in those first weeks trying to discover if perhaps the Circle had made a mistake after all—and coming reluctantly to the conclusion that they hadn't because they couldn't. That was the purpose of the rods. The rods could not lie nor be suborned. A conclusion she assumed the Grand Seneschal had equally (and equally reluctantly) come to or she would not have remained Chalice.

That, and writing to the priests of Fire, were the only subjects upon which she and the Grand Seneschal had ever agreed. The letter to the priests had happened before she had been found as Chalice. She had often wondered about the meeting for the finding of the new Master. The rods were absolutely reliable within their own demesne—one of the tales of their origin was that they were fragments of earthlines made material, created in the days when the demesnes were first shaped and magic was wilder and more brutal than it was now—but far less so when the answer they sought lay outside it. She knew that many, perhaps most, of the rest of the Circle were not happy with the Grand Seneschal's choice, and she wondered how he had carried his point. The rods at least must have supported him. Or perhaps the rest of the Circle was as afraid of him as she was.

Despite her weariness she usually woke before sunrise; lately it was her hand that woke her, for it was often worst when she wished to sleep. This morning there was a meeting in the East Hall during Dawnspan, which meant it had to end at a given time and could not drag on forever as last night's, with no defined term, had. Yesterday evening's sky had told her that the morning would be sunny, so there would be no excuse of not noticing when Dawnspan ended.

She picked up the cup of tranquillity—she'd been using that one a lot lately—and mixed the Ladywell water, young spring wine, grey clay, willow and cherry ash, six herbs, and two kinds of honey to go in it. It was almost the standard recipe for Connection, and one of the first an apprentice Chalice would have been taught, except for the honey, which was Mirasol's idea. She propped the book of common incantations up where she could glance at it while she dressed. She already knew the invocation for Connection by heart, but she felt painfully stuffed full, however erratically and inadequately, of new things, and preferred not to rely on her memory if she didn't have to. Although the open book was more a gesture than an opportunity for study, since it was still too dark to read. But it was comforting to have the book out too, like having a friend in the room with her. She didn't have many friends any more; her old ones were afraid of her, and the people around her as Chalice didn't want her among them.

Her way to the House from her cottage lay across the expanse of parkland where the great party for the investiture of the new Master had been held. The traditional place for the Master's investiture was a much larger piece of open parkland at the front of the House, instead of in the smaller stretch between the House and the beginning of the eastern woodland. Clearseer—who was the only member of the Circle willing to gossip with the Chalice—said that the rumour was that their new Master had said that his banquet could be held anywhere but where his brother's had been.

"The reasons given vary from his hatred for his brother to wanting to signify a new beginning to a realisation that since his people are afraid of him they probably won't turn out for

his party and a smaller space will make this less embarrassing."
Clearseer frowned, then shrugged.

"Which reason do you favour?" asked Mirasol. She wished she
felt more comfortable with the Clearseer. She had no reason to
mistrust his motives but, as the newest member of the minor Circle in a time of great strain and disorder, he was second only to
herself in unpopularity with the rest of the Circle. And as a minor
member, he could do worse than to curry favour with the second
most powerful member—however unpopular. On the other hand,
as Clearseer he should be trying to keep—or restore—honesty
and openness in the Circle. Good luck to him. Even a stronger
Circle than the one in place could be expected to be wary and
suspicious after the seven years they had had under the previous
Master.

"The new clean beginning, of course," said Clearseer promptly.
"But I'm afraid there may be something to the reason for choosing a smaller space."

Mirasol remembered the investiture feast for the previous Master. It had been wilder, the games and contests more reckless, and
the wine unwatered and over-liberal, than felt either appropriate
or safe. She had come with her parents, but they had not been
happy or comfortable, and neither had she been; she remembered
that many of the people she spoke to were wondering uneasily
if this was a foreshadowing of what was to come. She remembered—she had thought of this often in the last months—how
she had thought the Chalice looked regal but fragile, and several
of the other Circle members as if they weren't sure what their

duties or responses should be. The Prelate had been fawning and the Grand Seneschal had been grim—and she had been very glad that she need have nothing to do with any of them.

She remembered the Master's younger brother too. He seemed to stay as far away from his brother as he could, to take part in none of the games, and to drink no wine.

The new Master's party had gone off without incident but it had not been an enormous success either—or perhaps she was only too tired to notice after the investiture, which had required three different cups of her, a complex invocation, and far too much contact with both the Grand Seneschal and the Prelate. What she remembered the most was the way the Master had sat isolated, in the middle of what should have been his own people. The inaugural party was the one time, sometimes in their entire lives, when all denizens of his demesne could approach the Master directly and for no reason but to congratulate him and ask for his blessing, and usually there was a crowd of people doing just that. There had been for his brother's feast, although she had not been among them; he was kissing all the young women, and she hadn't wished to be kissed.

There had been few enough brave souls who had asked for this Master's blessing. She had stood by or near him some of the time—several times changing her mind whether her conspicuous presence would make things worse or better—and she knew a few of the people who did come: her woodright neighbours Selim and Kard, the herbswoman Catu and several farmers whose lands opened out south and west beyond the forest, although she didn't see Faine. She also saw from her eastern quadrant the sunny-natured shepherd Lody, who was a favourite with everyone who knew him; she was glad to see him so conspicuously casting his vote for the new Master. She recognised several Housefolk, including one or two of the House gardeners and Naz from the kitchens, who had been one of her best customers for honey for years and whose honey-glazed bread and biscuits, she had been told before she became Chalice, were locally famous.

The Master didn't try to touch any of his supplicants, which was unusual but not unprecedented. Instead he made the signs for joy and prosperity in the air between them. Mirasol noticed that he was wearing his gloves again. The gloves were daunting, but she thought of his ember-red fingertips and the blazing heat of his naked flesh and felt relieved. Once when she stood beside his chair she noticed that the gloves were no longer laced, but wrapped round and round and tied in place like bandages, as if, perhaps, he wished to do it himself, and had chosen an easier method to learn one-handed.

She guessed that when those present began to feel more certain that he would make no attempt to touch them with his dangerous hands, a few more of them began to come to him for his blessing. But he was undoubtedly an eerie figure. He sat on a tall chair carried out from the House for this purpose, and which looked almost as out of place sitting on the park grass as he did sitting on it among ordinary ambling humans: and Masters usually walk among their people on feast-days, rather than sitting broodingly still. The hem of his black cloak still moved to a breeze no one else felt. A single magnificent tree stood in this parkland, and the Master's chair had been set at the edge of its canopy and so, thought Marisol, with the tree as background, the Master looked majestic as well as eerie; but this did not make him seem any more approachable. He looked, she thought, like the model for one of the paintings in the long gallery at the back of the House, which were of scenes from the ancient days, when the demesnes were first being created. The Master might have been one of those early magicians: powerful, perhaps too powerful for the mundane world, and for good or evil no one could say for certain.

Enough musicians had come to make a good energetic noise, although there was little dancing, and Mirasol felt that too much of the music was mournful. The mountains of food on the tables had disappeared by the end of the evening; how much of it went home under coats and cloaks for the people who hadn't wanted or were too frightened to come, she didn't know. A lot of it had seemed to go rather suddenly and rather late, although that could be merely that it had taken a while for most people to relax and realise they were hungry. But at least when midnight came and the Circle piled up the remains of the food in the ceremonial salver—which was more of a small travelling hearth, and had to be effortfully carried by four Housemen—and the Chalice poured the dregs of her last cup over them and the Talisman broke one of her wafers over them and the Prelate gave thanks as the Grand Seneschal set fire to the little mound, there were only the correct few handsful left. And—despite the Master's presence—the bonfire burned sedately and, having burnt itself out, politely collapsed. There were barely even any sparks to stamp out, and the Housemen, noticeably wary as they took hold of the handshafts to carry the salver away again, visibly found them no hotter than they should be.

※　※　※

The inaugural ceremony was months ago now, and the parkland where it had been held showed no trace of it, although Mirasol always glanced at the old tree standing by itself where the Master's chair had been. This morning it was a silhouette from another world: no earthly tree's branches could reach so far, as if it were trying to protect the entire demesne. From what?

She was the first in the Hall for the morning's meeting, where the great windows were still twilight-grey. The early fog was beginning to burn off, but at the moment it still lay so thick upon the grass that from the House the trees on the far side of the drive were barely visible, and her shoes and cloak were wet from the walk from her cottage. She set the cup of tranquillity on the window-ledge, sat down beside it, unlatched one of the panes and welcomed the breeze into the big room to do what it could to dispel the heaviness of the air, heavy here as it was everywhere in the House. She had never been inside the House when the old Master had been alive, so she had nothing to compare with, but she hoped that one of the things having a Master again would do was make the air in his House light and free. After only the few moments needed to slip through a side door and make her way to the Hall she already felt the need of the reviving fresh air.

Just the fact of sitting down was a treat. When she was bearing Chalice, she had to stand. She could lean—she wondered if the traditional Chalice habit of lurking in doorways had anything to do with the fact that it was usually possible to lean against a door-frame—but she couldn't sit down. She had very nearly thought she wouldn't survive the sheer physical strain of all the standing; but about three months after the Circle had found her, she discovered the handful of pages stuffed into the back of one of the chronicles describing exercises to strengthen the back and legs for long hours of standing. For muscles accustomed to exercise their strength in movement—a woodskeeper's job was not physically easy—to bear motionlessness instead was a strange discipline.

But that was only one of the aspects of the life of the Chalice she had thought she might not survive.

She didn't know he could move silently. It wasn't till he was standing in front of the fireplace that she noticed him out of the corner of her eye, and then, as she turned, startled, to look at him, she couldn't remember whether he'd made any noise coming up the stairs to the front door on the first day or not. She was sure that his aides had made ordinary-footstep noises, as they had taken ordinary footsteps. What she remembered about him was his strange, awkward, rolling gait, but nothing about any sound he made.

In the meetings of the last weeks that he'd attended and she'd stood Chalice to, he'd either been seated before she arrived, and had not moved by the time she left, which often happened at the House; or when they met at one of the Circle points there were always enough people milling around and holding low-voiced arguments about order and hierarchy that any individual sound—or silence—was defeated. Sometimes he did not speak during the entire meeting, letting the Circle member in charge of this or that ritual or this or that Circle position carry leadership, although if she looked at him, she could see his red eyes flickering back and forth among those who did speak; and when there were rites to be performed, he performed the Master's part in them. And he performed them correctly, even when it was obviously very difficult for him to do so. There had been certain adaptations; he still appeared to have little physical strength. She wondered about this: Did the priests of Fire transmute their flesh into literal flame? There was no doubt that Elemental priests, were, eventually, no longer human, but beyond that there was little known outside the Elemental abbeys but rumour.

There had been attempts at discussions toward some general changes in the pattern of ritual to allow for the singular situation of the new Master, but his silence in those cases had drawn attention, and the brave, reckless, or disaffected persons who had tried to open the topic fell silent themselves.

All the Circle were nervous of him, but the Prelate was the worst. After the Prelate had dropped the staff of command during the sacrament of covenant at the ancient willow coppice that gave Willowlands its name, he sent a message via the Grand Seneschal that the Chalice should take his role in public ceremonies in future; that the Prelate's more all-encompassing spiritual power was upset by the Master's stronger power over his own land, confused as that was by seven years of Fire, and he, Prelate, was better off walking the Circle alone, at least for the time being.

She could have refused; the Chalice accepts orders from no one but the Master. But there was a precedent for what Prelate had done; sometimes the local Prelate and the Master—or, for that matter, the Prelate and the Chalice—could not work together, and the traditional alternative was that the Chalice pick up the Prelate's public duties. The Prelate was fourth in the Circle hierarchy, after the Grand Seneschal, but the Grand Seneschal's duties were practical, earthbound, corporeal, unlike the Prelate's—and the Chalice's. She didn't like it—she was barely holding her own, and she didn't need any extra obligations—but she did it, even if she didn't believe it had anything to do with a clash of powers and everything to do with funk. At least she didn't drop anything. Maybe Prelate needed some exercises to strengthen his shaking hands.

What worried her more was her guess that fear made the Prelate less willing to support the Master. Perhaps more willing to . . . what? Was she imagining it that he spoke rather too much to the Overlord's agent, Deager, when he came to Willowlands? She was sure neither of these men was the Master's friend. Was there a direct cause and effect between fear of the Master and the amount of time any Circle member spent chatting with the agent? (Sardonically she thought, By that reckoning, I am not afraid of the Master at all. I wish that were true.) How many more of the Circle would she have to count as against the Master? And herself in his favour—and the Grand Seneschal? How would he vote? She had no idea. The only thing she knew about the Grand Seneschal was that he had written to the priests of Fire after the death of the old Master, and that could have been no more than a final desperate gesture before accepting the inevitability of—and the havoc of—an outblood Master. Was the Grand Seneschal weary of his gesture yet?

Who else might she count for? Clearseer, who spoke to her occasionally when he didn't have to? Talisman, who spoke to no one? Weatheraugur, whose only contribution to the oblique conversations about adaptations for a Master who was also a priest of Fire was to ask the Master what he wanted to do? She saw none of the others outside the Circle meetings, spoke to them rarely in anything but ritual words.

The little breeze coming through the window was sweeping away the morning fog and in the few moments she stared dumbly at the Master standing by the hearth his figure seemed to brighten, although more as if some fire in him was burning more strongly than that the daylight was increasing. He still wore his long hooded cloak, but after the first day he'd folded the edges of the hood back till it only framed his face. She still didn't know if he had hair; the blackness of his skin and the blackness inside the hood made either hair or not-hair invisible. She knew that he'd sent his aides and his coach away three days after they'd arrived, so she assumed that he'd—what? Regained some little of his human strength, his human responses?—enough for him to move around on his own, to dress himself, to eat, to wash.

One of the rumours about the Fire-priests was that they neither ate nor washed: that they bathed in the Elemental Fire, which cleaned and nourished them. She doubted that plain, homely fire on an ordinary hearth would suffice. She hadn't heard any rumours of other helpers being assigned to him—not even a body servant, to help with the dressing and the eating and the washing. And she would have heard, with the mark of his touch on her hand. And while the Master ate little in public, she had seen him put food in his mouth, chew and swallow: there had been a plate at his elbow during his inaugural banquet, for example, and she'd seen servants refilling it. Clearseer had told her that the Master never ate in his dining hall; he had food sent up to his rooms, and the trays returned empty to the kitchens.

"And the only ash in his fireplace is wood," he added. "Although he gets through a lot of wood. There's a story that he chose the rooms he did—you know he didn't go into his brother's rooms?—because of all the private rooms in the House, they have the biggest fireplaces. Even the bedroom has one you could roast a bear in, and the sitting room's is big enough for a party."

The Master was alone now.

She was so startled that it took her much too long to come to her feet and bow. "Master, I give you first day's greeting."

"First day's greeting I return to the Chalice," he responded, correctly. He was always correct—had always been correct as far as she knew what the Master's actions and responses were supposed to be. She wondered what the Fire-priests said to each other, and whether he remembered the old demesne usages, or whether he had to study for his new role as she did for hers. Did he stay up nights cramming as she did? Did he read the old chronicles not only because he had to, but because he could not sleep? At least she did not have to fear scorching the pages when she turned them. But she burnt more firewood now herself, from sitting up late.

"Sit," he said. "I am sure you grow tired of standing."

She couldn't quite bring herself to sit, even at his suggestion; no one sat in the presence of a standing Master. As if reading her mind he said, "While I grow weary of sitting. At least this morning we are declared for Dawnspan, so we know it will be over in two hours."

This was so like what she had been thinking she laughed, and turned it into a cough. As Chalice she probably did have rank enough to laugh at something the Master said, but she would not have had the privilege in her old life, and she was still caught between her two worlds.

As he was caught between his.

The dawn breeze, still blowing through the open window behind her, now felt cold, and she shivered. She didn't know if he saw her shiver—would he remember what a shiver was, or was a Fire-priest always cold away from his Fire?—but he turned to the fireplace. She was watching him intently without realising she was doing so, and so she saw his chin drop, and a faint smile turn up the corners of his mouth, as if he were addressing a friend. And the ready-laid logs burst into flame.

She went to the fire and stood beside him without considering if this were permitted or not; she couldn't help herself. The fire looked and smelled and gave off heat like any ordinary fire; it did not burn too fiercely nor were the flames the wrong shape or colour. The rumour about Elemental Fire was that because it was the living fire of the living earth and air it both protected and aroused, it was nothing at all like the fire produced by flint and dry wood—except that it was hot, and it burned.

The day would grow warm later, but it was early enough in the morning now that the heat of the fire was pleasant. She held only her left hand out to it, and turned the back of her right hand away from it.

"Your hand does not heal," he said.

"It is in an awkward place," she said quickly, ashamed, snatching her left hand back as if she had done something discourteous.

There was a pause only long enough to register as a pause, and then he said, "I guess . . . it does not heal because it does not heal, and not because it is in a place where the skin is too thin and too flexible."

He held out one of his own hands toward the fire, and she saw that he wore no glove. She tried to remember—as she had tried to remember if he walked silently—if she had seen his hands since the day he had burned her, and she could not remember that she had. All she remembered was that he kept his hands hidden in his cloak when he could. At the banquet following his investiture, he had been wearing gloves—that was when she had first noticed they were tied instead of laced—and when he had to handle anything during the Circle rites, he wore gloves, and yet he still touched even stone and steel cautiously. When in the course of any meeting she held a cup to his lips, he let her do it, but he did not raise his hand to direct her. That was not unusual; many people believed that the binding work of the Chalice was more effective if only the Chalice's own hands touched the cup; and whatever the cause it was a compliment to her as Chalice. The other members of the Circle, before the Master's coming, had always firmly grasped the cup with her. She made it easy for them by always choosing among the long-stemmed Chalice cups, because it was forbidden to touch the Chalice herself if you were so fortunate as to be receiving a cup at her hands. To her surprise a few of the Circle, since the Master's coming, no longer held the cup with her. The Grand Seneschal was one of these, which was the greatest surprise of all.

He turned his hand over, palm up, fingers lightly curled. Then those fingers gave a little flick and recurl, a come-here gesture, as to a friendly animal; one of the ordinary-seeming flames of the ordinary-seeming fire streamed toward him, and the tip broke off, and jumped into his hand, like a tame bird coming for birdseed. It heaped itself up and swirled there for a moment—a nestling, making-itself-comfortable sort of motion—and then, almost as if rejecting some pleasure for a known duty, elongated itself and crept up his arm. He raised his other hand then—also glove-less—and began to sweep it together again, as if it were straw. No: as if it were feathers, light and fragile. He bent his arm as if its own weight would make the fire settle into the crook of his elbow, and easier to collect; and so it seemed to be. He cradled it there for a moment, gathering the last shreds together with his other hand, and then held it gently. It made a bundle about the size of a small skein of yarn. She could see it gleaming through his fingers.

"I might be able to heal your hand," he said.

She fumbled, getting the bandage off. She had to do it quickly, before she lost her courage. She'd been able to stand without flinching when he'd burnt her, but then she'd only half known it was going to happen, and she wasn't already hurt. To allow him, by sheer will, now, to do it again . . . because he *might* be able to heal her hand . . . because she believed he should be allowed to be Master if he could. . . .

She held her burnt hand up toward him. It began to throb at once, in the heat of him, or of the fire he held, or to the sudden hard beating of her blood in her veins.

She heard him inhale sharply, and in his strange voice she heard surprise as he said, "Honey!"

"It is good for burns," she said simply, trying to hold both her hand and her voice steady. She did not add: and this is the first wound, since I first learnt beekeeping from my mother, that it has failed to soothe, even when it could not cure.

His fingers closed on the skein of fire, and it sank, or subsided, or melted, and its colour grew less red and more golden. He picked the much-reduced nub out of the crook of his elbow and squeezed. When he opened his hand again, something thick and amber-coloured lay there. It looked rather like honey: perhaps a little too viscous, a little too ruddy. But it looked far more like honey than it did like fire.

He moved his hand till it was over hers, and turned the palm, so that the honey-fire ran off the edge and onto the back of her wounded hand. It had a hot sweet smell. . . .

Her hand stopped hurting the moment the honey-fire touched it. But that wasn't . . . that didn't begin to describe what happened. It was exhilaration, exaltation; it was the finest, purest, best moment of her life expanded into something unrecognisable and almost unbearably joyous. No rumour of any power of Fire had suggested anything like this.

She felt as if she came back to herself with infinite slowness, but some fraction of her mind had remained behind in ordinary time and was sure that it was all over in a matter of seconds. Still when she came back she discovered that she was being supported by a hand caught hard up under her left arm, so that her shoulder was nearly at her ear as she raised her head from her breast and gasped for breath.

"I'm sorry," he said. "I wasn't taught the proper forms for healing, and I was so afraid of hurting you further."

She looked up at him. She recovered her sense of up and down, and where her feet were, and stood on them. He let go of her arm. He had been holding her through both her cloak and the heavy Chalice robes, but there was no smell of singed cloth. She looked at his hand, and then glanced involuntarily at her sleeve.

"I can control it, a little, now," he said, understanding her look. "And I guessed you might. . . . It is one of the things I am trying to learn if I can control enough. Or not. I was . . . very tired, the day I arrived. But . . . once you learn to live in Fire, you do not return. I had not, quite, when the summons came. But I had entered Fire farther than I realised. I began to find this out on the trip here. I think I would not have dared, if I had realised."

"I am glad you did not know," she said. "That you came. You are—you *are* adapting. You are coming back to us. To your demesne. You have just said you can—you can control it." She could not bring herself to describe what "it" was. "You—you could not have borne so much of my weight, as you did just now, when you first arrived."

He said, "Fire helped me, just now. I could not lift the stone bowl at the Lower Water last week. Fire had no place there—as it rarely has any place in the functions of the Circle—and I could not call on it."

The memory of joy was draining away, leaving her in the too-familiar place of worry and frustration and ignorance and helplessness. She shook her head, to clear it, to shake loose something she could say to him, something that would convince him—something that would draw him further into the human world—where Willowlands needed him. "You are remembering the ordinary things." As she could not bring herself to describe what "it" was a moment ago, she could not now bring herself to say "the ordinary human things."

He bowed his head and spread his black fingers, and looked at them. She looked at them too; the tips were not ember-red today. "It is a capital offence to harm a Chalice, even for a Master," he said thoughtfully.

She said sharply, "I think no one else knows. Do not tell them."

"You are the only one I have hurt," he said. "I knew I was tired, but I did not know . . . remember . . . how delicate human skin is. I should have; I knew that the two young apprentices they sent with me could not touch me, and that the coachman avoided me. But I was . . . overwhelmed by the world. I had not seen it in seven years. I did not know how much I had changed.

"And the first thing I did upon arriving at my demesne, where I had come to hold as Master, is burn my Chalice when she gave me the cup of welcome."

"It was an accident," she said fiercely. "Anyone can have an accident, from a king to a scullery maid."

There was a pause. "Chalices are usually great believers in fate and omens," he said at last. "As are Elemental priests."

She didn't notice that she had reached out both her hands and seized his cloaked arm. She did not notice the oddness of the texture of the fabric beneath her palms—the fabric that could contain a Fire-priest's heat. "I am probably a bad Chalice," she said. "Certainly the three men who greeted you first on your arrival believe I am. It is true that I have only been Chalice eleven months, and that I was plucked out of my woodright without warning and without training. But the Circle's finding rods chose me and I have not seen nor heard of any record anywhere of a Circle finding the wrong Chalice. I'm sure the Grand Seneschal at least has tried to find such a record, for he would be rid of me if he could. Chalices feel the pull of the land strongly, you know—more strongly than any of the rest of the Circle save the Master himself. With nothing to shape itself to, that pull was tearing me apart when the Circle came for me, eleven months ago. I wonder sometimes if I feel it the more strongly because I had no training—because I went from woodskeeper to Chalice with nothing between. So I ask you to listen to me now. I *know* it is better for you to be Master of this land, blood Master, than to have the Overlord's this year's favourite set in your place, to unshape the land in grief and pain and chaos, and reshape it to a frame that is not its nature." She paused to catch her breath, saw her own hands on his arm, as if they belonged to someone else— and jerked them away.

51

"Master, forgive me," she said. "I speak out of turn."

"I thank the Fire you have spoken so, whether it is out of turn or not," he replied. "I—I am here to learn to be Master and I am failing even to relearn to be human." He glanced at the fire again, and it gave a little leap and flicker, like a smile and a wave. "It is not surprising no one can treat me as human, for I am no longer human. But what the people of Willowlands and I still have in common—should have in common—is Willowlands itself; and yet I hear nothing anyone says to me, about the great work of Willowlands, consultation after discussion after ritual after debate—I hear nothing, except as if clumsily translated from a foreign language. I see my Circle's mouths moving and I hear the clatter their tongues make: and I understand nothing. Till I have begun to believe that I have indeed forgotten the language—the language of the land. I cannot be Master here if I cannot hear my people; when I can barely remember to say 'yes thank you' when a table servant offers me food." He murmured something she could not quite hear, full of hissing syllables, which she guessed was the language of Fire, and then he continued, "Any Elemental priest would say we are all one beneath the three humours of the world; but the priests of each humour relinquish the other two . . . as if, perhaps, if we went out into the world again, we would hear only one word in three of what any ordinary human said. Perhaps I have heard only one word in three of what anyone here has said to me.

"I was prepared for this or something like this; I thought I was prepared. But I believed that we would reconnect in the land—I would not have come otherwise—and that has not happened. I have begun to fear that perhaps I do not hear the land any more either."

"Do you?" she said. She did not think that this speaking out of turn was much worse than her last, although to ask a Master if he could feel his own land was beyond any conceivable breach of etiquette, of law; if she had thought of it, she would have expected lightning—the Fire of the sky—to strike her dead before she finished saying *you*. But she did not think of it. She thought of her land—their land—which so badly needed its Master, and what she heard in Willowlands' Master's voice was despair. She knew despair, and she would draw him away from it if she could, both for the land's sake and for his own—and for hers. And perhaps if a Chalice could not speak openly to her Master, no one could. "Do you hear your land speak?"

He was silent; silent long enough that she might have thought of what she had said, of the perfidy and faithlessness of the query she had dared put to her Master. But she did not think of it. She thought only of what he might answer her; and prayed for him to say that he was still Master.

"I believed I did," he said at last. "I felt—something—the moment the carriage bringing me here crossed the boundary from Talltrees. I have thought that part of my exhaustion was not merely that a priest of Fire can no longer live as human, but that the land— my land—drew me back toward it so quickly that I was torn in two, between it and my training in Fire; that it needed my strength, and drew it remorselessly from me, when I had little to give. I lay awake all the first night here, listening, when I was so weary I could not stand, and when what I heard seemed half dream. . . ."

His voice trailed away and she said quickly: "No, it is often like that for me too, still; I have thought it is because I am so new to it and because I was not called to it and bred up in it the proper way, but snatched, almost stolen, out of my old life and thumped down in this one. I think perhaps it is like dreaming, but like dreaming as a breeze is like a storm wind. If all you know is breezes then your first storm wind is—" And then finally, belatedly, it occurred to her to whom she was speaking and what she was saying, and she stopped and caught her breath—half in terror, half in shame—but even as she did she thought, *He speaks to me clearly enough*. Tentatively, because this was neither the time nor the place, she felt for her own landsense, and it was right there, close, solid, steady—closer and steadier than she would have expected it to be, if it were not also responding to the presence of the Master.

He said: "This morning, now, your words to me, have been the first human words I feel I have truly heard since I arrived five months ago. I thank you. You give me hope."

And then the Grand Seneschal appeared in the doorway, and glared at them both as if he couldn't help himself, before coming to make his obeisance to the Master with a smooth, respectful face. His apprentice, Bringad, followed him, looking worried; Bringad always looked worried. Then several more people arrived, Circle members and attendants and a few more apprentices; then the factors for farmers and woodskeepers, for whom this meeting had been called; and more bows and greetings were given. The woodskeepers' factor, Gota, to whom she had once reported, had never once looked her in the face since she became Chalice. She acknowledged his respectful greeting with a hand gesture that his downturned eyes should be able to see, and sighed. Soon everyone who was to attend this meeting was present, all standing behind their chairs, waiting for the Master to sit first.

The Chalice took up her goblet and hesitated; she had thus far always chosen to stand by the main doorway during all House meetings, in whichever room they were in. This was the least controversial place for the Chalice to stand. She hadn't yet had time to learn the rules about standing by a window, which were complex, to do with the cardinal directions, the seasonal angle of the sun, the position of the House, and the earthlines that ran through the demesne. The maths oppressed her, though she often thought wistfully of being able to stand in sunlight.

It was also perfectly proper for the Chalice to stand by the Master's right hand.

But when she looked at him, with the thought barely half formed, she saw him with a little shock, for it was as if the conversation they had just had had not happened—and yet the absence of pain in her right hand told her that it had. But the great cloaked figure standing by the fire held power and authority as it held darkness; their conversation could not possibly have been what she seemed to half remember it had been about. He might be strange, alien, no longer human; but he could not be doubted. This was the Master. She turned toward the doorway.

His voice stopped her. "Stand by me," he said, and took two long, loping, silent steps to the tall chair at the head of the table. Two Housemen stood by it, waiting to slide it forward as the Master sat down. He sat, and the Housemen stepped back—a little too quickly, a little too far—and the Master raised his right hand, and the cloak fell back from it. She saw, in the low morning light, that a few fine hairs grew on the back of it, just as on a human hand. She shifted her grip on her goblet, proudly turning the back of her own unblemished right hand toward the company, and took up her place at the Master's side.

* * *

She heard the plans being made to visit the Well of the Red Fishes that afternoon, but she did not pay attention. The Chalice would not have to attend; the Well needed neither binding nor calming. She could go home and sweep the floor and chop the wood and talk to the bees—and read more hand-sewn books and crumbling piecemeal manuscripts about Chalicehood.

* * *

There was another meeting tomorrow she would have to stand Chalice to; and another one the day after that. And soon the Overlord's agent would be coming again, to see how the new Master was settling in to his responsibilities. This is what Overlords' agents did, they visited their Overlord's demesnes and discussed any problems a Master might be having, in his own lands or with a neighbouring Master; and in a difficult Mastership—as for example when a Master died while his eldest son was still a child—a responsible Overlord would send an agent to that demesne more often. But in this case she mistrusted the Overlord's motives. She wondered again what Prelate said to the agent; and were not Prelate and Keepfast increasingly friendly? And on the last occasion of the agent's presence in Willowlands had she not felt Keepfast had spoken too long and too animatedly to the agent also?

She would bring the cup of unity to the meeting with Deager, and she would sprinkle a little of its contents around the table before anyone arrived.

Once the Grand Seneschal had realised that he was stuck with her—once all the Circle had become resigned to her as the new Chalice, that there was no escape through deciding that the omens had been read wrong or the rods had fallen incorrectly—they had tried to persuade her to move out of her small cottage and into the House. Chalices lived in their Houses. But she did not want to move, not least because the Grand Seneschal and several of the others of the Circle, including Keepfast, did live at the House; and there was no rule that the Chalice must live at the House. She was still afraid that such a rule would turn up somewhere, even though she doubted any of the Circle were still actively searching for it.

One of the things she'd learnt on her own ragged, bemused, zigzag way was that the best sources of useful information were often in strange places, and she wondered if any of the Circle were imaginative enough to guess this, after they'd run their fingers down various indexes and inventories and failed to find "Chalice, living quarters, requirements of" anywhere. She wanted to feel that none of the Circle were imaginative enough, but she didn't dare; hope was dangerous, and might make her reckless or more vulnerable—about where she lived or anything else. She wondered what she would do if she herself found a rule about the conduct of a Chalice that she did not want to—could not bring herself to—conform to. She was sure the Grand Seneschal and the rest of the Circle didn't really want her at the House either; the attempt had been to make her look more like what they believed a Chalice should look like—and perhaps living at the House would indeed seep into her awkward woodskeeper's ways till she looked like someone who belonged there, if perhaps not someone as illustrious and irreproachable as a Chalice should be.

But the attempt had failed, and living at a distance had never made her late or careless of her duties (although it often helped make her short of sleep). She thought too that the time it took her to walk to the House and back again was a kind of mind-clearing, mind-composing exercise . . . perhaps even a protection. She thought of the weight of the mere air of the House—and of trying to live somewhere not only constantly surrounded by people, but constantly surrounded by people who would not meet her eye. She also thought that the Circle could not have guessed how much easier they would have found it to intimidate her if she lived at the House or they would not have given up so soon.

Sometimes she regretted her odd sources of information nonetheless: one of them had been where she had discovered the story about the Master having been put to death for harming his Chalice. She had read it shortly after the Grand Seneschal had received the letter saying that the priests of Fire were allowing their new third-level acolyte to return home to be Master, while Willowlands waited for his arrival—while she was urgently reading all the crabbed and fusty old records she could lay her hands on, for anything she could learn about Chalices and their circumstances. She had read this tale with a shock, but it had not occurred to her then that it would bear any relevance to her or to her Master. Would I really rather not know the law existed? she thought. Wouldn't I just have invented something like it—and worried about where I'd finally find proof?

In some ways it was not so preposterous or absurd that she had been chosen; and if she had been chosen as apprentice at ten or eleven, she would have been ready when the Chalice came to her. (She wondered if the Chalice had ever failed to go to the accepted apprentice. That involuntary Chalice would be even less to be envied than herself.) A well-established, well-rooted Chalice was *Chalice,* and all else about her was forgotten, was inconsequential. It was true that the last three Chalices at Willowlands had been Housefolk; but her family was one of the oldest on the demesne and almost everyone in it had some landsense, and had had for generations, as did all the members of all the old families, those both in and out of the House. She felt the blow when the old Master and the old Chalice had died, but that was hardly surprising. Almost everyone had felt so extreme a calamity to the land, even those families who had moved to Willowlands in their own generation. And her landsense hadn't told her what had happened, only that some great and terrible cataclysm had occurred. When Selim had come to tell her the news she had not only been shocked and appalled but astonished.

Although Selim had been living with the news for a day and

a half, telling it over still shook her so badly that she had to sit down. "Branda brought the news to me," she said, "and I told Marn yesterday. She said she would tell Kard. . . ." Her voice trailed away. She watched Mirasol moving as if blind around her own kitchen, as if trying to remember what you did when you had a visitor, and said, "If you're going to offer me something to drink, Mirasol, tisane would be nice, but your mead would be better."

Mirasol shook her head to clear it—it didn't clear—and then tried to smile and didn't do that much better. She'd brought Selim indoors and put her in a chair before her news had really sunk in, and, now that it had . . . she found herself standing, staring at her hands, which had frozen on the cupboard door handles, the cupboard where the mead lived. She opened the door and reached in—hesitated—and instead of mead, took down the honey brandy. She stared at the bottle. She had put down the mead that had become this brandy nine years ago: Her parents were still alive and so was the old Master, and the folk of the demesne were worrying what kind of Master his elder son would become. Her hands were shaking. The Master and Chalice both dead! No wonder the groaning of the land had been keeping her awake at night—giving her nightmares that followed her around during the day and hid in the shadows.

She managed to pour two fingers of brandy for Selim and herself by holding the wrist of her right hand with her left, and then said abruptly, "Let's go back outdoors again. The sunlight still falls unchanged." And there are fewer shadows for nightmares to hide in, she thought, but did not say this aloud.

They sat on the worn stone chairs some forebear of Mirasol's had built several hundred years ago, when the family had first moved to Willowlands and been granted this woodright. The chairs had been among Mirasol's favourite things all her life, and she felt she needed their solidity now. She dropped a cushion on one of them for Selim but settled on another one herself without; she didn't mind the hardness of the stone and liked the way the seat seemed to have been worn to a shallow human-buttock-shaped cup. She liked to think this was from all the years of sitting but it was more likely her ancestor had had the luck or foresight to choose saucer-shaped stones. She thought of hundreds of years of rain and sun falling on these chairs. . . . In all those years they would have seen the deaths of many Masters and Chalices . . . but never both at the same time. And never in such a terrible way.

Selim was watching her ironically over the brim of her glass. "You nestle into that seat like a cat on a blanket—your dad and his mother did the same. I've always thought the family name that ought to go with this woodright is Hardbutt."

Mirasol laughed. She knew she was supposed to—the Hardbutt joke was very, very old—but she was grateful to Selim for dusting it off and bringing it out on this occasion, when there was so little to laugh about. Laughter went on and on, like sunlight and stone, even if the human beings who laughed did not.

Selim sipped a little of her brandy and gave a great sigh and stretched out her long legs. "Thank the gods for honey," she said. "Your honey in particular. Just so long as your bees don't decide to object." There were bees in the foxgloves near the chairs, and

Selim glanced at them uneasily. Most of Mirasol's visitors glanced at her bees uneasily; they were unusually large, and they had the disconcerting habit of coming, as if to say hello, to Mirasol and—even more disconcertingly—going on to investigate any company Mirasol might have. But Mirasol's honey was the best in the demesne; several people had told her that they thought it was even better than her mother's. *The bees like you,* they said, and bore with the bees' discomfiting behaviour.

As if they had heard, two or three bees broke off from exploring the foxgloves to fly toward Mirasol. They settled first in her hair and then walked down to her shoulders. Two or three more bees joined them, strolling down her arms and then creeping over the rim of her tumbler to taste the brandy. As well as being unusually large, only their bellies were striped yellow; their backs were a black as velvet-glossy as a fine horse's. One bee flew on toward Selim. Selim made a noise.

"Don't worry," Mirasol said mildly. "They're not going to say 'what are you doing with my honey?' and be angry. The most amazing honey they've ever made was after I put some mead out for them one winter when I'd got some other stuff wrong and didn't have anything else to give them. Put your hand over your glass if you don't want bees walking in it."

Selim nervously put her hand over the rim. The bee flew round Selim twice without landing, and went back to the foxgloves. Selim was accustomed to ordinary bees—many people had a hive or two tucked away in a corner for their own use, including Selim's nearest neighbours—but no matter how often she visited Mirasol she never quite adjusted to Mirasol's bees. "You have been stung, haven't you? Even you," she said.

"Of course," said Mirasol. "Every beekeeper is stung. Hasn't your cat ever scratched you?"

"That's different," said Selim, but she sat back in her chair.

Mirasol found the hum of her bees soothing—bees and honey were two more things that went on and on—but neither sunlight, stone nor bees could distract her long. Distantly she still felt the land lamenting its loss—an almost tangible drumming under her feet. The earthline that ran through her meadow had the restless, unhappy, unseeing manner of a horse pent and pacing in its stall when it is used to being able to run loose outdoors. "What—what will happen now?"

Selim knew she was asking about the news Selim had brought. She shrugged. "I don't know. Branda said he'd see Gota today." Gota spoke to the House for all the woodskeepers, because his woodright contained Willowlands' ancient willow coppices and was thus the most important of all the demesne's woodrights. "So if there's anything to know Gota will tell us."

"The Master's brother . . ." Mirasol began, and didn't know how to continue.

After a pause Selim said, "Yes. We're all thinking about him. But nobody comes back from the Elemental priests. He's been there seven years; that's too long." She didn't have to add, Downbrook was given an outblood Master sixty years ago, and it has still not recovered from the shock of the change. Nor did she have to add, And Willowlands was already under strain, from seven years of an increasingly bad and careless Master and a Chalice who put no check on him.

* * *

And when, almost immediately after Selim's visit, things had begun to go wrong for Mirasol, the truth never occurred to her. She guessed it was to do with the devastating loss of Master and Chalice, but assumed that equally strange and punishing things were happening to everyone in the demesne.

She lived in a small cottage in that corner of Willowlands' old forest which she tended; whose tending was her inheritance from her father. Ordinarily she saw Selim or Kard or Marn at least every few days; their woodrights bordered on hers, and the woods-keepers were a close group throughout this and every demesne. Two days after Selim's visit Kard had stopped only long enough to tell her that despite the unlikelihood of any result, the Grand Seneschal had written to the priests of Fire about the younger brother of the dead Master.

Kard had looked worried and preoccupied, and had been in a hurry, and Mirasol asked no questions. She was worried and pre-occupied too, and also in a hurry, because things had already begun to go wrong. And after that some time passed when she saw no other human soul. But she was too busy—and too distressed—to go in search of someone to talk to. The loss of Master and Chalice would have thrown all the demesne's workings into con-fusion, but she soon felt that she did not want—did not want to risk—telling anyone what was happening to her for fear that she would be one of those whose landrights did not survive the current wreck.

She had guessed that her axe would not strike true, so she had put the heavier work aside for the present. There were always smaller tasks mounting up that she never quite kept up with the way she wanted to, although she knew that was normal enough. But the day Mirasol came home from tending the ash grove which the Lady had blessed, she found that one of the big crocks in the cellar where the end of her winter's mead remained had foamed up and run over. This in itself was annoying and wasteful and had to mean that she had set it up badly and been trapped by her own incompetence, but it was also surprising. If this had happened five years ago she wouldn't have thought beyond finding out what she had done wrong. But she knew—mostly—what she was about by now. That this should happen was almost frightening.

And then it was indeed frightening when she realised that it had not merely run over, but had covered the cellar nearly knee-high in froth and mead—which was frankly not possible. Even if she'd tipped the crock over herself what it contained couldn't have done more than make a large sticky puddle.

She spent much of the next several days scooping the mead-lake into buckets and hauling the heavy buckets to the roots of favoured trees—and being followed by clouds of interested bees. They landed all over her—anywhere the mead might have splashed, which was everywhere, and in the buckets, on the ground, and especially the tree roots where she poured the mead, where the tiny cracks and irregularities in the bark made tiny reservoirs—but none of them stung her, even when she heed-lessly and impatiently brushed them away. At least, she thought grimly, her inconvenient windfall should not go entirely to waste; she remembered the honey the bees had made from the mead she'd given them the first winter after her mother died—when she had made a mistake. Although that mistake was merely that she'd found she couldn't bring herself to kill any of her bees, which was the system all the northern demesnes used, and so had to get them through the winter somehow. She'd been cold that winter herself, after wrapping up her most exposed hives in all the blankets she had.

Perhaps the trees too would like their improbable drink enough to produce especially rich blossoms for the bees next year. It seemed remarkably strong mead, for all that it had no excuse for its existence. She never tasted it, but the mere smell rose to her head and made her dizzy.

As a result of the mead-lake and its aromatic effect she took to sleeping outside at some little distance from her cottage. While the earth floor of the cellar had been beaten hard enough by many generations of feet to prevent the mead from turning it into a bog, the reek remained, and she found this gave her wild, terrifying dreams of fire and water, which were no im-provement on the nightmares she'd had since the deaths of Master and Chalice. She asked the Radiant Pines, whose resin was used for perfume, if they could spare her some boughs, and when they said yes, distributed them across her cellar floor, but even they were not enough. She wondered how long she would be exiled; it was all very well now in summer, but by next winter, she would need to be back in the cottage, with its sturdy walls and stone hearth—and next winter's mead in the vat in the cellar.

But by the time she had done what she could to rescue her cellar, other things were going wrong. Her two goats, Nora and Spring, were suddenly producing so much milk that they baaed miserably for relief twice and even three times a day, which meant that she had to stay near the cottage to get back to them, and that meant she could not tend the full extent of her woodright. This would become another trouble for her as soon as anyone noticed; but she was already unhappy at the idea of neglecting her trees, especially now, when they needed reassurance, as did every living thing in the demesne. Nor was she equipped to handle so much milk; she had nowhere to keep it, let alone time to turn it into butter and cheese and hilliehoolie.

But what hurt the worst of all was the fact that the beehives near the cottage, incredibly, were literally running over with honey.

The mysterious excellence of Mirasol's honey had probably held her woodright for her. By the time her mother had died only two years after her father, she should have married someone without a landright of his own, to help her with her bees and her woods; it was not proper she maintain both alone, even though she was capable of the extra work. And so by clinging to this impropriety she had grown used to the sense of needing not merely to serve but to placate the Housefolk and the lesser Circle members—most of whom also bought her honey—who were more concerned in the everyday lives of the common folk of the demesne. A surplus would have done her good with those who had the power to injure her—if she had had the time to collect it, strain it, bottle it and take it to the House. Yet if she tackled the honey glut, she would fall even farther behind in her woods-keeping—and the demesne's woods were growing ever more restless with no Master holding the earthlines steady and no Chalice to bind and calm.

She began to take her goats with her when she went off to tend her trees. They slowed her down when she couldn't afford the time, but she could at least get to the boundaries of her lot that way. She'd stake them somewhere the browsing was good, and come back to milk them halfway through the day. She couldn't bear to let the milk spill immediately lost on the ground, so she carried a bucket or a bowl with her, and left the milk for anyone or anything that might like it. She knew this was ridiculous but she did it anyway.

She had more buckets and bowls than she needed, for her family had been keeping the slightly awry ones through generations of making buckets and bowls out of odd bits of wood too good for burning. But losing one a day was rather extreme, so a few days later she went thriftily to where she'd left the first, expecting a sour, stinking mess and a polluted bucket. The bucket was where she'd left it, but it was empty—it didn't even smell of milk—it smelled as clean as it would have if she'd just scrubbed it out ready to use. She hoped the foxes or the badgers or hedgehogs or whatever had enjoyed the milk, but she'd never thought of any of the sharers of her woodland as being such tidy drinkers. It was as if whoever it was were saying thank you.

But this is what happened with all the milk she left: the vessel shining clean and exactly where she'd left it when she went back to fetch it. She didn't believe this was fox or badger or hedgehog conduct. She began to look warily at the milk she left behind when she took her goats back to the cottage; but it always acted like ordinary milk when she was there, and the milk she used at home still behaved itself as it should. She told herself she should let the magic—or whatever it was—work unmolested; but her curiosity got the better of her and at last she went back to where she'd left a big shallow basin of milk only the day before . . . and found the surface of the milk invisible under a carpet of her bees. "Bees don't drink milk," she said to them. When they lifted and flew away the basin was empty and clean.

When human beings first discovered honey, they had hunted the wild bees and followed them back to their nests. Some enterprising honey-lover must have noticed that bees often nested in hollow trees, and so, perhaps, rolled or dragged or hacked out a suitable log nearer home, left it at a convenient spot, and hoped a passing swarm might settle in it. Eventually someone began experimenting with making hives out of straw, mud, clay, pottery, and with sowing the seeds of plants bees were seen to like; and eventually with breeding more docile bees.

But the basic facts of beekeeping hadn't changed that much: bees still made wax honeycomb to store their honey in; and a beekeeper had to both break into a hive and cut into the honeycomb to retrieve the honey.

Mirasol went home then and there, that day (the goats dragging sulkily behind her), and lifted one end each of all her movable hives, propped it and at the lower end sawed, pried or hammered in a hole—knowing as she did so that this was exactly the sort of drastic human behaviour that would upset the bees. Except that it didn't. They flew placidly around her and the note of their humming never changed. She put a grass mat for a sieve under each new opening and a bowl under that, and left them. It was a nonsensical thing to do, but much of what was happening to her—and to her animals—was nonsensical.

And the daunting thing was—it worked. The honey streamed out in such quantities she almost ran out of bowls for milk. When the three hives in two old trees beside her little meadow began to drip honey down the boles, she merely tucked buckets among the tree roots. The buckets filled up too.

This was almost as distressing a problem as too much milk— no, more distressing, because honey was much more valuable than milk. And then her bees swarmed; again and again; big, healthy, vigorous swarms longing for places to build their nests and produce more honey. She, like every beekeeper on every demesne, wove spare skeps for just such an eventuality; but her mother had showed her how to use wooden or clay hives, and once she had decided she would kill none of her bees she'd found that straw skeps made the least satisfactory bee homes. Nor had any beekeeper she knew had to deal with swarm after swarm after swarm. A month after the deaths of the Master and Chalice she had bees living in all four corners of her roof and another swarm in the eave of the hearth inside; she had to leave the window near it open all day, and keep an eye out for returning stragglers in the evening if she closed it. Many of the trees round her clearing had at least one bee home in them, and the huge triple-boled hollow tree that had contained two bee families since she was a little girl now had six. By then she could no longer hear Nora and Spring bleat through the humming of the bees. Nor could she hear anything else.

And so she did not hear them when the Circle came to her cottage at the beginning of the fifth week after Selim had brought her the news. When she looked up from her midday milking—she had stayed home that day to empty the honey buckets—knowing that she was unkempt and wild-eyed, and with the remains of the still-sour stink of the cottage cellar easily penetrating to the bare bit of ground where she did her milking, queasily mixed with the intense sweet reek of the honey and the warm animal smell of the milk, her first thought was that they had come to turn her out of her woodright, and she burst into tears. She did not consider that the full Circle would not have come to deprive an obscure woodskeeper of her livelihood; all she could think of was that she was no longer doing her job, that the Circle must have gone past some of the recently neglected woods she was responsible for, and had detoured from their proper business to pass sentence on her failure.

part
TWO

The day the Circle came to her seemed a century ago now, although it was only a year. Once Nora and Spring had joined Kard's small flock of four their milk production settled back to normal, although she heard later from Selim that it was two months before they stopped eating as much as the other four goats together. She could guess that Kard hadn't dared complain—inheriting the goats of the new Chalice, who no longer had time for them, had to be an honour—but no small woodskeeper has much to spare, and if the new goats had gone on eating their heads off, Kard might have had trouble getting through the winter; profits from additional cheeses wouldn't have come in time. Mirasol had been distressed at this story, declared that Selim should have told her sooner—"Why didn't Kard say something to me himself, when I go to him now for my milk?" she exclaimed, even knowing what the answer was. But Selim smiled one of her new, uncomfortable smiles, said that Kard was very pleased with his new goats which were now both in kid, that probably she shouldn't have told Mirasol at all except that this was a story that had a happy ending and she thought . . . and then her eyes slid away from Mirasol's and she hadn't finished what she had been going to say.

Then the new Master had returned but there was no happy ending for the demesne. Or perhaps for the new Chalice. Selim was the only one of Mirasol's old acquaintances who made an effort to remain in contact, to be welcoming when the Chalice managed to snatch an hour away from her responsibilities. And Mirasol had lost her woodright after all: she had known that she could keep neither it nor her goats once she was Chalice, and so she gave them up because she had to. The woodright had been divided among the three other rights it bordered on; Selim was one of the beneficiaries and claimed, with a believable manifestation of sincerity, that the extra work was worth the extra result.

But Mirasol had dared try to wield some of the power of the Chalice to keep her cottage, and her bees. She had declared her preference in a meeting with the rest of the Circle—declared it officially after having borne a series of unofficial attempts to persuade her to move into the House—and had worn her most gorgeous robes, and used the cup of decision, to bind the meeting. It was bad enough that the meeting itself had been at the House, with its heavy, disapproving air—and while no one but the Chalice should know the proper names of the Chalice's vessels, any Circle member who chose to pay attention would be able to predict, over time, which cup came out for which sort of occasion. She was sure the Grand Seneschal guessed by the damning look he gave her when she offered him the cup of decision, but even the Grand Seneschal would not dare refuse a cup offered him by the Chalice. The Circle drank—and Mirasol kept her cottage. And her bees.

It was possible that the overwhelming presence of her bees had discouraged Landsman from deciding to reassign her woodright whole, which would have included the cottage for its new incumbent, when he came to view the situation and decide on his recommendation for its future. The bees seemed as integral a part of the scene as the cottage and the trees. Landsman had not stayed long nor said much, but he had bowed to her so resentfully when he left that she felt his decision couldn't be against her or he would have been happier about it. And saying little could have been merely conservation of effort: the Circle had had to shout over the rumble of bees to make her hear their original news, especially since she couldn't believe it even after her ears had taken it in.

Perhaps it was her bees who kept other, more ordinary visitors away. She reminded herself that even Selim had found her bees disconcerting when there had been far fewer of them—before the Chalice had come to her. At least since she had accepted what she could do nothing about, her bees had stopped swarming, and the rivers of honey had slowed to mere streams—and you could begin to hear yourself think again, and eventually conversations no longer had to be shouted—as if by her acceptance the power of the Chalice had begun to run in the channel where it belonged. However ill suited she felt herself to contain it. She tried to think of it sometimes as she thought of her bees, something apart from her that it was her duty to tend; but it was like trying to tend the sea you were drowning in.

If it was her bees that were keeping her old friends away at least this new attribute seemed to include keeping unwelcome visitors away also. The Grand Seneschal had once come to her cottage alone, to try to convince her, he said, that she would be better taking the Chalice's quarters in the House. The underlying message was, she felt, that he wanted to keep an eye on her, and that would be easier at the House. Yes. And of the entire Circle she found him the most intimidating of all, so that at Circle meetings she had to keep reminding herself not merely that she was Chalice, but that she was also Second of the Circle. When she thought of meals taken daily either in the small House dining room, which was still large enough to seat twenty-six, with several of her fellow Circle members—either that, she supposed, or immured in her room with a tray like the Master—no. Or being *walking* distance from the outdoors—from grass and trees and weather and bees—instead of the other side of a single plain door: no again. It wasn't possible. It was one of those things that she, Mirasol, within the Chalice, could not do.

She was aware also that none of the Circle, most especially the Grand Seneschal, wanted to believe that the particular vessel of her Chalicehood really was honey, and she was not pretending something so ridiculous (and unheard of) from perversity—the personal perversity of wanting to keep her cottage and her bees. She wondered which was the chicken and which the egg: did the Circle wish her to be an ordinary Chalice so that they felt justified in trying to bully her into moving to the House, or did they hope she might yet become a proper Chalice if she gave up her bees—by moving to the House?

But her bees had promptly stung the Grand Seneschal—twice—and he'd left in some confusion. She'd chased after him with salve for the throb and the swelling. She hadn't stopped him leaving for a fear a third bee would sacrifice herself to drive the interloper away. But since she needed the stingbalm so rarely herself, and since her bees were usually very well behaved (no matter how uneasy about them the visitor was), it had taken her a little while to locate it.

She'd insisted (panting from having run after him) that she put it on at once—although in hindsight she was surprised he'd allowed her to insist. He had one sting on one hand and the other on the opposite wrist. As he stood there with his hands held out they could both see the swellings subside, and he admitted (with a curious edge in his voice that might have been surprise, or indignation that he'd needed the healing, or that the healing had come from her) that the pain had stopped immediately.

She went home again slowly, hoping that he wouldn't decide to order her to get rid of her bees. He couldn't, in theory, order the Chalice to do anything, but in practise the Grand Seneschal could do just as he liked, and often did. He could certainly contrive to overturn the Landsman's decision to let her stay where she was.

She took a big pot of her most popular honey to the Grand Seneschal the next time she went to the House, as an apology. It seemed to have worked. If anything—and she found it difficult to believe that the Grand Seneschal would have deliberately done her any service—it had benefited her, for she suddenly had more orders for honey from the Housemen and -women, almost as if some permission—even encouragement—had been given. And although the honey yield had subsided since the first flood after the death of the old Chalice, she continued to have more than she could sell to her usual buyers in and out of the House, so this was very useful—especially when the Circle members who had once been her customers dropped away. Only the Weatheraugur and the Talisman still bought honey from her. The Talisman, she knew, used it in some of the tokens she made for her Circle work; the Weatheraugur merely liked it on her bread.

One day the new Clearseer bought a pot of her honey, and when he came back a month later for a second pot he said he was using it in his scrying.

"I didn't know honey was ever used for scrying," she said tentatively.

"It isn't," he said. "But it is customary to use water if your Chalice is a water Chalice, and a little wine if she is a wine Chalice. At the moment everything looks unnaturally golden and wonderful—which is no bad thing, but perhaps not practical—but I still have hopes of creating a tradition." He smiled at her: hopefully? Beseechingly?

She smiled back, and sold him a pot of her palest, clearest honey.

And Mirasol was glad of the money. She was going through quantities of paper taking notes and paper was expensive. (Sometimes she wondered why she found her increasing stacks of notes and notebooks such a solace, when the more of them there were the harder it was to find the annotation she was looking for.) Occasionally she'd been offered old manuscripts of Chalice records.

She guessed they were black market, but she had no one to ask, or no one she was willing to ask (it was the sort of thing the Grand Seneschal would know how to find out), and she so longed to know *everything*. She'd once bought a particularly old mouldering one, because of its superlative oldness and moulderingness, and it had taken every penny she had. It had perhaps been worth it: it had been where she'd read of the one occasion when a Master had been put to death for harming his Chalice, which meant that she held the copy of that dangerous story, and not someone else. On the other hand it had rather put her off buying any more, because she felt a bit cautious about what else she might learn that she'd be glad to be spared.

She wondered where the Master had learnt that story; if another telling of it might be on some shelf in the library she had not come to yet. She doubted she could ask him, nor say: hide it, or I will.

And her bees kept making honey, and her buyers kept coming back for more (even if they looked around uneasily and tended to walk rather quickly back down the path from her cottage), and her tiny money pot had refilled by the time she needed more paper.

She also wondered if the Grand Seneschal had told anyone he'd been stung. She couldn't imagine him doing so; surely it was an admission of a loss of face? Perhaps here was why she had been left alone; but the Grand Seneschal would not need to give a reason for (for example) suggesting that the Landsman turn the new Chalice off her old landright. *Stop,* she told herself. The important thing was that he hadn't. The Grand Seneschal could no more order the Landsman to do something than he could order the Chalice, or any other member of the Circle doing their bloodright business; but it was a rare person who was brave, stubborn or desperate enough to resist his suggestion. Drily she thought, It has cost me sorely to be that rare person.

Her bees often landed on her—not just one or two or several any more, but dozens. When she came to take the honey away and replace the bowls and grass mats with new ones she had the extremely odd sensation that they were trying to help her. "Well, if you ate all this, you'd be too fat to fly," she said to them. She moved slowly so as not to startle them, but she no longer bothered to use smoke first to make them sleepy. This was foolish, but then harvesting honey by cutting a hole in a hive and putting a bowl under it was foolish too. Perhaps the reason her honey was so popular now was that it was so clear and clean; even sieved ordinary honey was never immaculate. But the honey still flowed—clear and clean and shining, in all the shades of golden from palest primrose to darkest amber—and her bees never stung her.

She worried about the combless honey, however, worried about how her bees were feeding themselves, till eventually she pulled the back off one of her mother's old pottery hives, the way she had done when she harvested honey by the usual method, and found the back full of normal sealed-up honeycomb; so she put the pottery plug back in, and daubed it round with mud and clay again to make it secure, and tried to stop worrying. She had noticed that three of the hives near the cottage produced no honey through the ridiculous holes in their bottoms, although she saw bees flying in and out of them apparently no differently than they flew in and out of all the other hives, and for a while she left them alone, thinking only that those bees had retained their normal bee sense and good for them. But eventually her curiosity got the better of her—why those particular hives, so close, as they were, to her cottage—and she pried the back off one of them too and discovered . . . rows and ropes and webs and columns of empty beeswax. She was initially shocked—there was something terribly wrong with these bees, and what was it, and would the rest of her bees catch it, and would they all die, and what were these bees living on? . . . And then the panic subsided and she felt so light-headed she had to sit down, and when she sat down she began to laugh. Guessing what she would find this time, she got out her comb knife, and began to cut out just enough of the clean comb to let her see through to the front and yes, as if in reverse to the honey-river hives, there were the tidy rows of full honeycomb.

So she had beeswax candles to sell again too. Her mother had made beautiful ones, but the Chalice didn't have time. But she made them, and put a little honey in them too—a little of the honey Chalice's honey—and sold them. Beeswax candles were even more valuable than honey.

She had always been aware of the influence of the seasons on her bees' honey, but in the year since she had become Chalice she had begun to realise that the individual hives' honey had qualities which seemed to remain constant through the different seasons of nectar-producing flowers. She'd always tasted her honeycomb as she divided it up, so the different flavours—and colours and textures—over the year as different plants came into flower were familiar to her, as was the fact that these differences were quite marked enough for marked preferences, so for example the honey she liked best on bread was spring honey, and the honey she wanted with a winter stew was the last rich almost chestnut-coloured honey of the autumn.

It had also seemed to her for some years that different families of bees seemed to specialise in different flowers, and in different flying ranges to look for their preferred flowers, and that this tendency too had grown more pronounced this year. All honey was good for wounds and burns, but there was a lengthy folklore of specific honeys which declared, for example, that oak honey was the most nourishing for invalids and lavender honey was an appropriate gift from a lover to his or her beloved—and the honey from Willowlands' willows was for wisdom and decision-making. (She used a lot of this in her Chalice mixtures and wondered sardonically how much worse the Circle's relationship might be if she didn't.) It was this honey she had put in the Master's welcome cup. But this year the difference in taste and other qualities of the Chalice's bees' honey seemed much more extensive and distinct.

The majority of her honey was still just honey (although to a beekeeper honey is never *just* honey), so that when someone wished to buy some she didn't concern herself about what else she was selling besides golden sweetness. But she began to taste what came out of her bowls more attentively and discovered that there was the honey that made her feel sleepy and the honey that made her feel full of energy. There was honey that cured headaches—she'd tasted it the first time when she had a headache, which had snapped off like a branch breaking, which inspired her to taste it again the next time she had a headache and it had had the same effect.

But more and more she had somehow *felt* what a honey was good for as she bottled and labelled it; and as she grew accustomed to the discipline of—she called it *listening*, as she thought of *listening* to the earthlines—to the honey, she often heard quite complex things. There was a honey for stomach-aches and a honey for baldness; the stomach-ache honey was also good for bed-wetting and night terrors in children, and the honey for baldness was also good for too-heavy bleeding during a woman's monthly and for persuading a broody chicken to stop plucking her breast feathers out and get back to laying eggs. (This particular combination made her laugh.) And there was a honey that was particularly good for burns and wounds. There was also a honey to stop a well going dry, to stop a dog barking and to make fruit trees crop more heavily; and one that seemed to be to make the weather hold long enough to get the hay cut, dried and stacked. She stood looking at the last of these and wondered how it was supposed to be applied: did the farmer eat it, or put it in a bowl by the threshold of his house or his barn, or drop it in the corners of his hayfields, or did the scythesmen rub it on their scythes? The next time a farmer's wife bought honey from her, should she send her home with the haymaking honey?

And all of them tasted glorious on bread.

Still her mind kept reverting to the fact that her honey, which had never before failed her, had been able to do nothing for the burn the Master's touch had caused. She tried to tell herself that that had happened before she'd discovered there was a honey that was particularly good for burns. But she found herself doubting that it would have succeeded either. Maybe she had not yet discovered which honey was best to counteract a Fire-priest's touch? She thought of this when she remembered their conversation: that he himself had said he was no longer human. Was there a honey that could cure that?

She was thinking about the Master again one afternoon when she noticed the hum of her bees changing its note. It was a warm sunny day, so she was outdoors, with her books and papers scattered over the old stone chairs. She'd absorbed without really identifying the information that, since she had become a honey Chalice, the bees' note changed not only when they were angry or frightened but when they were making some kind of comment. . . . She resisted thinking that they were telling her something, but perhaps they were telling themselves something. She hadn't yet figured out (or perhaps let herself figure out) if different notes meant different things.

In this case she looked up and saw the Master coming toward her.

She stared at him blankly for a moment, believing he must be a mirage of her thoughts; perhaps her bees' next trick was creating three-dimensional pictures. She blinked, but he remained the

Master and did not dissolve into nothingness, or into a cloud of bees. She did not think even her bees could create the blackness of him.

She jerked to her feet, for you cannot remain seated in the presence of a standing Master, even in your own front garden, and even when he arrives unexpectedly. She didn't think the Master was supposed to come to the Chalice; he was supposed to call her to come to him. But then she should be living in the House with him, where a message sent and answered involved no more than a few corridors and a flight of stairs or two.

She looked behind for the cart and driver which must have brought him, for she knew he could not walk so far, and saw a face she knew: old grey Ponty, who might have retired years ago, except he went on being sound and healthy and happy to see his tack appear—and as steady a pony as had ever carried a rider. He gave dogcart rides on feast-days to children who were fascinated by a smaller, quicker, more graceful version of the big farm horses most of them knew best. He looked fat and sleek and untroubled as he browsed the edge of her little clearing for savoury grasses. As she looked at him he raised his head and took a step forward into the sunlight as if appreciating the warmth, or as if to say to her: "All is well." She couldn't see his eyes through his thick forelock, but his ears, themselves barely visible, were pointed straight at her.

"Ponty," she said stupidly.

"Most horses prefer to avoid me," said the Master. "Ponty came straight up to me and asked for apples, which I have been careful to provide since then. He is also the image of his mother, who taught me to ride."

A memory she had no idea she had rose in her mind's eye: she was a very little girl going to the House with her mother—possibly for the first time, which was why it came to her so clearly. Her mother was carrying the pack Mirasol still used for transporting honey; when it was full of jars, you walked slowly enough for even quite a little girl to keep up with you, if she was a good walker, and Mirasol was, because her father often took her with him when he tended his trees. As they reached the drive from the forest track two older boys on horseback came trotting round the far side of the House and turned toward them.

Mirasol and her mother had already turned toward the back of the House but Mirasol had wanted to stop and watch; she liked horses, and knew the names of the work-horses and occasional riding pony whom she saw when she was out with her father. These two were from the House stables, and the one in the lead was very beautiful, although it threw its forelegs out in a nervous way. The boy on it suddenly gave it its head, and it shot forward, the boy easy and graceful in the saddle. It galloped past them, and Mirasol noticed that the boy was beautiful too. They made a splendid picture; but there was something in the way he ignored them that, young as she was, she did not like. It was not arrogance, but a kind of deliberate performance: he knew the effect they made and gloried in it. She turned her attention to the other boy. He was younger, and the horse he rode was only a pony. He followed the first boy, but remained trotting, and as he passed them he smiled and nodded, neatly but unshowily balancing the gesture against the motion of the trotting horse. He was ordinary-looking but he also looked—nice, Mirasol thought, a little wistfully; she missed having other children to play with. He was older than she, and he was from the House, but for a moment she had felt they might have been friends.

Her mother had stopped and was staring after the two boys. "That's the Master's two sons in a nutshell," she murmured.

"Mama?" said Mirasol, but Mirasol's mother shook her head and went on toward the House.

It was that ordinary boy who stood before her now. Half in the old memory and half in the shock of the moment she stumbled into speech: "You—you might have sent for me—or—or—Someone—anyone—would have been honoured to have been asked to bring you—anywhere—"

"Honoured?" he said. The sunlight fell upon his black cloak and disappeared in its folds. A small breeze stirred, although the cloak moved oddly in response, and as the fabric brushed against the body it concealed she was again reminded of her sense that even the shape of his body was no longer quite human.

There was a brief silence, and she realised, too late again, that this was not how a Chalice, or anyone else, greeted a Master. Was it herself, her own worries and preoccupations—her own inability to fit into the skin of the role she now played—that kept making her behave so, or was it the strangeness of him? Or was it the unexpected memory of him as a boy she would have liked to have had as a friend?

Breathlessly she said, "*I* am honoured by your presence here. You are most welcome. . . ."

He'd come halfway across the meadow and had stopped, waiting, as it seemed, gravely.

"Welcome," she said again, still feeling dizzy and confused, but realising she meant it. He *was* welcome. "May I offer you—" She stopped. She had no idea what a Chalice was supposed to offer a Master who visited her at her home. There must be a tradition, a right thing, even perhaps a rule. But it was not an eventuality it had occurred to her she needed to prepare for. And perhaps there was no rule after all, because the Chalice should have lived at the House, at the House with the Master.

"Honey," he said. "Will you offer me honey?"

"Of course," she said, still wit-scattered. "Anything—anything I can offer you."

"Honey, please," he said politely, as if he were anyone—as if he were one of her customers.

She looked at him bemusedly. Which honey? Not the sleepy. The energetic? One of the ache-soothers? Which one? One of the ones she hadn't figured out yet (maybe they were just to make dull bread or porridge taste wonderful)?

"Of course," she said, and went indoors, as much to hide her confusion from him—but what did he see with his uncanny eyes?—as to fetch the honey. She went to the shelf where she kept the jars in use, and put her hand out blindly, choosing by not choosing: and so her hand reached itself, and took down a jar.

It was one of the mysterious ones: she knew neither what it was for nor what it was made of. It was an early-summer honey, and she could taste the yellow singers and the wild cherry, but there was something else in it as well. Perhaps it's a confusion-tamer, she thought, and the choice is really for me.

She took two spoons, which is what she would normally do for a friend—or had done when she had had friends. But it was only as she picked up the second spoon that it occurred to her that this honey was also her secret favourite, and that she liked not knowing what was in it, and had silly fantasies about what it might be for, besides making dull bread or porridge taste wonderful. Would a Master eat honey straight out of the jar? She dithered a moment longer, and then made up a tray, with a half loaf of bread and a knife, and two cups, and a pitcher of water drawn that morning from the cottage well—whose water now had the faintest sweet taste, as if a little honey were leaking into its source.

He was sitting in one of the stone chairs when she came back outside again. She had noticed before that he rarely stood for long; she wondered if the Hardbutt family furniture was to him any improvement on standing, but he looked, she thought, almost relaxed. More relaxed, anyway, than he had ever been during all the gatherings she had stood Chalice to.

She paused in her doorway to look at him a moment longer. Even when there was not the slightest breeze the hem of his cloak stirred faintly, as if in response to some intangible air. Or flame. As she watched he raised his hands and put his hood back, tipping his face up to the sun and closing his disturbing red eyes. She'd never seen him bare-headed before and in the strong sunlight she had confirmed what she had suspected since the first time she saw him at the front door of the House, when she had given him the cup of welcome: there was a peculiar, somehow indefinite quality to his features that was not only to do with blackness seen in shadow. The lines of his face seemed strangely mutable, as if they flickered, almost like flames.

But she also saw that he had hair: black and straight, pulled back from his face, and tied at the nape of his neck with something she could not see, lost in the folds of the hood. The boy who had smiled at her and her mother as he trotted past on his pony had had curly brown hair. But many straight-haired people had curly hair as children.

She had to kneel to move some books out of the way before she set the tray down on the wide low stone that served as an outdoor table. He opened his eyes again and looked at her. She risked looking at him for longer than a glance. She could not discern pupil from iris—if perhaps a third-level priest of Fire still has ordinary irises and pupils—which were as lightlessly black as his skin. What should have been the whites of his eyes were red—red as fire—red as the embers that will set flaming anything that touches them. Reddened eyes in ordinary humans look sore and sick; his looked uncanny and fathomlessly deep. What might he see with such eyes?

As she had done the morning he healed her hand, she heard herself asking a question she had no intention of saying out loud: "Do you see differently?"

"With my red eyes?" he said, equably enough, and blinked. His eyelids stayed closed a fraction longer than a usual blink, and when they opened again that sense of burning embers was even stronger, in a face that seemed itself to flicker slightly, like a hot fire burnt low. "I'm not sure. It's a gradual process, being taken by Fire. I still see the leaves of the trees as green, and a cloudless sky as blue. But I see heat, in a way I remember I did not, when I . . . before I entered Fire."

"You see heat," she said, not understanding.

"You are warmer than the surrounding air," he said. "I see—or read—that. I read Ponty as a warm space too. A warm solid space—a Ponty-shaped space. His heat outlines him, and inside . . . within that outline there is movement, swirls, billows, like a stream in wild country over a rough rocky bed . . . the movement of his life force. It moves clearly and strongly in him, like clear water. It is rarely so strong or so clear in humans. There is a rabbit in the brush over there; I see the curled and curling shape of its warmth, its body, behind the leaves, which screen it, I think, from your sight." He looked around. "You can probably pick out the singing birds in your trees by tracing the sound; I can see the silent ones. I can see the ones invisible on their nests, and I can see how many eggs they sit on, for this late brooding. I can see where there is no life inside a shell, that it will not hatch."

"And the bees?" she said, fascinated.

"Yes. The bees are tiny golden sparks, as of fire."

"Of honey."

"Yes. Of honey. The hives glitter with the movement of the bees."

"I wish I could see them like that," she said wistfully. "It must be very beautiful."

He made no answer and—again as she had done that morning before he had first asked her to stand by him—she suddenly recalled to whom she spoke, and looked at him quickly, her mouth already open to apologise. But he was looking at her with what seemed to her was surprise. Her mouth stayed open, but no words came out.

"It is very beautiful," he said.

She looked down, at her tray, at the little lopsided jar of glittering honey.

"I don't know much—I don't know as much as I should—about Chalices," he said. "Isn't their usual susceptibility to water?"

"Or wine," she said. "Occasionally beer or cider or perry. Perhaps once every other century a woman who is pregnant or nursing when the Chalice comes to her finds that she holds her Chalice in milk, but that is not considered lucky for the demesne. Occasionally in a demesne near the sea it has been brine. I've read about the finding and naming of many Chalices now and I've not read of another one whose gift was honey. Never honey. I suppose that's one of the reasons that it never occurred to me what was happening, in the beginning, after . . ." She knew she was talking too much, but it seemed to pour out of her, like honey from a jar: it wasn't only the overwhelmingness of her life that made it lonely; it was that she had no one to share with how enormously interesting it also was. "And the coming is not usually so . . . melodramatic. That will have been the unsettled state of the demesne, I know, but. . . . You do get things like wells overflowing, but it was mead and honey everywhere here, and my goats were fountaining milk, and usually it's not quite so . . . You know the Lady of the Ladywell was our first Chalice—that was her house well originally—her well overflowed, but all that happened, according to the records, is that it was the herald of a drought ending, and so very welcome.

"This demesne has usually had water Chalices—maybe because of the willows. The last Chalice, the one who—who

94

died"—she glanced up at him briefly and away again—"she was a water Chalice. I think that may be part of why . . . and part of why I . . ." She had babbled on too much already, but she did not want to stop there. "There's a very old story about a blood Chalice. She must have had a horrible time. But she brought her demesne through a series of wars that destroyed the demesnes around her, according to the story, so maybe it was worth it to her. I've never found any record of her, though, only the story. In the story her demesne is called Springleaf-turn, and there isn't one."

"'Part of why,'" he said. "Part of why she and my brother died?"

"I don't know," she said. "I should not have mentioned it."

"You have the right to know how your predecessor died."

"I have the *right* to have been apprenticed to the Chalice I was to succeed! I have the *right* to have known I was her heir! You have the *right* to have lived here and supported your brother as Master and learnt what you needed to know as his acknowledged Heir! Our land has the *right* to be cared for by a Master and a Chalice who know what they're doing and—and are able to do it!"

"And Willowlands is in trouble because these rights were not honoured."

"Yes," she said wearily. "Yes." She did not say, And it is why two—lame, faulty, unfit, what do you call a priest of Fire exiled from his Fire? What do you call a small woodskeeper suddenly ordered to be great?—unsuitable, unready people were made Chalice and Master, and why they cannot make a damaged land whole. It is all wrong; and the frame, the pattern, the yoke that holds us all, is not yet broken, but it is breaking.

"Tell me why you said what you did. That being a water Chalice was part of why they died."

She was silent a moment. At last she said, "They died of fire and wine. I—I guess—and it is only a guess—she might have shaped the way better if she had had more strength for wine. Willowlands has always been very—" She tried to think of an adjective that would fit. The only ones that came to her were "pure" or "clean" or "clear" or "simple" and she could not say any of them to the brother of the man who had made it not so. There were other demesnes whose strength was not in clarity or purity, but she did not know how to make her own another of them, even to heal it. She thought, If the land chose me, then it cannot want to go that way. The only thing I have to offer is simplicity—dumb, harassed simplicity.

"He was holding one of his—parties—I guess. Yes, he had begun them before he sent me away; indeed it was because of them that he did send me away, because I could, or would, not keep silence about them. No, no one has told me this, but it was the old pavilion that burnt, and it was there I know he held his first assemblies, because it suited his purposes. How can a Master and his Chalice be so insensible as to be overcome by fire, in their own demesne, unless they are drunk—or drugged?"

Quickly she said, "At least we did not lose the House."

"The House would not have borne such usage as his carouses were," he responded just as quickly. "He had to hold them elsewhere. I am sorry the pavilion was not stronger."

"But——" she said. "The——the old magic, before the demesnes were made, the old magic still lives close under the earth there. You know this—you must have felt it too. The pavilion was power to use, for good or ill, without rule."

Another silence, while he looked at his hands. "I apologise for the violence of my words. I did not—do not—hate my brother. The bitterness I feel is the bitterness of my own frustration—my own lack of power to pull our land together again. Or rather, the power is still there, but it has been turned to, or into, Fire, and I cannot turn it back, however I try." Savagely he clapped his hands together, and when he opened them, a pillar of fire roared up from between them—he closed them again and the fire disappeared. "That is only a trick to frighten children, here. Here I cannot be sure, if I reach out to grasp a goblet, that I won't miss, and grab the air, or burn the hand of her who holds it out to me. It is the same when I reach for the earthlines. I miss, or do harm."

"You healed the burnt hand of the woman who held the goblet for you. It is not all tricks to frighten children," she said, hoping he had not seen that she had been frightened just now. "I hear the earthlines too—I not only must, as Chalice, but by being Chalice I cannot help it—and I have felt no harm done lately."

He raised his eyes and looked at her. "Would you? Would you feel it? Could you say to yourself, 'Yes, here is a break—a roughness, a troubling—that was not here a sennight ago'?"

She returned his look and refused to look away. "I don't know. That is what you are pressing me to say, is it not? I don't know because I don't know what the earthlines should feel like, should sound like—what they would feel like if the land were settled and content—whether their constant plaintive murmur would at last fall silent. *I don't know.* It is only one of a thousand thousand things I don't know. But I know the land lies quieter now than it did a year ago—than it did six months ago. I know the earthlines lie softer than they did."

He shifted his gaze away from her, as if looking through the woods to the House and then beyond, across the long leagues of the entire demesne. She sat staring at him, and was so far away in her thoughts that when he looked back at her she did not move her eyes quickly enough.

"What do you see?" he said.

"I remember seeing you once when you were a boy," she replied, not adding that she was trying to find that boy in his face now, and failing. "You trotted past my mother and me, and nodded and smiled at us. It could have been Ponty's dam you were riding; I always noticed horses when I was a child, and Ponty looks much the same as that pony did. Your brother had cantered on ahead."

An expression crossed his face so fleetingly that had she not been staring at him she would have missed it: it was the expression of the little brother whose older brother had just cantered on ahead of him—again. For that tiny, fleeting moment not only did he look fully human, but she saw the boy he had once been, and knew it was the same boy she had seen that day with her mother.

"Yes, he would have cantered on ahead. He was an excellent rider from the first time he sat alone on a pony; but any horse he rode immediately wanted to gallop. He had a similar effect on everyone. Except perhaps me. He overwhelmed his Chalice."

It was not a question. She could think of nothing better to tell him than what she guessed was the truth. As Chalice, her guess came from sources no one else had, although her conclusions were no different from what everyone knew, whether they spoke it aloud or not—which they did not. She stood to all the important meetings of the House and the Circle. Neither they nor their new Master spoke in the terms he and she spoke in now. "He—chose—her to be flexible. To be responsive. The old Chalice was old before he became Master, and your father was a man who—who deeply believed in tradition."

"Narrow-minded and intolerant," he said. "The trouble did not begin with my brother."

"I guess," she said slowly, "that the land did feel some—imprisonment, under your father. And your brother wished to open the prison door. He knew his—his own mind soon enough that he was able to—to will the land to choose a—a supple young girl when the Chalice wished to take an apprentice. A girl who would grow into a Chalice who would help him unlock the door."

"My brother wished to run wild with no hindrance from anyone or anything."

"He helped create a Chalice who would accept his lead."

"Who would provide no obstacle to his self-indulgences."

She was silent. She would have liked to disagree, to honour the memories of the Master and the Chalice they had received their sovereignties from, but . . . Master and Chalice were always grievously hard burdens to bear. What she and her Master had been given wasn't even the onus of building bricks without straw; the bricks had existed and been shattered. You can't make bricks out of broken bricks.

"By wine and fire," he said slowly. "Therefore the land would have a Chalice neither of water nor of wine. And it drew me back from a place farther into Fire than anyone has returned from."

"I am not strong enough," she said. She had never said this aloud to anyone before—anyone but her bees. "I know too little, and I do not learn fast enough. And there are not enough hours in the day." And the land has been bent away from true too far and for too long.

"I do not believe that," he said. "At least—it would not be if you had a Master you could rely on, who could sustain you as a Master should."

"I do not believe *that*," she said firmly. "I—"

"No," he said. "Let us not have another exchange of compliments. You have chosen to support me, and I tell you that I support you. I do hear our land about some things, and I feel it respond to you—it responds as a frightened horse does to the rein in a kind hand, when the brute that hurt it has gone. It is skittish and uneasy yet, but it listens to you. It is listening hopefully. There is good heart in our land; it will return to us if it can.

"So I suggest there be a pact between us—that we accept that we are Master and Chalice here—and that we are each other's Master and Chalice. Will you assent to this?"

While they were talking the bees had, as usual, come to see who Mirasol's visitor was. But a more than usual number of them had settled on him, and had not flown away again. This was not their usual behaviour, but she was too disturbed and confused by the conversation to have paid proper attention; nor had she noticed that their humming note had changed. "Oh—I did not think," she said. "The bees—they probably do not like the smell of fire on you."

He made a sudden movement—exactly the sort of sudden movement you should not make when surrounded by half-agitated bees. His hand had gone to his forearm, bare above the wrist, and she realised one had stung him—stung the *Master*. Several thoughts flew frantically into her mind simultaneously: this was why a Chalice was never of honey; but no Master had ever smelt of fire as this one did; what law was there about a Chalice who caused injury to her Master? "Don't—don't—"

But he hadn't tried to crush the bee that stung him. He was holding her, very gently, against his forearm, with the tip of one finger. "There, little one, that's not necessary. Don't wriggle so, you'll do yourself fatal harm. Your sting is barbed, you know, you have to tease it out slowly. . . ." He raised his finger, and one rather tired and dazed bee flew away. None of the others had stung him, and after a few seconds they all too began to fly away, in little groups of twos and threes; and their hum had steadied and deepened again to its usual note.

"You know something of bees," she said.

He looked at her, and something more like a human smile than the last time she had seen the corners of his mouth curl upwards changed his face. It seemed to quiet the flicker, as if the hum of the bees had a calming effect on this too. "A bee sting is very like fire, is it not?"

She smiled too, hesitantly. "I suppose it is. Are you—"

"Hurt? Harmed?" he said. "No. It is very difficult to burn a priest of Fire, although it can be done."

She said, "I am glad that when you were sent away you went to Fire." Again she had spoken unthinkingly, in the carelessness of relief, but he replied readily:

"A bee could not sting a third-level priest of Earth any more than she could sting a thirty-year-old oak. A bee could not sting a third-level priest of Air any more than she could sting a sunbeam."

Think before you speak, she said to herself fiercely, but aloud she said immediately, "A thirty-year-old oak cannot be transplanted and live; and what happens to the light when a cloud passes in front of the sun? I am still glad, if you had to be sent away, you went to Fire. You walk on the earth and you cast a shadow; you speak in ordinary words and—and you can be stung by a bee. You are more human than you fear."

She could see him considering how to refute her words; but the silence stretched to a minute and at last he said only, "Thank you."

"Honey—" she began again.

"Yes. You were going to give me some honey."

That was not what she had been about to say, and she was bewildered for a moment. Then she recalled herself, and gestured at the tray. "I didn't know how you would like it."

"What would you recommend?"

She opened her mouth, closed it again. Opened it again, said resolutely, "Straight out of the jar." She handed him a spoon, and the jar.

"There are two spoons."

"I will have some too, if you permit."

And he laughed. It was a creaky, crackly noise, and if she had not been already much accustomed to the strangeness of him, she might not have realised that was what she was hearing; it sounded rather like the noises a fire makes burning sappy wood. But she did realise, and she smiled. "You are Master," she said.

"And you are Chalice, and the first, so far as we know, Chalice of honey, and it is your honey. I am honoured to taste it, and will it not . . . will it not make the bond necessary between us stronger to eat a little of your honey together?"

Involuntarily she glanced at the back of her right hand, where, sometimes, when the light was just right or just wrong, there was a faint scar visible. "It is not fitting nor desirable that the bond began with hurt," she said. "But it did begin then, when your hand slipped on the cup of welcome."

"It is a strange Mastership and a strange Chalicehood," he replied. "The last Master and Chalice died ill, and without Heir or apprentice. We are making new ways because we must. We have had one burning between us. Let us have the sweetness now."

Two, she thought. Two burns and two sweets. For it was a strange sweetness when you healed my hand; and one of my bees burnt you. Do you fear to overwhelm me? You shall not. And the land chose me without your will—while you still lay in Fire. Yes. Perhaps what we do *is* possible.

Possibly I am strong enough.

She realised she was smiling, and looked at him again, and when he smiled back, this time, it was unmistakably a smile, not merely the remains of an old human reflex not quite abolished by Fire. "Does honey always make one smile?" he asked, as if it were a serious question.

"Yes," she said firmly. "Yes, it does. With your permission, Master, I will give you some to take back to the House with you. Do not let Ponty know you carry it!"

The night the Onora Grove burned she had been sleeping fitfully, for there was a ferocious storm tearing at the landscape, and the earthlines were uneasy. When the lightning struck not far from her cottage, she was out of bed and dragging on her clothes before she had thought of anything she might do. Even after it had occurred to her that she needed to have thought of something to do—and could still think of nothing—she went anyway, snatching up the smallest and plainest of the Chalice cups off the shelf as she passed, one that had no specific meaning or duty, and stuffing it down one pocket in her cloak; a small jar of honey went into the pocket on the other side.

When she opened her door and stepped out the rain felt strangely warm against her face, but the wind buffeted her like a blow from a fist and she stumbled, holding on to her door-handle for balance. She scuttled down the path from her door, leaning against the blustering gusts. The wind was behind her as she turned onto the main path, which was wide and smooth enough for wagons, so she ran, clutching her skirt and the ends of her cloak against the force of the gale. The rain drove against her, through the cloak, through her clothing, to her skin. The sky was turning red as she sprinted toward the grove, and through the roar of the wind she began to hear the hissing of the rain-lashed fire. The wind slewed around and the fog billowed out to meet her; her lungs hurt from smoke as well as running.

She almost hurtled into the Master; in his black cloak he looked like more smoke and fog. She had not come far, but her legs were trembling with effort, and with fear. The Master was standing, apparently merely watching the fire; but he turned to her at once and said, "Good, you're here," as if he had been waiting for her— expecting her. "Can you bring me water from the stream?"

It should have been hard to hear him through the sound of wind, rain and fire, but it was not; and his voice sounded calm and strong. Bewilderedly she turned around, realised where she was, and went to the stream. It flickered a macabre, almost phosphorescent red; it did not look like water. Nor could she hear its usual cheerful murmur as it tumbled in its bed. She dipped a cupful up and returned to the Master.

"You have brought honey too?"

Wordlessly, she pulled out her jar. It was the calming honey, and she saw it, as she tugged the stopper out, as the tiny frail thing it was, absurdly so, to set against a forest fire. The flames were now leaping taller than the trees, seeming to erupt out of the strangling smoke, and the increasing heat, as close as they were, was no longer only heat but pressure, squeezing her like a giant's hand. But she felt as if she were already on fire: the flick of her hair against her neck must be leaving welts; the brushing of her own fingers against her skin burned; she expected to see flames licking up the sides of her heavy, sweltering, rain-sodden cloak. But honey was the thing she could do, to mend a rent in the landscape, to put out a fire. And here she had a Fire-priest with her. This time it was not all up to her.

After a moment's hesitation, as she had not remembered to bring a spoon, she scooped up a little honey on one finger—it felt pleasantly cool—and stirred the finger through the water in the cup. Still wordlessly she held it out to him.

"Can you come any closer to the fire?" he said. "I can protect you, I think."

It was a little like that day he had first said "stand by me," the day he had healed her hand, when she had had to pull the bandage off quickly and hold her hand out toward him quickly, before she lost her nerve. Rain, wind and red fire-heat beat and tore at her; the last thing she wanted to do was go nearer the heart of the maelstrom. She knew that lightning fire was hot enough to burn, even through rain, but it felt all wrong—it felt like the end of the world. Was this what Elemental Fire was like—the end of the world?

She turned away from him and stumbled in the direction where the heat and redness were the most savage, with her wet and steaming hood pulled as far down as it would go over her face as protection against sparks, and her hands tucked under her cloak— one holding the cup and one covering the open top. She did not dare fall, and she could not see her way; her feet felt for each step blindly, and her heartbeat in her ears was almost louder than the fire. She had to open her mouth to breathe, but the smoke scorched her lungs, and her mouth felt as hot as if she were swallowing fire.

The Master walked behind her. She could not sense him doing anything, but when he said "this is far enough" and they halted, the fire was raging all around them, and either the rain had stopped or it was evaporating before it had a chance to fall. Her cloak and hood were dry, and despite the intense, aggressive heat she shivered as if she stood in a blizzard of snow, not fire. Everything around her was fire-red: the air, the earth, the sky, the poor burning trees—the Master himself was red, his black cloak as red as his red eyes.

No way out, she thought. The fire's come round behind us, and there's no way out.

Again she held the cup out to him, but she needed to hold it, small as it was, with both hands, because her hands were shaking so. He held his hands over it for a moment and then said, "No. You will have to pour the water into my hands. I'm sorry—there may be a bit of a—sudden reaction. I believe I need the Chalice's hands to do the pouring, but you will want to step back quickly, I think."

She thought she might be weeping, in terror or despair, but

her tears too evaporated before they touched her face. The heat was indescribable—unbearable—and in that moment she knew that the Master was doing something, or she would already be dead. She took a deep breath—slowly, because of the heat; still it felt as if her lungs were boiling in her breast—and poured: steadily, not too fast, not just slopping it into his cupped hands, trying to let the weight of the cup stop her own hands from trembling. She remembered having done this with the cup of welcome; but this one was too small. In the smoke and the shadows and the glaring red light she could not see if the water was pouring or not . . . perhaps it was only steam erupting out of the mouth of the cup . . . and then she stepped back, as quickly as she could without, she hoped, leaping like a rabbit. In any Chalice work you had to do it gravely and unfalteringly or it didn't incorporate properly—like not letting the sponge work if you were trying to make bread—I wish I were at home now, with the dough rising and a nice little fire to heat the oven—those are all I know, the ordinary, commonplace things, those are what this Chalice works in; I was not made for this—oh, I can't breathe— my face is burning—my hands—

This is still a rite like any other, she told herself, even if it isn't in any of my books, even if I don't know what it is, even if it is in the middle of a holocaust. I am still Chalice; I bear the cup; I bind and I—I calm—and I witness.

She was half prepared for the pillar of fire that shot up from his hands as it had done that day at her cottage, although this was much more frightening, a red-gold, dazzling-bright column as big around as a man, roaring even louder than the fire. And smelling faintly, mysteriously, of honey. And of . . . *wet*. The backwash of heat that slapped her face was damp.

And the fire went out. The column that had leaped up from the Master's hands simply rose up and disappeared, like a falcon from the fist of the falconer; when it had gone, the fire in the grove was gone too.

Nor was there any wind, and the rain fell gently, softly, with a quiet susurration; it was now little more than a mist, a drizzle. Even the lingering smoke seemed benevolent, and barely stung her eyes and throat. In her astonishment, and in the sudden release of fear, she staggered, and fell to her knees; the earth she fell on was cool and moist. Hastily she scrambled to her feet again; the Master was looking in the other direction, and had not seen.

In the near silence she heard a shout, and then another. Of course: many other people would have seen the red sky and smelt the smoke, and they would be coming, with their buckets and spades, to see what they could do. It was only a few years ago that Mirasol had been one of the members of the water-chains when Cag's barn had caught fire from another lightning strike; she remembered the weary, terrifying boredom of passing the buckets hand to hand to hand with the fire towering over them—but they had saved the barn.

She guessed what the Master would do, so when he slipped away among the trees she followed him closely, that he might not lose her. It was difficult because she was exhausted by what had just passed, and her feet refused to obey her. Her head swam, and she had to keep stopping and putting her hand on a cool wet tree, till the dizziness passed. She would not have been able to keep up with him if he had been an ordinary human, even an exhausted ordinary human, walking at an ordinary human speed. But he did not—could not—move quickly, so following was a matter of recognising which set of oddly shifting shadows was him. This was strangely difficult to do, partly, she thought, because he still did not walk as most folk walked. His gait was half a shamble, half a kind of rolling lurch, not unlike that of an old sailor, permanently home from the sea; even landlocked Willowlands had a few of these.

She was not surprised when they arrived at a small clearing and Ponty was waiting for them. He appeared entirely unperturbed by the fire; he had been dozing, and calmly raised and turned his head to watch them approach.

She did not ask her Master why he had left before any of his people saw him; she knew why. His people—his own people—would not like it that their Master, who was still too visibly a priest of Fire, was the first person there when lightning set fire to a wood. This did not—could not—trouble her as it might trouble them, but for her own reasons she had to ask, "How did you know? How did you know the storm would come, and lightning strike, and strike here?" She did not add, And Ponty is no racehorse.

Ponty was wearing a rope halter, but when the Master had lifted the loop from the tree-stump it was tied round and gave it a tug, the headstall fell apart. If the Master had been wrong about his ability to stop the fire's advance, Ponty would have been free to flee as soon as he tried. She wondered if a Fire-priest also had

110

a charm to enable a slow, elderly pony to outrun a forest fire. Would the folk with the spades have dug a fire-break in time to save the Chalice's cottage and her bees?

"I didn't know," he said. "If I had guessed wrong I might not have been here—somewhere—in time. But lightning is often mischievous, and I did hear this storm coming toward us and the lightning"—he hesitated—"bragging. I knew it would strike somewhere in Willowlands, and—we are not so far from the ruin of the old pavilion here, you know. I thought it might be drawn here."

"The pavilion did not burn by lightning," she said.

He hesitated again. "It holds the memory of fire," he said at last. "Lighting is young and strong and thoughtless, but it could also wish to visit the site of some particular victory of one of its kind—as a young soldier recently commissioned might visit the scene of some great battle—and leave some token in memory of the members of his regiment who fought and died there." With a hand on Ponty's withers he moved the pony into position beside the tree-stump, clambered awkwardly up the stump and then eased himself onto the pony's bare back. For another of those unexpected moments, as he settled himself, he looked fully human: someone accustomed to riding, and fond of his mount. The angle of Ponty's ears, as they tipped back toward him, said that he found his strange rider agreeable. "May Ponty and I save you a walk home?" said the Master, as near to light-hearted as she'd ever heard him. "I—er—I don't weigh as much as you think. Fire doesn't, you know," and he wasn't light-hearted any more. "Ponty would find you no burden."

"I—oh," she said. Her first impulse was to refuse, but then she thought, I'm tired, and—why not? Ponty was built as if from oak; he wouldn't mind a second rider even if the Master did weigh as much as a human man. "Thank you." Nonetheless she slid gingerly behind the Master, trying to keep a little distance from him, difficult without a saddle. Her exhaustion overcame her and when Ponty stopped outside her cottage door and she groggily dragged herself awake again she found herself snuggled comfortably against the Master's back. The rain had stopped, but she was cold from weariness; the unusual warmth of her riding companion was very pleasant, although her cheek felt chafed from the peculiar fabric of the Master's cloak, and possibly from the heat beneath it. It was a bit like being pillowed against a frying pan.

When she took a deep breath her throat and lungs felt as they always felt. Even her eyes were no longer sore. And there was a faint, lingering dream-sense like the memory of the ecstatic sweetness of the Master's healing of her hand.

It took her a moment to get herself down—long enough for Ponty to turn his head to watch, which made her laugh. "Good night," she said. "Good night and—thank you."

"I am sorry for tonight," he said. "I was clumsy. It should not have been necessary to frighten you."

"I should not have been frightened," she said. "You had said you would protect me."

"It is to be an exchange of compliments between us again, I see," he replied. "Therefore I will say that your courage astonished me."

"Courage," she said. "I was too frightened to run away. If there was any safety, it was to stay with you."

"It was your presence as much as the water and honey from the Chalice cup that enabled me to do what I did."

"You put out the fire."

"You came. Alone with a pot of honey."

"I am Chalice," she said simply. "You came too. You are Master. What else could we do? Thank you for the ride home."

"My pleasure," he replied, after a pause, and she wondered if he was talking about the fire, or the ride, or the conversation. He added, "I will see you tomorrow at noon, for the clearing of the well."

"Oh—the Journey Well. Yes. Yes. . . ."

He nodded, once, his red eyes eerie gleams in the darkness above her head, and Ponty took a step away.

"Won't they"—she hesitated, not sure how to ask what she wanted without saying bluntly "if they knew you were at the fire they might think you set it"—"won't they miss you? Have missed you?"

"I go out often at night," he said. "With Ponty. It is—it should be no worse that I was out the night of the fire than any other night."

part
THREE

Two days after the fire the Overlord's agent came to the House, and another man with him. She already knew she did not like the agent, Deager, and she disliked the new man immediately, although at first she could not be sure she disliked him for any reason other than the company he kept.

He gave her reason soon enough, however, in the proprietorial air with which he looked round. He was introduced to her with a tremendous flourish, although no reason was given for his presence; which, with the air and the flourish, was explanation enough, and her heart plummeted. By the time the Grand Seneschal informed her, stiffly, that this was the Overlord's choice for the next Master's Heir, she didn't need to be told, and in her anger and frustration she said, "That is *hasty*," before she remembered to whom she spoke, and she bit her lip, waiting for the rebuke. But none came. She was so surprised she looked into his face. He scowled at her at once, the familiar contemptuous, disapproving scowl, but when she ducked her head and then glanced back again a moment later, his face had relaxed into what looked a lot like sadness.

The new man's name was Horuld. She paid little attention to his breeding, that several of his forebears' lines ran directly from Willowlands, and several more had crossed in the ensuing generations, and which Deager was very eager to tell out, over and over and over, even to such unworthies as the demesne's shabby and erratic new Chalice, who was herself one of the indications (Deager didn't say this but he didn't have to) that the demesne was still in trouble, over a year after she had taken her place in the Circle.

So far as she knew no Chalice had ever been deposed. But she had never seen any record of a Chalice chosen when there was no Master to hold the land steady while the Circle did its work either. It had very occasionally happened that an apprentice died with or before her Chalice; but then too there had always been an experienced Master. And there were stories of Chalices who had not been able to bear the work they were called on to do—even those who had had their proper apprenticeships—and broken under it. There were only a few of these stories, but one was too many, and there was more than one. She believed that one such Chalice was the Chalice she herself followed.

She was surprised—even more surprised than she had been at the Grand Seneschal missing a chance to reprimand her—when Horuld seemed disposed to talk to her. There were other, more prepossessing and conversationally skilful members of the Circle he could address himself to; demesne hierarchy declared that Chalice was Second of the Circle, but that had to be remembered only when there was work to be done. Her Circle recollected it only when they had to, as did the Overlord's agent—or they always had done previously. She was, as Chalice, compelled to be present for the agent's visit, and—as Chalice—she would serve whatever Master fate set over Willowlands. That was enough. Perhaps the training she hadn't had would have included how to hold superfluous discourse with people she would rather avoid. When she was standing Chalice or performing a ritual she did not have to chat; but Horuld's first visit was informal. In other circumstances this would have seemed friendly and considerate; as it was it seemed ominous and coercive.

Deager, having proved to his own satisfaction, if not all of his audience's, that Horuld's bloodlines were an excellent choice, wished to make it clear—he said—that the Overlord was merely anxious that an unambiguous Heir should be in place, after the recent disaster. If such an accident should happen again, the demesne might fall apart entirely. It had been without a Master for seven months; it could not survive this a second time.

She tried to tell herself that a declared Heir was a sensible precaution; their present Master was the end of his family. The previous Master should have declared an Heir when he sent his only brother to Fire. She wondered why the Overlord had not obliged him to do so; she had only been a small woodskeeper then, and small woodskeepers heard little about Overlords' decisions. The demesne gossip said merely that the Master was a young man, and hale, and he would produce Heirs—had probably produced a few already, the uneasy joke went. But they would be bastards, and prohibited. By the time the ordinary folk of the demesne had begun to realise that their young Master seemed to have no intention of marrying and producing a proper Heir, especially in combination with his increasingly alarming general behaviour, the fear of what this meant also meant that no one wanted to talk about it.

And then the worst had happened.

Perhaps she should try to believe that the Overlord was merely doing the responsible thing—the responsible thing he had failed to do before—but again she wondered. It was too soon to tie an Heir to the present Circle; Willowlands was still too precarious. However necessary an Heir was, forcing him upon them now would unbalance it further. Would the next thing be that she was obliged to take an apprentice? She had no energy for the binding that would entail. Leaving aside that she had nothing to teach one.

Perhaps it was only her dislike of both Deager and Horuld that made her feel the agent was making it clear that Horuld was being introduced to Willowlands as the Heir only after he had made something else even more clear, if not in so many words: that the Overlord would like to see Horuld taking up this inheritance soon. She was too quick to feel she needed to defend the Master, she told herself. But what she had taken from the agent's description of Horuld's bloodlines was that if he was the best that could be done for her poor demesne, the Overlord should be straining every muscle to support the present Master. Did the Overlord want to break Willowlands entirely? Surely not. The disruption would damage the Overlord's grip too . . . no. He would be counting on riding it out; might he, more, be betting on the huge increase of his own power the successful changeover would produce? She knew almost nothing of the politics among Overlords. Demesne folk did not travel to the crown city nor visit the court of the king; and as practising Chalice she was furthermore indissolubly tied to her land.

But whatever else she knew or thought of the Grand Seneschal, he would not have kept such a piece of news as a visit from the Heir from the rest of the Circle; and Deager glossed, or slithered, over the question of why Willowlands had not known who was coming with him, which made it plain that there had been no message that had gone awry.

She had mixed the cup she would offer to the company before she came. She had mixed it for the visit from the Overlord's agent, and that was all. That was how it was done; that was why it was important that a Chalice know in advance who would drink from her cup, and for what reasons. Last-minute changes were destabilising, which was why battlefield cups, which were perforce rare, were also notoriously volatile.

It should not have been a good omen, that a Master's Heir should be left out of the first cup he received from the Chalice. Perhaps the Overlord, or some other of his plotters, had decided that being left out was better than a Chalice throwing her weight against him, which a loyal Chalice might be suspected of doing upon the presentation of any outblood Heir. Chalices were parochial by definition; of all the Circle, only the Chalice could not set foot across her demesne's boundaries. Some of the oldest records called the Chalice *the Landtied*—and because of this literal overidentification, the Chalice's response to outbloodedness in any member of the Circle was considered crucial. This perhaps explained why Horuld was interested—indeed eager—to talk to her. Perhaps she could be disposed to include him kindly in her mixture for his next visit, after he had been careful to make a good first impression. She would not need to be disloyal. Any Master's Heir was an important part in the demesne structure; most accepted Heirs attended at least some Circle gatherings; and under the present circumstances the only possible Heir was an outblood. A Chalice must at least punctiliously include her Master's Heir in any cup he was present for; of course it would be better if she felt at least benign toward him, or even generous.

But she did not feel benign or generous. She listened, smooth-faced, when the agent pronounced some blather about how the surprise of presenting Horuld unannounced would create "clarity" in an awkward situation; that he would be more able to see where he would best fit into difficult circumstances if no one was trying to soften the truth. She knew that a properly schooled Chalice would have some matching blather to offer in return, but she was not a properly schooled Chalice, and it gave her a little meagre pleasure that her silence discomfited the agent, and by his discomfiture he exposed that he knew his action had been dishonourable.

Did she loathe Horuld because Deager was a toad? No. Sun-brightener was a toad, and his antics merely made her feel tired and sad. Or because the Chalice was repelled by outbloodedness? She looked at Horuld and every particle of her recoiled. No. She bore the Chalice, she was not engulfed by it.

Mirasol had arrived a little late at the House for the meeting with Deager. Just as she was leaving her cottage a young mother had burst into the meadow carrying a wildly weeping child. Mirasol knew them, Kenti and her daughter Tis; they were neighbours. Tis had pulled a kettle of boiling water over. Fortunately it had only been half full, but the child still had a badly burned arm; and the local herbswoman, Catu, was gone to a lying-in, Kenti did not know where. Mirasol hadn't spoken to Kenti or her husband Danel properly since she had become Chalice, in spite of the fact that Danel and she had grown up together; she had been jealous when he had been apprenticed to a ploughman, for the horses.

Kenti said breathlessly, "Can you do anything? Can you help?" Her eyes went to the back of Mirasol's right hand, which was holding the edges of her cloak together over the cup of congruence in her left hand, and then hastily rose to Mirasol's face. But she couldn't meet the Chalice's eyes the way she had many times met Mirasol's, and they dropped away again. Poor Tis was weeping in a miserable, exhausted way that was painful to hear.

Mirasol brought them into the cottage and took down a small pot of the honey especially good for burns and smeared it carefully over Tis' arm. The little girl cried out at the first touch but by the time Mirasol had finished she had fallen silent, and leant back against her mother's body staring at Mirasol with huge still-wet eyes. Even as Mirasol looked back at her the eyelids drooped, and Tis was asleep.

And then Kenti burst into tears. Mirasol led her to the big soft chair by the fireplace where Mirasol did much of her reading and let her collapse. "It was my own carelessness—I know what she's like—I let myself be distracted—it was only a *moment*—and then I heard her scream—and I knew Catu was away—I didn't know what to do—it was *awful*" and then she couldn't say anything for a while.

Mirasol made a tisane—a spoonful of her soothing honey with a spoonful of the calming herbs she'd had from Catu herself; in the early months of her Chalicehood she'd drunk it by the bucketful. When she brought a cup to Kenti, Kenti laid Tis tenderly down beside her on the chair, sticky arm uppermost, and took it. She breathed in the steam and gave a little half laugh: she recognised Catu's mixture.

"I've used honey for littler wounds—your mother taught me that when I wasn't much older than Tis—but this one was so dreadful. And then I remembered—I remembered your hand. I thought, if your—if the Chalice's honey can cure what a Fire-priest can do, then perhaps it can cure Tis' arm."

Mirasol said gently, "The Master cured my hand."

"He—?" said Kenti unbelievingly, and Mirasol saw the fear in her face, the same fear she saw in the Housemen's faces before they bent nearer their Master to slide the chair under him as he sat down; the fear she saw in the faces of most of the others of the Circle when their part in a rite brought them too close to him—the fear of him that made the Master leave the burnt grove before any of his people saw him there.

"Yes. He." She wanted to say, Tell Danel. Tell your mother. Tell all your friends. But she watched Kenti's face and knew that she would tell the story—if she believed it. Kenti's face said that she wanted to believe it—she wanted that hope, not only for herself, but for her demesne.

Kenti sat looking at her daughter for a long moment and then said wonderingly, "Look—the mark is already fading. Your mother's honey could not have done so much so quickly. It is the Chalice in you, I know, but perhaps—perhaps—perhaps it is also that we have a Fire-priest for Master. . . ." Her voice had sunk to a whisper.

Mirasol was still thinking about the hope in Kenti's face when she walked up to the House. She knew she was late, but it was only Deager, the agent, coming for a—snoop, she thought uncharitably. Overlords' agents were supposed to visit their Overlords' demesnes, but she didn't like the way Deager's nose twitched, the way his eyes darted around, as if he were hoping to smell something rotten, to see someone doing something illicit or disgraceful.

And then she arrived, and there was a surprising number of people churning around in the big hall behind the front doors, and a youngish, weaselly-faced man she had never seen before standing a little too close to Deager's elbow.

The situation was uncomfortable enough to begin with, when it was only Deager and Horuld, herself and the Grand Seneschal and the Seneschal's apprentice Bringad, and four of the minor Circle (the others were hastily sent for when Horuld was revealed as the Heir) plus the attendants the visitors brought and their own Housefolk. As the word spread about Horuld, more and more people streamed in, and both the noise and the tension level, it seemed to Mirasol, rose, and the ever-worried Bringad looked more worried than she had ever seen him. But when the Master arrived . . . she did not know how to understand it, explain it, even to herself. It was as if the level ground tipped a little in one direction and the high curving sky changed its arc just a little in some other direction.

A Master was not expected to greet a mere agent on his arrival; the Grand Seneschal did that. But as the representative of his Overlord, a Master would be churlish as well as foolish not to see him at some point during his visit. She assumed the Grand Seneschal had despatched a message to the Master about Deager's unexpected companion; it was impossible to read any trace of surprise or disquiet on the Master's shadowy black and strangely mutable face when he made his entrance. Mirasol heard with what was beginning to be a familiar sinking of the heart the conversation falter and then stop as he was noticed, before the head Houseman announced him. Perhaps all Masters are greeted with a respectful hush, but she doubted that most demesne folk drew together as if for protection when their Master appeared.

When Deager (his voice positively quavering as he addressed the Master) described Horuld as the Overlord's candidate for Heir, the Master merely bowed his head. There was a disagreeable pause, and then the agent rushed to begin telling Horuld's bloodlines over again, speaking too loudly and too quickly, and at first forgetting his flourishes. But when a Master has no son nor other suitable close relative, the meeting between the Master and the Master's newly declared Heir was as laboriously and ponderously formal as centuries of tradition could make it, including, in this case, the tradition that an unexpected situation should be treated even more formally than the same situation when everyone knew what was happening. The Grand Seneschal managed to insert an orotund phrase or two (rather like a pole through the spokes of a wheel, Mirasol thought) into the agent's barrage of genealogy, which had a steadying effect. When Deager finally fell silent, his concluding bow was as elaborate as if he were being presented to the king. But Mirasol found herself thinking that the Master had bowed his head so very ceremoniously indeed that perhaps he had somehow known of Horuld's coming before the message from the Grand Seneschal.

Most of the initial gestures among any group that required the presence of the Chalice were stylised, just as her offering of the cup was, but during Horuld's first visit to Willowlands they all seemed to move as if they were puppets in a puppet show, their limbs made of wood, the pulling of their strings performed by a puppeteer. If there had been an audience Mirasol felt they would not have found the performance convincing. Although Deager had insisted in a manner that was obviously meant to be magnificent but came over as merely presumptuous, that this first informal meeting with the Heir should proceed as it would have if Horuld had not been there, this was not possible, as Deager would have known it was not possible. Furthermore any meeting involving the Circle to which the Chalice stood should be precise about the number of people present, the number of people who would be offered the Chalice's cup—which Deager would also know.

And the Willowlands folk were doubtless awkward with surprise. They had known an Heir would be chosen, and Mirasol had held Chalice during the gathering when the Master had acceded to the Overlord's wish, as presented by Deager, that the Overlord do the choosing. But that had only been a few weeks ago, and they had heard nothing of the progress of the search. She had begun reading about the meeting of a Master with an unknown Heir, so she knew that if it had been a proper meeting she should offer her cup first to the Master and second to the Heir. After a moment's invisible dithering behind the face she tried hard to keep in an expressionless Chalice mask she did so anyway: let Deager assume this was a manifestation of magnanimity and support; she considered it buying time.

The contrast between the Master and an ordinary human had never been so marked, she thought, as between the Master and his Heir when she took the cup from one and offered it to the other. She had directed them to stand on either side of her—which would also have been the correct form for a planned first meeting between the two of them: she could see Deager smiling with satisfaction, but she ignored him. The Master seemed to tower over her, and his natural heat, as she stood close enough to him to hold a cup to his lips, wrapped itself around her as if claiming her—and briefly and disconcertingly she remembered riding home with him after the fire in the Onora Grove. Horuld, who was no more than average size, seemed puny and frail in comparison; and the fact that he was obviously struggling not to flinch away from the Master added to this impression of weakness.

She might have helped him, as she often helped the Circle members who were still reluctant to approach the Master, by stepping toward him, by allowing him to maintain a greater distance; but she did not. She offered the cup to the Master with a bent arm, and then turned and offered the cup to Horuld, again with a bent arm, and waited, forcing him to step close, not only to her, but to the Master. He did not try to take the cup from her, but he did raise a hand to grasp it, and she could feel him trembling. There were beads of sweat on his upper lip which she doubted were only from the heat. Before she took the cup on to Deager and the rest of the Circle, she bowed, to the Master, and then to Horuld. The Master must receive the deeper bow, of course, but the Heir might have had one nearly as deep; her bow to the Heir was only enough more than perfunctory not to be offensive. She let her gaze pass as if carelessly over Deager, and saw that he had stopped smiling.

She could feel, before she had got halfway round the Circle, that it was not a good binding. When she made her final bow it was almost difficult to stand upright again, and she was exhausted. She had to make a great effort to meet the eyes of Horuld and Deager; the Grand Seneschal's eyes looked glassy and unfocused, and the Master's were as unfathomable as they had been the first day, when his hand had slipped and burnt her, and his face was only blurred shadows. She tried to remember the sudden surprising joy of his healing of her hand, of talking to him about what he saw, about her bees being tiny golden sparks in his strange vision—of the night that she had helped him put out the fire in Onora Grove, and the ride home after. But she remembered these things as she might remember something out of a book, a story told of someone else.

Even if, by some extraordinary accident, the Chalice had not known beforehand all those who would drink, a well-mixed cup should have had a more positive effect than this. Perhaps she had mixed it injudiciously; that was likeliest. Even without his bringing an unannounced Heir, her dislike of Deager made it onerous for her to mix a cup that she would have to offer to him. But even if a more experienced Chalice might have done better, it was still true that introducing an Heir without proper advance warning was like throwing a boulder on one side of a delicate scales and expecting them still to balance.

But perhaps the lack of binding and balance in this gathering was because Horuld was *wrong* . . . wrong for the demesne, wrong as Heir, wrong even to be here. It had been known in the past that an outblood Heir was rejected by the demesne, however carefully the humans had tried to make the best choice. Perhaps the Overlord had overplayed his game by giving the Master and his Chalice no forewarning that the Overlord's choice was coming to be introduced to his hoped-for inheritance.

By the end of the day, when she could leave the House and make her way back to her cottage, she was shaking and sick. She pulled her hood over her head and held it bunched round her throat with her hands, feeling that what she really wanted to do was disappear: if she wrapped the ends of her cloak around her tightly enough and then tighter still, eventually there would be no one left inside. . . . Usually the gentle thumping of the empty Chalice cup against her hip was comforting: another ritual got through. Today it was not; she felt that she—they—Willowlands had indeed not got through the ritual of the introduction of the

Heir. She concentrated on the thought of sitting in the last of the daylight in the clearing by the cottage, listening to her bees.

She was still ten minutes' walk from the cottage when some of her bees came to meet her. She stretched out her arms to them and they landed on her hands and forearms, stroking her skin as if the tiny hairs were sepals they expected to secrete nectar for them. She shook her hood back, and several landed on her face and neck; out of the corners of her eyes she could see more landing on her shoulders. As she walked the last few minutes to the cottage she found herself thinking that her head felt strangely heavy, and that the hum of the bees was unusually loud; and then when she came out of the tree-shadowed path into the sunny clearing around the cottage she saw a great cloud of bees lifting away from her and dispersing, and she realised that she had been wearing a hood and cloak of bees. She watched them scatter about their proper bee business, and wondered.

Horuld came twice more in the next few weeks with Deager, and then a third time he came alone. When he came with Deager their visits were announced in advance; but now as the acknowledged Heir, he might come as he pleased—and stay as he pleased. She was in the House library when he came that third time, and the first warning she had was a shadow falling across the open door; she was deep into her research and would not have noticed, except that a half-familiar voice said, "Chalice," and her body had recoiled before her mind had recognised who it was.

She turned the recoil, she hoped, into a mere startle, and stood up at once to make a ceremonial sign of greeting, saying, "Forgive me, my mind was lost in what I was doing."

He said smoothly, "And I have interrupted you; forgive me."

She bowed her head and waited, hoping his appearance was a formal signal only and that he had no business with her. The demesne's folk were growing used to their new Chalice, and they were now coming to her more and more; this was a relief in some ways, and she knew she must be grateful for the good this was doing Willowlands, but she often had to put aside what other work she had planned on doing. She had fled to the House library today and was hastily reading up on the behaviour toward and reception of outblood Heirs. Part of her problem, she thought, as she had thought many times since the Chalice had come to her, was that she was not by nature a formal sort of person; she found that side of the duties of the Chalice so difficult as sometimes to feel incompatible with her private self. She wondered if this was anything like trying to live in the human world when you were a priest of Fire.

She had waited what seemed rather a long time with her head bowed, hoping that he would go away, waited until she began to worry that there was some ritual gesture that was now hers to make that he was waiting for. She raised her head at last, reluctantly, and found him staring at her with an intensity she disliked a great deal.

"I hoped," he said with a diffidence she was sure was feigned, "that you might have a little time for me."

Involuntarily she glanced at the book still open on the table.

The driest record of a thousand-year-old court award ceremony would have been preferable to spending time with Horuld, and what she was reading did not merely interest her but drew her almost feverishly. She had not seen the Master for private speech since his first meeting with Horuld, although she often felt his presence in the earthlines, and she wondered what he thought of his Heir, and what he was, or wasn't, doing to make his Heir acceptable to the demesne. She realised in the shock of Horuld's unexpected and unwanted presence that part of her feverishness to learn about outblood Heirs was that she suspected the Master of trying to persuade the demesne to find Horuld satisfactory, even desirable. This was only what a responsible Master would do, but. . . .

"Of course," she said, after too long a pause. "Chalice and Heir must"—she stumbled over her attempt to find words she could bring herself to say—"be acquainted."

And she went with him. But when he offered her his arm she pretended not to see, and instead folded her own arms in the ritual shape of a Chalice without a chalice, elbows tucked closely in, wrists crossed and hands loosely clasped. It had only ever been something to do with her hands on those fortunately few occasions when the Chalice was expected to attend but with no cup to present; today it felt like warding.

He had nothing to say to her; nothing of substance. She kept waiting for him to reveal his purpose—the purpose that was keeping her away from her reading—and answered as briefly as possible, almost falling into monosyllables and then remembering with an effort that she had to be polite to him; trying to prevent her mind wandering from his pointless remarks about the weather, about the picture or ornament in this or that hallway of the House, about that bird which had sat singing outside the House when he arrived. At each new topic she would jerk her attention back to focus, expecting to hear what he wished to speak about at last. The weather? Was there an omen in it? There were those who could read the future in the shape of the clouds, or said they could—although the Weatheraugur, whom Mirasol thought wistfully she rather liked, said this was nonsense. The painting of the yellow fruit outside one of the lesser meeting rooms—she'd always thought it rather dull herself—had it perhaps belonged to the forebear Horuld could trace his Heirship to, and he was suggesting that it should be more prominently displayed? The bird—he couldn't be talking about a redsong, could he? Redsongs were commoner than mud in a wet season. If he was trying to imply that a redsong singing for his arrival meant the demesne welcomed him, he was a fool.

He went on and on. As Chalice—and she did not plan ever to be Mirasol for this man—she could not be asked to sit and chat, so they had to stand or keep moving. They paced slowly through the House and then he took her for a stroll around the gardens, remarking on a shrub or a flower as if imparting some new perception, while she felt half mad from boredom, and from his extreme ignorance of plants. It occurred to her to wonder if anyone so ignorant could be Master; no garden would flourish under the weight of such ineptitude, which would put a greater burden on the gardeners and the rest of the Circle. And yet Horuld's animation seemed to increase the longer he held her prisoner. He caught her eye every opportunity he had—and she felt she had to meet his eyes occasionally—and smiled as if he believed she was happy in his company.

Once or twice she caught him looking at her in a way . . . she had to be imagining it; no Chalice and Master, nor Master's Heir, could . . . but the look made her long for the heavy camouflaging Chalice's robes, when ordinarily she was extremely grateful to be free of them for a day.

She finally managed to stop at one of the gates to the garden and resist being swept any farther. She did not know how she could take leave of him; she'd been clutching the formality of the Chalice to her with her clasped hands against her breast and therefore had to maintain the Chalice's character. She was sure a Chalice could not dismiss an Heir, but she didn't know how to get rid of him, and he gave the impression that he would cling to her forever if she did not. So she stopped and stood and bowed her head and refused to meet his eyes for several minutes—her heart beating in her throat in fear of the terrible insult she might be offering—and at last he thanked her for the noble condescension of her company—*ugh*, she thought, keeping her face blank—and bowed several times as he backed away from her. *Backed* away from her, she thought, troubled, when he finally seemed to have gone away and left her alone, and she risked raising her head again. *Backed* away. What had she given him that he was so pleased with?

She half ran back to the library, but her concentration was gone. She read a little more, about mixtures to be thought of when dealing with outblood Heirs, when the Master was present and when he was not, how both to delimit and to integrate such an Heir's place in the demesne. And then she shut the book and picked up another, smaller book that she could take with her back to her cottage. Perhaps reading within the sound of her bees would help bring her mind back to her business again; she would be positively glad of some ordinary unexpected visitor hoping for help or honey. . . . She didn't understand why she felt such a sense of doom. All that had happened was that she had lost two hours to a nonentity . . . except that he wasn't a nonentity. He was little enough in himself, but he was the Overlord's pawn and a danger to her demesne, and to her Master.

The walk back to her cottage settled her nerves a little; enough, at least, that she could open her new book and begin to read it without missing every other word. The amount of reading she did now was yet another of the strains of being Chalice. Her mother had taught her to read, and she had a few record books of this little corner of the demesne's woods (she kept telling herself she should pass these on to the new keepers, but she never quite got round to it), her father's account books, and one of the lives and meanings and symbolism of the trees of the demesne. She had used this when she had planted trees for her bees—birch, beech and hawthorn, but also a parasol tree. There hadn't been a parasol tree outside the House gardens in generations, but the one at the edge of her meadow was already twice as tall as she was, and her bees adored its flowers.

Most important she had her mother's receipt book, which had been her grandmother's and her great-grandmother's before that. It contained brisk notations of three generations of beekeeping which backed what her mother had taught her and therefore made some of the inevitable moments of learning by experience a little less overwhelming. It furthermore included things like how to tan leather and how to mix clay and straw for bricks and then how to bake them, useful things that any member of the small folk of the demesne might want to know.

But barring a little burst of winter weeks when she had studied the tree book she had never spent real time reading. Till she became Chalice. Her eyes were often tired now, but worse her mind was tired; she felt that the shape of her memory had been laid down when she'd learnt bees and woodcraft, and that neither shape readily held books or Chalice. She was not old, but she was old for learning something that should have begun when she was young.

It was cold early this year. She got up to close the door and the windows and to light the laid fire. Other years she might have worried that her bees would stop producing honey too soon, and that she would have difficulty bringing them through the winter. Perhaps there were advantages to being Chalice after all. But then bees which had (apparently) stopped building combs for their honey so as to let it pour out for their Chalice might not remember how to start again in time to manufacture sufficient winter stores. She would have to count how many colonies she was taking honey from and do some sums. I don't think I have enough shelf space for that much honey, if I have to feed them, she thought, let alone enough jars.

The memory of the time she had spent in Horuld's company still lay like a burden on her. But would it have been any better if she were still only a woodskeeper who also kept bees? She had always cared passionately about the demesne. Not all its folk did; some of them figured demesne business was for the Master and the great folk of the House and the Circle, not the ordinary small folk of barn and field, woodright and lake, even House kitchen and stable. But then many of the ordinary demesne folk did not feel the earthlines as she always had—as her parents both had, although not as strongly as she did. If she had not become Chalice, she would have been one of the people standing around the House doors the day the new Master had come home from Fire.

And she would not have liked the look of the Heir, even as a woodskeeper. And as a woodskeeper she could have done nothing about it. The problem was that she doubted there was anything she could do about it even as Chalice. Why did this afternoon with Horuld lie on her so, as if it would stop her breath? She shivered.

She went to the door and opened it. She could not hear her bees any more; they had wisely withdrawn into their warm hives. She took a deep breath of the suddenly winter air. There were even a few snowflakes falling, nearly a month earlier than usual. She found herself worrying whether the early cold had anything to do with a new Master who used to be a priest of Fire.

She went back indoors again and moved the kettle over the centre of the fire. She'd have hot water with a little mead and a little honey in it, which she liked better than any tisane, and keep reading. The terrible *need* to learn—to learn something, she did not know what—about Heirs continued to pull at her. She didn't know if she had brought the right book with her, but it had been the book her hand had fallen on, and she'd come to follow such signs, now she was Chalice, having no mentor to give her better guidance.

It was late when she found it. She should have gone to bed over an hour before, but in her mind there was still the little nagging voice telling her to keep on, that she hadn't found it yet, that she had to find it. And so she kept on. She was so blind to everything by then—blind with reading, blind with anxiety, blind with a too-narrow focus of concentration—that she almost missed it.

And so it was that the Heir was installed to great rejoicing amongst all the folk of the demesne, and all saw that the choice of Heir had been a wise one, for all that his outbloodedness had been great, and there had been those who had doubted he could be made of the demesne as a Master must be. But the Overlord had chosen his seers well, and they had read the earthlines truly, and the earthlines had told him where to look, that the Heir-blood ran to this man and not some other. And the demesne flourished from the moment his hand was laid upon it, and there was no hindrance nor turbulence, no discontent in tree nor well, no revolt in beast nor human. And the Overlord was pleased, because this gained him both praise and power, that he should have chosen so perfectly; but there were those who had watched and considered all, who said that it was less to do with the sagacity and good judgement of the Overlord and his seers than with the profound pragmatism of the marriage of the Heir to his Chalice. This convention is not well known, for it is so awfully and fearfully against what is well known, which is that the Master must not *marry nor otherwise fondly touch his Chalice in any analogous manner, for the Chalice's power is to bind and the Master's to rule, and mixed they create an abominable disharmony, for they make weight and stillness when there should be lightness and motion. But in a state of disharmony, as an outblood Master conjoined to a demesne, such a tie is the pair's highest work, and creates a small harmony from a larger disharmony, from which a larger harmony may grow, in the shape of the child of their coupling who shall next be Master, and who shall call from the demesne by the strength of his inbred harmony the perfect Chalice to complement him.*

She had already begun to study the directions for the preparation of the cup that would enable such a connection to be made between Master and Chalice when it finally sank in what she had read.

Marry Horuld!

That was the reason Horuld wished to speak—had been directed to speak to her. *That* was the reason he had looked at her—

She went to the door again and opened it, and half flung herself out into the cold clean-smelling darkness, away from the warmth of the cottage and the book she had been reading, which she suddenly felt must smell rotten, must be polluting the room it lay open in. She went back inside just long enough to shut it, tipping its cover over with the end of one finger, as if greater contact might make her ill. Then she wrapped herself in both her shawl and her cloak and went outdoors again, and walked, walked away, any way at all. . . .

There was still snow in the air. She guessed it had been falling lightly, laconically, since she had first noticed it, but the ground was still too warm for it to lie. Some of the trees had a dusting of snow on their leaves. There had been no clear signs of a hard winter, and the harvest had come in safely with no more than the usual number of sudden storms. Thunderstorms, so long as they were not too destructive, were a sign of good luck; the very violence of them showed the strength in the harvest they raged over. In a harvest season with no storms the saying was that the crops were weak, and would give little nourishment. Fire of all things, she felt, was strong; she in common with many other of the Willowlands folk had feared too many storms at harvest rather than too few.

The only lightning-set fire had been the one at Onora Grove.

She lifted her face to the snowflakes and let them brush her skin—they felt a little like the feet of her bees—till they had swept away the murk of too much reading, till she felt like herself again. Marrying Horuld was no worry of hers. The demesne had a Master.

She turned around, returned to her cottage, put an extra blanket on her bed, and slept dreamlessly.

In the morning she tucked the book under her arm as if it had no power over her, and took it back to the House. There were other books to read, and she still needed to know as much as she could about outblood Heirs. The fearful little voice that had driven her to keep reading the night before had fallen silent;

what she now wanted to know was if there was a way for a Chalice to say "sorry, I'm busy" to an outblood Heir who wanted to waste her time.

When the shadow fell again across the door of the library, she gave an involuntary shiver, nearly a spasm, of revulsion—*not again!* But it wasn't the Heir. It was the Grand Seneschal.

It was no good reminding herself that a Chalice had only to stand for a standing Master; she had scrambled to her feet before she'd thought anything but *uh-oh.* Once standing all her possible ceremonial gestures deserted her and she merely blinked at him and tried not to worry. The Grand Seneschal did not like the library. This was a fact well known to the Housefolk, who also knew they were therefore unlikely to be caught up for it if the books were not tended properly. The result was that Mirasol had to wipe the dust, and occasional spiders, off almost every book she took down. Fortunately the House cats had no such reservations and there were no mouse nests (at least that Mirasol had found) behind decapitated bindings. She stood and blinked some more. If the Grand Seneschal had come to the library there must be some unexpected urgency for the Chalice. Uh-oh.

But he only stood in the doorway and looked at her while she stood and looked at him. She was tired—she had had a very late night the night before—and she always had trouble dragging herself out of anything she was reading back into the real world, perhaps because reading was still difficult for her, or perhaps because, since she had become Chalice, she liked the real world less than she had. Eventually she tried a small bow. She'd never known him not to address her with grimmest formality, and here he was only standing there, as if he did not know how to begin. She finally thought of a suitable gesture, and touched her fingertips together and held her hands out toward him, in the ritual giving of first speech to another.

Still he hesitated. At last he said, in a curious, almost jerky way, as if the words were ripped out of him, as if he had not chosen to speak at all, "I had thought you . . . concurred in my choice of Master. In my attempt to bring our Master home. Even that you welcomed him. That despite his formidable priesthood his true blood as the younger brother of the former Master was proof that he was yet best for our demesne. . . ."

She was so amazed at the Grand Seneschal saying *I* and *my* and *you* to her that it took her a moment to translate what he was saying. The Grand Seneschal had never spoken to her directly before; he spoke forbiddingly and exclusively in the third person when he had to address her at all, and had never—she felt—let it be anything but clear that he only addressed her because she had somehow, incredible as it seemed, become Chalice, and the Grand Seneschal was, unfortunately, too often compelled to address the Chalice. And now he spoke to her directly—and as if in great grief.

In *his* choice of Master? Those very early days of her Chalice-hood were vague in her memory, with an overwhelming confusion and disbelief that even in retrospect made her wince and wish to avoid them. The Grand Seneschal's letter had already been written and sent by the time she had begun to bear Chalice to the gatherings of the Circle, but even in her dazed and muddled state she'd been aware that not all the other Circle members had agreed with the Grand Seneschal's decision. She could only remember hearing Prelate and Sunbrightener say as much aloud, but she was sure they were not the only ones. Perhaps the Grand Seneschal had been in the minority—he might, she thought, almost amused, be the only one, and had won his victory by mere force of character. The Grand Seneschal ranked third in the Circle hierarchy, after the Master and the Chalice, but he could not overbear the other nine—unless they let him.

She had been surprised to discover that the Grand Seneschal had written to the priests of Fire, because it was not a level-headed, dispassionate thing to do. In other circumstances it might have made her like him. But there had been no level-headed thing to do, because the Master should not have died with no Heir. What else was there to do but seek his nearest blood relative?

How could the Grand Seneschal think she did *not* support their Master?

She dropped her hands. "But—I do—I would have no other Master." She glanced at the book she had been reading, much as she had done when Horuld had interrupted her the day before; but she was not thinking that she wished to dismiss the Grand Seneschal because he disturbed her, only that she had not yet found a way to dismiss the Heir if he disturbed her again.

"It is all over the demesne that you spent the day with the Heir yesterday."

"The *day*," she said, appalled. "It was two hours—it felt like a century—if it had been an entire day I—I would have run away from Willowlands before sunset." She did not think of how irresponsible (and impossible) a thing this was for a Chalice to say; only how best to express her revulsion against the Heir.

Something that might almost have been a smile appeared on the Seneschal's face, but disappeared again immediately, and the grief seemed to deepen. He did not sound accusatory when he spoke, only sad. "And that you held your hands clasped, as Chalice."

"Ye-es," she said. "Yes—but I—I did not want to be Mirasol with that—man," although as she said her own name she wondered if the Seneschal even knew it, or if he might think that *Mirasol* was some strange low slang common among minor woodskeepers.

As if he did not know what else to do, the Seneschal wandered over to the table next to the one she stood beside, pulled out a chair and sat heavily down. She was clearly not bearing Chalice, so anyone might sit down in her presence without consequences, but this was still as out of character as the *I* and the *you*. Also the Seneschal always behaved with great precision, and he sat down with a thud, as if exhausted.

"I feared it might be something like this," he murmured. Louder he said, "Why did you not merely send him away?"

"Send him *away*?" she said. "Send away the *Heir*? I only wish I could—that I knew how." She looked at the book again. "I was hoping some book would tell me how, in case he comes back."

"How could you send away the Heir?" the Grand Seneschal said, almost gently. "By telling him to go. You, Mirasol, are Chalice. He is only Heir."

"But—"

"By spending time in his company—as Chalice, as you did—you were giving him your favour—your warranty. He will have gone away to send word to the Overlord that the Chalice of Willowlands supports him. Do you not know—you spend so much time *reading*"—and in his voice at last was the tone she was used to hearing when the Grand Seneschal spoke to her—"can you possibly not know that there is a move to put our Master aside and set the Heir in his place?"

"No!" she cried—although she had feared as much. "No, *no*—how could you think it? I would myself die, if it were necessary, to keep our Master; but the only story of a Chalice doing so, it was at Stonehollow, twelve generations ago, and it did not work and so . . ." Without thinking, she turned to glance up at the shelf where the book that had told her that story stood, and when she turned back again she was suddenly angry. "*Reading.* Yes. Yes, I *do* spend a tremendous amount of time reading—I should have known that I was giving that lizard Horuld my blessing? How was I to know it, please? When did I serve my apprenticeship, and with whom? Who speaks to me at all, since I became Chalice, except those who must?" She glared down at the sitting Seneschal. "I am far too strange and grand now for my old friends, even if they knew that a Chalice might send away an Heir with no form but the bare words of command—which I rather doubt they do know. All I have is *reading*. The books do not scorn or avoid my company, and they tell me plainly what they know."

"Forgive me," he said.

She heard him say "forgive me" and had a sense of dislocation and preposterousness almost as great as she had had on the day the Circle came to tell her she was chosen Chalice. She sat down with a thump as abrupt as the Grand Seneschal's had been.

"I guessed that," he went on, "yesterday, when Zinna brought me the news of the Chalice and the Heir—followed by Dora and Mallie and Sim bringing me the same news. I guessed that you did not know. You are right. I have blamed you often for the things you did not know. My only excuse, and it is no excuse, but I have only seen that now, last night and this morning"—and she realised, looking at him, that he had probably had even less sleep than she—"my only excuse is that I too have felt beleaguered by events. It is hard enough to lose a Master; harder yet to lose him unexpectedly and in such a way. . . . There are not even any folktales of how a Seneschal may best fulfil his obligation when his demesne has neither Master nor Chalice." Softly, draggingly, almost dreamily he added, "The last years of our Master's brother's Mastership taught me only to rely on no one; it did not teach me how to be a Grand Seneschal with a broken Circle; it did not teach me to lead when there was no leader. . . ."

Unwillingly she thought: And he carried our demesne for seven months while I staggered blind and stupid in his wake; certainly our Prelate gave him little help, and the rest of the Circle little more. How could he not resent me, even though it was not my fault? Willowlands has been lucky to have such a Grand Seneschal—Willowlands who so gravely needs a little luck.

"I even believed that the most I could do for an inexperienced Chalice was to—to spare her the weight of a Grand Seneschal's advice. I know that my manner is not—is not cordial. But I could leave—try to leave—her—you—free to find your own best way.

147

Our Circle has never been a true Circle. Our previous Chalice could not bind us and we grew more separate still, less aware of each other, under the—the curious strains of the last Mastership. Those of us who were very—involved with the old Master have I think never quite . . ." His voice trailed away. More strongly he went on, "It had not occurred to me, till yesterday, that there might be things a Grand Seneschal would know that would be useful to a Chalice struggling to invent her own apprenticeship. That, for example, a woodskeeper become Chalice might not guess an Heir might seek her validation for his own power.

"I knew you supported our Master. I knew it because you never said one word about the burn on your hand. That is why I guessed—finally—yesterday, about what had really happened." He smiled again. This time it lasted long enough to be identified as a smile, but it was more wintry than the snowflakes still drifting down outside the library window. "Let it be, perhaps, set in my favour that it was my support of your silence, at the beginning, that enabled you to go on being silent. Deager wanted to declare that by that wound the Master was no fit Master."

She whispered, "He cured my hand. The Master. It would not heal, and he healed it."

The Grand Seneschal put his hands on the table, palm up. "I beg you give me leave to tell that story."

She thought of Kenti and Tis, and her conviction that Kenti wanted to believe that same story, that a priest of Fire can cure as well as harm. "Will it help?" she said. "Will it help us keep our Master?"

"Yes—it will help. I do not think it will help enough."

He looked up at her, and the grief was still in his face, but it was a different grief. "We should have had this conversation months ago—when we first knew that Fire would give him back to us. No"—he put his hand up against her, although she had made no attempt to speak—"you need not reproach me; it is my blame that we did not. I know. I know. What I do not know is what to do now. And whether or not it is too late."

"It *cannot* be too late," she said passionately. "I—we—we won't *let* it be too late."

Then he did smile, a real smile, if still a sad one. "Then we will not let it. I must think. We will begin—I will tell it that the Master healed your hand; there is nothing to gain by pretending the accident did not happen, since everyone knows it did. And you—you must find a subtle way to tell everyone you can that the time you spent with Horuld . . . dispirited you; that you felt compelled to it because . . . because everyone of our demesne must bind themselves together in every way possible, to support our Master; the Heir must not feel shut out, however unworthy the Heir might be; that the situation at Willowlands is not traditional and so tradition is little help."

"I can't say that—be subtle, you say?—gods of the earthlines, how do you expect me to say that subtly?"

But the Seneschal only said grimly, "Those books you read—I have read some of them, and it has given me a distaste for reading, because it seems to me that most of them are full of unpleasant things said pleasantly. I'm not sure what else dead written words can teach you except the trickiness of words. Find a way to say this unpleasant thing pleasantly, from your books. I do not deny that I am asking you to walk the edge of a knife blade; you must condemn the Heir, who is human, that our Master, who is not, be seen as the better choice; and how to condemn him when at least the whites of his eyes are white and his clothes hang on his body the way clothes do hang on a human frame? And yet you must also condemn him in such a way that you may still welcome him if the worst happens and he becomes Master."

He stood up again. "I am sorry. I am older than you; I should have . . ."

He didn't say what he should have, and impulsively Mirasol said, "You were Grand Seneschal for our Master's brother. What . . ." And then she could not think of a way to ask what she wished to ask. "I—I—you see, I am not good at subtlety. I do not want to ask about the bad times, about the end. Only what it was like, having a—an ordinary Master."

The Grand Seneschal stood silently for some moments. "I wonder if there has ever been an ordinary Master. No—I think I do know what you are asking. But I don't think I can help you. I had my apprenticeship, you see. I learnt to hear and feel what a Seneschal must hear and feel of the demesne, to best serve his Master: I learnt this because the Seneschal who was daily, hourly, thus listening and feeling taught me and watched over me as I learnt. I was apprentice under the Seneschal for our Master's father, and indeed my first years as Seneschal were under him, under a Master who had held the land steady for fifty years and more. And in those years the Circle was also a Circle. Then our old Master died and his elder son became Master and all began to change, to . . ." He stopped. "But now, with this Master . . . a Master who is struggling to engage with his land without hurting it, as he hurt his Chalice when she gave him the welcome cup . . . there is nothing in my experience for that, any more than, I guess, there is in your books." He looked at her. "I daresay an apprenticeship—having had an apprenticeship—is better than no apprenticeship, even in these circumstances. Because I know that it does not help the situation I find myself in—I know the situation is not the fault of my ignorance. But that does not change the situation."

"It is the fault of my ignorance that I have been seen to sanction the Heir, when that is exactly what I did not want to do," she said bitterly.

After a pause the Seneschal said, "I came here to tell you that, yes. But I wonder . . . we have had a strong harvest. The Wildwater running over its banks after the seed went into the ground this spring—shortly after our new Master came home—looked like a bad sign. But the second sowing grew better than the first sowings have for several years. The Onora Grove has given us firewood and timber; it was not an area of the wood Oakstaff had thought to open up, but you know the Circle has decided it will open well. And we were lucky with it; even from the House the sky was red with the fire, and those who were there say there was a sudden heavy downpour that lasted just long enough to put it out. The earth tremors have all but gone; I can't remember the last report of a wall being knocked down—or of chasing animals so terrified they will break through a fence themselves. And no other demesnes—not even those who share a boundary with us—have been troubled. It has not been an easy transition. But even blood Masters have done worse, when the change has been sudden or unexpected. And outblood Heirs have done very much worse, I think."

Mirasol smiled a little. "Flood, fire, famine and war. I could tell you stories."

"Perhaps you should tell them."

"But subtly."

"Yes . . . but what I am thinking now . . . we have had too many disasters in too short a time, and we have begun to think in disastrous terms. When the Onora Grove burned, I wondered if it would take the demesne with it; and yet instead we have a new meadow with a pond where the stream bank fell in, and most of the trees are still fit for good use, in the hearth, or under axe and lathe, or. . . . Perhaps this disaster comes to you for you to shape."

"The only lathe I know is the feel of turning pages," Mirasol said forlornly. But she thought of the things she knew that even the Seneschal apparently did not. If anyone might have ferreted out the truth about the fire in the Onora Grove, she felt it would have been the Grand Seneschal; but he gave no sign of knowing it. He would have mentioned, she thought, the law that a Master can be put to death for harming a Chalice, if he knew of it; he would have mentioned that an outblood Heir might marry his Chalice to prevent the demesne from tearing itself apart from the stress of the blood change. She shivered. "Has the Grand Seneschal—have you had your disaster? And have you shaped it?"

His look was bleak. "I am shaping it now. My disaster is that I did not speak to you long before. If I hadn't—as I should have— when the priests of Fire first agreed to send our Master back to us, then I certainly should have spoken after he burned you and you said no word against him. Bringad has thought well of you from the beginning: I should have listened to him. And, Mirasol, it is not that you are—were—a woodskeeper. My grandmother was the daughter of a kitchen maid—got by the Master's fourth son. My great-grandmother was turned off the demesne before the baby was born, because it was the fashion in those days to do so, because the child might be able to cause trouble if it wished, on account of bearing the Master's blood. The Master I had my apprenticeship under—our Master's father—learnt of the story and set his Seneschal to track the line, and bring them home. My mother and father and I came here for the first time in the back of an ox-cart, and were shown into the Grand Seneschal's office smelling of dirty straw and too many weeks on the road, carrying a few ragged bundles that were our only possessions. I was eight, and could barely stand or speak, because I was overwhelmed by my first experience of my landsense, which had met me at the boundary of Willowlands. I had no idea what was happening to me; I thought I might be dying. When I turned nine the Seneschal took me to apprentice. I do not know why the earthlines speak in your blood so strongly, but that they do is all that matters. But I had twenty years' apprenticeship. You've had a year of reading— and of bearing Chalice perforce."

"You have held the demesne together, while I read."

"You have been Chalice since the day the Circle came to you. Your presence in the earthlines is strong; you were easy to find. This is why I hoped I could convince you to live at the House. We've needed your strength whether you knew how to use it or not. But I've come to realise that your bees were right not to let you go; a honey Chalice should live among them.

"Come to me if I can help you." He smiled again through his bleak look. "I will talk to you." And he turned and left the library.

It was snowing harder when she walked home that afternoon. She had not had a great deal more time for reading about outblood Heirs. There had been several messages for the Chalice—dragons take it, she thought, they're learning to look for me in the library. One, however, was an interesting query from the Housekeeper about the Chalice's beeswax candles. She knew that the Chalice put a little honey in her candles—you could smell it when they burned (and very pleasant it was, added the Housekeeper punctiliously) and she had furthermore heard that the Chalice also had different honeys which she used for different purposes. The Housekeeper wondered if she applied this to her candle-making? Might there, for example, be candles that, burning, helped you stay awake, if you were, perhaps, up late over your accounts?

"I haven't the least idea," said Mirasol. "But it's an intriguing thought. I shall experiment, and bring you the result, and you can tell me what, if anything, happens. Thank you."

The Housekeeper, looking slightly bemused (I daresay Chalices aren't supposed not to have the least idea, thought Mirasol), bowed herself out.

The last message was a reminder that her presence was necessary tomorrow evening for a meeting of the Circle with the Master, here at the House. If the weather continued as it was she might have to stay overnight there. She had done this several times when she was first Chalice, and more inclined to take other people's suggestions, because she found it difficult to say no—to keep saying no—to other people's advice. But she had learnt very quickly that she slept badly away from her own cottage, as if it were the one safe quiet place in a world suddenly in pandemonium.

She remembered one of the few times—before today—that the Grand Seneschal had showed her, she thought, any understanding. The Chalice moved from one person to another, but they were all Chalice; and as little changed outwardly as possible. And so a new Chalice took up residence in the old Chalice's rooms. The rooms were stripped to the walls and cleaned from ceiling to floor before the equally purged and polished furniture was replaced. When she was first shown the Chalice's rooms the walls positively glittered, and the sheets on the bed crackled with, she guessed, not merely washing and ironing but sheer newness; she'd never had the luxury of new sheets herself. Even in the midst of her own crisis she had been able to wonder at the time spent, in the middle of the demesne's crisis, on the task of scrubbing the Chalice's rooms. She supposed it showed respect—even for an unapprenticed woodskeeper Chalice—or perhaps terror: cleaning might be the only thing the Housefolk could do to clear the residue of the catastrophic end of the previous Chalice and help the new one to find her way.

But despite the shining walls and spotless furniture and new bedsheets the Chalice's rooms had been haunted. Mirasol had barely been able to stay alone in them long enough for the footsteps of the Housewoman who had showed her there to fade away down the corridor. She never so much as sat down. She left and went in search of the Grand Seneschal; she thought the head Houseman might have been enough, but he was new in his job too, and she did not wish to get him in trouble if he were not authorised to requarter a Chalice. So she looked for the Grand Seneschal. It had been less than half an hour since the end of the meeting, and she had left him still arguing—or rather listening and refusing to argue—with Prelate and Landsman. He could not be asleep yet, although she did not relish the thought of knocking on the door of his private apartments. But she had found him—despite the lateness of the hour—in his office.

She thought she did well not to stammer or squeak when she said she could not remain in the Chalice's rooms and that if he could not offer an alternative it was still not so late (it was past midnight) that she could not walk home, which was probably the best idea after all, but she did not wish to leave without informing him. She hadn't stammered or squeaked, but it had all come out in a breathless rush, like a small woodskeeper forced (for some inexplicable reason) to speak to a Grand Seneschal.

He stared at her in the blank, forbidding way she was already accustomed to, but his answer, when it came, was in no more oppressive a tone than usual: "You may have the Yellow Room." She had followed the Housewoman (a different one) in a daze. In the first place she had expected some dispute, even a silent one, when the Seneschal let her know that while he would accede to the Chalice's wishes, she as the woman within the Chalice was (again) failing to bear her new responsibility in a seemly or becoming manner. Furthermore, only the most important rooms at the centre of the House had colour names—suitable perhaps for the housing of a true, a satisfactory Chalice (supposing the Chalice's rooms had been somehow infested by tigers or chimeras, and uninhabitable), but. . . . As she thought about it now—the memory of their recent astonishing conversation at the front of her mind—the Yellow Room had since then not only been kept for her, but it was the most conveniently placed of any of the private rooms to the library. Either he had already noticed her spending every minute she could in the library, or he guessed that, unapprenticed as she was, she would have to. No—that her best choice was to learn what she could from the library's *dead written words*. Perhaps he had been trying again to influence her. She grunted a laugh. The wind was in her face, and several snowflakes fell on her tongue.

There were a few bees huddled under the peak of the little overhang that sheltered her front door. They flew, or fell, to her shoulders, and clung there. "It is too cold for bees, you silly things," she said. She hadn't meant to light a fire—only to go straight to bed—but her loyalty had its limits and while she didn't want to dump her bees to fend for themselves when they were already stupid with cold, she drew the line at taking them to bed with her. And so she stirred the banked embers and added kindling till a log would catch, and then sat down in front of the hearth to let it warm her and the bees still sitting bemusedly on her shoulders. As the fire began to work on them she had to help one or two free themselves from the tangling weave of her shawl, which made her think of the Master, the day he saved the life of the bee who had stung him.

She had to think what to put in the cup for tomorrow, and which cup to use. That the Heir would not be there meant she wanted to mix something binding—and exclusive. No longer did she have the luxury of merely wishing to make any gathering move as smoothly as possible; she wished to tie this truculent Circle and this singular Master together as tightly as she could, whether they moved comfortably and effectively within those confines or not . . . and then she had to hope that any such successful tie as she might create did not instead only rouse its members to split themselves more thoroughly apart.

She stared into the flames and thought, I am playing with *fire.*

She must have fallen asleep, because she dreamed. She was standing on the knoll where the pavilion had stood, the pavilion that had burnt to the ground, killing the Master and the Chalice and a dozen others, including the Clearseer and the head Houseman. The ruins were black and cold around her, and she felt nothing of those recent deaths, not even that of the previous Chalice. What she felt—or remembered—instead were the stories of what that place had been before the pavilion had been built on it. It had been a place of power since before the demesnes were made, and its power had been both used and subverted by the folk who lived here, and their Masters. But in her dream she remembered something she had not known she knew. Perhaps the lost knowledge was brought forward by the conversation she had had with the Grand Seneschal about the dreadful mistake she as Chalice had made in her behaviour toward the Heir. Perhaps she had never known this before, but the conversation and the urgency behind it had opened a way for the earthlines to speak to her directly.

Because, centuries ago, when the power of that place was still allowed to be what it was, and had not yet been dammed or forced into some channel it was not meant to be barred and bent by, it had given prophetic dreams to anyone who slept a night on it. It could not tell everything, and about some things it did not always tell the truth, or at least it told the truth so obscurely that it was easily misunderstood. But on a few subjects it most often spoke clearly: it would tell a man if his wife was faithful. And it would tell a woman whom she would marry.

And while the old usage had fallen into neglect, the power was still there.

Mirasol snapped awake. She could know now, at once—by morning—if her error in being gracious to the Heir was a critical error or not. If the oracle went against her . . . she couldn't remember if the story stipulated if, having learnt what the oracle would tell you, you could change your fate or not: keep your wife by persuading her to give up her lover, refuse to marry the man you did not want, whether the man you did want appeared or not.

Did Chalices ordinarily marry? In her confusion of mind she could not at present remember. Chalicehood was not passed down from mother to daughter as Mastership passed from father to eldest son, but it did sometimes run in families; a bloodline that matched well with the Masters' would find the Chalice returning to it again and again. The Chalice before her . . . the Chalice before that had been that one's aunt, Mirasol thought. So far as she knew, her own family, on neither her father's nor her mother's side, despite the fact they had long been of this demesne, had ever produced a Chalice, although her father's had produced both a Landsman and an Oakstaff many generations ago. But did Chalices marry and have daughters? Occasionally the Chalice came to a woman who was either pregnant or nursing, who then held her Chalicehood in milk; was the fact that this was considered bad luck for the demesne an indication that Chalices were encouraged to remain single and celibate? It was a clue to her state of mind, she thought, that she could not remember having read anything about this—although she knew she had not deliberately sought the information. She had never been in love, and her parents had not tried to force a husband on her; and since she had become Chalice, there had always been too much else of more immediate, more drastic relevance. . . .

She struggled to her feet, feeling dizzy and stupid, her mind still half in its dream. She pulled her cloak and shawl up over her shoulders again; they had slipped off as she slept and in front of the fire she had not needed them. She looked vaguely around for the bees that had come in with her, but saw no sign of them; perhaps they belonged to the hive tucked next to the chimney breast. She could feel the finger of cold draught that told her that the bee door she had hollowed out of the window-frame was still open.

She went to her own human door and opened it. The snow had stopped, although it was still cold. Much too cold to sleep—to try to sleep—outdoors. But the night was at least half over, she thought; she only needed to sleep long enough to dream. She needed only to dream of one face—or of no face at all. How might the oracle tell her she would not marry? She shook her head. It would find a way. But she had to go *now*. She could not wait— not even till tomorrow night. The cold weather seemed to have settled in, so it would be just as cold tomorrow night; and she'd already spent half of tonight warm, indoors, in front of a fire.

She pulled on one of her oldest, shabbiest winter woods-keeper's dresses, snatched up her shawl and cloak again before she had time to change her mind and left, closing the door gently behind her. Since it had stopped snowing the temperature had risen again; the wind against her face was almost warm. It was the week of the dark of the moon or she might have tried to guess what time it was. But she had to have slept a few hours by the fire, or she wouldn't have woken so fuzzy-headed.

It was a longish walk to the knoll of the old pavilion. She knew the way, although no one, herself included, went there any more—not since the death of the old Master. The grove that had burned was more to the east; from lightning's point of view it was close to the pavilion, but from a walker's it was not; from Mirasol's cottage there was a long detour round a rough scarp. One of the main footpaths of the demesne ran quite near it, and the heavy use it had was evident; the turn-off to the pavilion, which had once been just as wide and worn, was now mossy and overgrown; Mirasol had to duck under young branches and floun-der through banks of nettles.

She paused at the edge of what had been its parkland. It was rapidly reverting to meadow; from where she stood she could no longer see the carriage drive that had led to it from the House, on the side opposite the wood. She could still see the knoll, however, and the ruin of the pavilion; the grass and the fast-growing saplings seemed to avoid it.

Her walk had warmed her, but she still shivered, looking at the knoll. She waded through the autumn-brown grasses, and the crackling noise this made seemed to announce her presence . . . to what? Seedheads popped and flung their contents over her like the audience cheering a victor of some contest on a fete day. . . . Again she shivered, although she was not cold.

When she came to the crest of the knoll, the walls of the fallen pavilion seemed suddenly high and claustrophobic, shutting her in, though the highest of them were no taller than the top of her head, and most of them came no higher than her knees. It had been a curious shape, circular at the centre, but with arms like a star. It sprawled over the knoll as if it had been flung there; now that there was no level roof tying all together, the way the arms crept down the slope from the central plateau looked strange and eerie, and the few splintered stone stair-steps that had survived the fire looked like the teeth of lurking earth-monsters.

At first she was at a loss; she only knew you had to sleep on the knoll. But what part of the knoll? Did she have to lie down and close her eyes in the centre of the old pavilion? For a third time she shivered, and this time she told herself crossly to stop it. It wasn't that cold, and the knoll was empty. But it wasn't empty; or if it was, it was no use to her. She stiffened against the next shiver, and pretended it hadn't happened. What if what had occurred here a little over a year ago had broken the power of this place? What if she was here on a fool's errand?

She sat down on the top of the knoll, which was not, she thought, precisely at the centre of the pavilion. This was obscurely comforting. The tallest of the standing walls created a corner, and protected her from the prevailing wind. She lay down and curled up on her side, bending one arm beneath her head as pillow. She was not cold; she only had to sleep for a few minutes; it would be dawn soon, and daylight would wake her, daylight and birdsong. Surely the birds did not avoid this knoll. . . .

She was asleep when the temperature dropped and the snow started again.

It was not at all the dream she was expecting.

First she dreamed of a man, no longer young but not yet old, in heavy boots and leather gaiters and a farmer's smock, walking along a tree-shaded road, whistling. She could not make out his face clearly through the changing leaf-shadows, but she thought it was an open, friendly face. Who is this? she thought, but she was strangely unreassured that this man was not Horuld. He stopped by a well, and unhooked the bucket, and dropped it into the well, and wound it up again; in her dream she could hear every creak and splash, and the faint puff of the man's breath as he raised the bucket. He reached for the dipper, which hung next to the peg he had taken the bucket off. It had been an ordinary dipper—hadn't it?—he must have thought so too, because he didn't merely pull his hand back when he saw what he was reaching for but stepped back from the well itself. What now hung on the dipper's peg was a cup that looked like a Chalice's goblet, heavily worked in silver; dreaming, she tried to see what the forms and figures were, but could not, only that the work was so ornate it threw its own shadows across the bowl. No ordinary roadside well should have such a thing. The man looked at it for a moment longer, laughed, shook his head, and drank directly from the bucket, which, when he hung it back on its peg, he did so very carefully, that his hand should not brush the mysterious goblet.

No, she thought. Perhaps this man might have courted a beekeeper with a woodright, but he will have nothing to do with a Chalice.

As the man walked on down the road, she seemed to remain behind; and the shadows of the trees grew thicker and darker till she was in a cold grey place where she could no longer move her arms and legs; and then she thought, though she was not sure, the figures on the well goblet had come to life, and she was surrounded by the faces of angry, frightened men and women. She recognised none of them, nor did any one pause for her to memorise it so that she would recognise it if she saw it again, when she woke, if she was to marry an angry, frightened, unknown man. She struggled to wake or to move, and as if she had broken some invisible bonds, she seemed suddenly to be free; and now she seemed to be walking at the edge of a field under a night sky. The field seemed to be familiar to her but it was hard to tell in the dark. The almost sweet, slightly dusty smell of a ripe cereal crop was in her nostrils, and she knew it would be a good harvest. The stalks came to her shoulders, and she could see over them, to where someone else seemed to be walking at the edge of the same field at a little distance from her; as she brushed her fingers through the half-soft, half-bristly awns, she thought in surprise, *They're warm.*

And then the dream had shifted again, and she was surrounded by redness and heat. Where was the face of the man she would marry, or some sight of herself standing alone in an embroidered robe carrying a cup? She could see nothing but the peculiar un-differentiated redness. Not quite undifferentiated: there were streaks in it, fluttering, trembling, golden streaks, and a gentle thumping noise near her ear. Just one ear, as if her cheek rested against something that brought the echo of the sound to her.

She was still curled up, but she didn't seem to be lying down any more, and her head was resting against this gently thumping thing, her wrists bent round each other and hands clasped under her chin as if she were bearing herself as Chalice. Except that she wasn't bearing herself at all; something was holding her. Her legs were folded under her as if she were sitting in a chair at home, the chair whose seat had lost most of its stuffing, so you had to sit on the frame edge, with your legs bent under you, or half disappear down the unexpected well. . . .

There was redness all around her, redness and gold; they blended together, and they did not blend, for the red was hard and restless and spiky, and the gold was smooth and supple and flowing. She seemed to breathe it; her right nostril drew in red, and her left gold. Her Chalice-cradling hands instead cradled a rope of red and gold, whose individual threads wove in and out between her fingers, the red through the fingers of her right hand, the gold through the fingers of her left. She felt that the very hair of her head had gone red and golden, that the hair on the right side fell coarse and harsh and red, and on the left, fine and soft and golden. She wondered if the strangeness of what she saw, the way everything seemed both too shallow and too deep, was that her right eye saw only red and her left only gold, and they somehow could not put the two together as they had done all the ordinary things in her life till now. . . . She felt dizzy, except that she was being securely held, and could not fall. She thought she should be frightened, for she knew the world was not red and gold; but she did not feel frightened. The red and gold were very beautiful. She wondered if what she was held by was a red thing or a golden thing.

She didn't know when she realised that the Master was holding her in his lap. The chair-well was the space between his knees—she supposed—as he sat cross-legged. The thump was the beating of his heart. (Did priests of Fire still have hearts that beat?) His arms were around her, one round her waist, and the second gently holding her bent head against his chest. She wanted to tell him that she was awake, that he could let her go, that it was very nice of him to warm her like this—it was rather cold to be sleeping outdoors—but it wasn't necessary. But she found she couldn't. Indeed she couldn't move, even to drop her hands out of the Chalice clasp.

It is good that you are awake. But do not try to move yet.
What?

You are still dangerously cold. Do not try to move.

I—I'm not cold!

You are held by Fire. Let it do its work.

I . . . don't understand.

I found you half dead of cold. I do not understand either.

She stopped puzzling over the strange immobility of her body and tried to remember what had happened before she woke up. The warmth she felt now reminded her of waking up by her own fireside with the understanding that she had to go to the old knoll—suddenly she remembered that its old name had been Listening Hill—and go to sleep there long enough to dream. She needed a dream from Listening Hill to tell her if she was to marry Horuld.

This was not something she wanted to tell the Master.

She was beginning to be able to feel her breath going in and out. Her elbows were tucked so close to her body that they moved as her rib-cage expanded and contracted. She could feel her own breath on the backs of her hands, she could feel the long bone of her right thumb pressed against the bottom of her lowered chin . . . and at that point she found she could let her clasped hands drop. The red and the gold seemed to dim into the shadows, till all she saw was shadows. For a moment she grieved for the red and the gold.

The Master let go of her gently. She tried to sit up, and swayed a little. He uncrossed his legs and knelt behind her, his hands now under her elbows, and as he stood up he drew her with him. He's stronger, she thought fuzzily—no; he would say that Fire was helping him. But her thought added stubbornly, And his limbs seem to bend in all the ordinary human places, and he seems *solid*—like flesh, not like fire. She tried not to stagger. The billows of his cloak fell down between them. She couldn't remember now what she had been leaning against while he—and Fire—held her: his shirt? His bare skin? Is it only his face and hands that are black—is he red and golden under his clothes, like fire? But no hearth fire ever looked like what she had seen. Had he become Fire again to save her? She thought, I'm not burnt, I'm only warm.

Once she was standing unaided he bent and picked something up off the ground: her shawl, and then her cloak. He wrapped them round her, though at the moment she was so warm she did not want them. They were comforting, though, comforting in their familiarity. It hadn't been frightening when she woke up, but now that he had released her the idea of having been held by Fire was terrifying. She touched her hair; it felt as it always did. She held her hands out in front of her where she could see them, and they looked just the same as usual. They were not black, and the tips of the fingers did not glow red. And he had learnt not to burn human flesh. He had only burnt her the once, when he had only recently left his Fire, when he was exhausted by a journey he was no longer fit to endure.

It was only then that she noticed that it was still dark. Since they stood on open ground there was enough light to see by despite the cloud cover. She turned to look at him. His blackness was a silhouette against the grey sky; he seemed to grow out of the silhouettes of the broken stones of the pavilion. But she could see his red eyes, looking down at her.

"How did you find me?" she said.

He looked up, away from her. "I often try to read the earthlines at night, when the world is quieter, and most human beings are asleep. This last week I have been walking—with Ponty's help—the line that runs from the Ladywell to the crossroads by the golden beeches, but tonight I could not concentrate. Fire is very aware of heat and cold; I thought for a while that it was only dancing with the snow. Eventually it occurred to me that it would not—not—I don't know how to explain—at last I looked where it would draw my attention and saw one of my folk dying of cold on the pavilion hill. My Chalice. And so I came here." He looked at her again. "You were not . . . you were not trying to destroy yourself, were you?"

"Oh, *no*," she said, appalled. "No. Absolutely not." Was I? Would I rather die than marry Horuld? A tiny thought added plaintively, Who would take care of my bees? If I died, or if I married Horuld? she thought back at it, but there was no response.

He let out his breath in a long sigh that crackled like fire. "I thought, perhaps . . . being Chalice to such a one as I . . . might be too great a strain."

"*Gods* of the earthlines," she burst out, *"no."* She thought, And how would a Chalice who cannot bear her Master's Fire choose to kill herself? Very possibly by freezing.

He was silent for a moment and then said, "I have also thought, lately, that perhaps, it would be as well if I . . . removed myself. Ceded the Mastership to Horuld, presumably, as he has been chosen by the Overlord."

"No," she said again, but he did not seem to hear her this time,

and there was a lump in her throat so large she could not immediately say it again. She put her hands to her throat as if to squeeze the lump away and let her speak. "No—think of the hardship—even the annihilation—of any demesne when the bloodline is broken and another family must establish itself."

"That is only when the bloodline *is* broken. I do not know if anyone has ceded a Mastership before. My thought is that if the old Master can create a way for the new, there may be little disturbance. Less, perhaps, than the disturbance caused by a priest of Fire trying to become Master of a demesne, even if he is of the old bloodline."

"What disturbance has been so great that you must think this way?" she cried. "Do you know—do you not know—that the demesne has been in trouble for years? Perhaps no one will tell you—very well, I am your Chalice, *I* will tell you—your brother had been trying his best to shatter Willowlands upon the rock of his egotism. He grew much worse after you left—after he no longer had to pretend to explain himself to you. He could no longer be bothered even to listen to the earthlines, let alone walk them. He was fully absorbed in what he called his *researches*. I know very little about this, even now, because I was a small woodskeeper when your brother was Master, and such as I was only heard rumours, and since then I . . .

"But I can tell you what the small folk of the demesne experienced, the last years of your brother's Mastership. Mortar would not hold and walls fell down. Roof-trees cracked when they were sound and without woodworm. Saplings well-planted withered; seed put in the ground did not sprout. Sheep rarely had twins; cows were often barren. And every season there were *fires*. Brush fires, till the farmers who were accustomed to burning off their redberry moors no longer dared do so; chimney fires; lightning fires. The same year we in the east saved Cag's barn, two lightning-struck houses in the north and the west burnt to the ground. But the heat of your brother's energies beat out from the pavilion, night after night after night, till they too caught fire and *burned*."

He answered, "Yes, I have wondered about that fire. You are right that most people—even my Circle; even my Chalice—do not speak to me willingly of what happened since I went to Fire. But I can read, as I find my way slowly through this land that is unexpectedly my demesne, that there had been much fire here in those seven years. As unusually much, perhaps, as there have been unusually many quiet old horses overturning their carts or their ploughs and running away—although any horse may take fright and bolt—or as unusually many Housefolk being turned away for breakages and carelessness, although there are always people who do not pay proper attention to what they are doing, or do not care.

"I have never known why my brother chose to send me to Fire, rather than Air or Earth. Perhaps Fire runs in our blood: I did think, in the heat of my own fury, that he chose Fire from his burning rage against me. But as the priests agreed to take me he must have been right about what there was in me that Fire could fix on, could yoke to itself; they would not have taken me merely because my brother wished to be rid of me. Perhaps—perhaps we were born in the wrong order, and it was he who should have gone to Fire, where the fire that was in him could have been put to better purpose."

Perhaps we were born in the wrong order was so like what she had often thought that she could not reply. Perhaps his brother would have been a good priest of Fire; but Willowlands had had to live with his being a bad Master.

After a little he went on: "The Circle will not speak to me of what happened in the seven years of my brother's Mastership, but they speak to me much—if not very clearly—about what has happened since I returned. They will not say it outright, but they would like to see the Overlord's Heir as Master here."

"Not all of them," she flashed back at him. "Not I. Not the Grand Seneschal."

"That is two against nine," he said gently.

"And the twelfth?" she said. "What of yourself? Would you truly say against yourself?" She paused, and a dreadful thought occurred to her: "Do you miss your Fire so much?"

"Miss Fire," he said musingly. "I don't know. Isn't that strange? Do you miss your woodskeeping?"

"Yes," she said immediately. "Especially—" She fell silent.

"Especially now?" he said. "Why were you asleep on Listening Hill on a night too cold for human flesh and blood?"

She jerked as if he had struck her when he said "Listening Hill."

He waited, but she made no answer. "I do not think you would come here for the sake of recent ghosts," he said at last. "And I remember it had an oracular name, when it was still called Listening Hill. What foretelling was worth the risk—was so urgent it could not wait—with the snow falling?"

Almost at random she said, "I miss woodskeeping because I knew how to do it. The Chalice is a bloodright, like the Mastership is, but it seems to me much like finding water. The rods in the dowser's hands draw down till they crack, and when the hole is dug the water springs up, but one must still brick in the well or the channel or the pond, or the water will spread itself out and sink back into the earth again and be lost. I do not know how to brick my channel. I feel—I feel as if I am trying to hold back a river with my hands. The Chalice energy is *strong* . . . and I am weak and foolish. At first, when it only seemed to be about mixing cups and standing in doorways, I thought I could learn enough to—to *appear* to be Chalice. That part even made some sense to me: water is the basis of all things, the thing of all things we need to stay alive, and whenever I was in doubt I put a little honey in; and there were books that told me the usual, the standard mixtures for the usual, standard gatherings. By narrowing it down to the most visible, the best-known, of the Chalice's work—the bit where she dresses up like a mummer and stands around holding a big flashy cup with enamel and jewels on it—I could think about trying to learn it, despite the daily—hourly— sinking of the heart at the size of the task. Don't think about it; just put something in a cup and stir.

"At first, after your brother died, the demesne was in such disarray that the least gesture toward coherence seemed a great one. But disarray has its own destructive inertia and those small gestures have meant less and less; and my faith that I am learning to make them correctly is too slow and slight a thing to set against . . . and I have made a terrible error from ignorance."

His silence was a waiting and listening silence. And would he not have heard the story already, from someone else? Might not the thought that his own Chalice preferred the Heir have further urged him to consider ceding Mastership? What if he thought her someone who would say one thing to him—as she had just done—while saying, and doing, something else entirely when he was not there? And so at last she said, draggingly, "The Heir came to me. I spent time with him, as Chalice, as a way of keeping distance between us, because I did not want to spend time with him at all, and I did not know that the Chalice could send the Heir away. The Grand Seneschal told me—told me that I could have sent him away. I would not have known else.

"The Grand Seneschal told me that the Chalice had been seen alone with the Heir and had thus indicated her championing of him. I did not know. It is what I did not want—of all things what I did not want. The Grand Seneschal said it was a result of my lack of training; but that is something there is no cure for. I see no comfort—nor useful penance—there. The Grand Seneschal has said he will try to counter the damage I have done with a tale of my shameful ignorance, and that I must—must make up— some tale in support. But I cannot see that the revelation that your demesne's Chalice is inept and imprudent is going to be seen as a satisfactory situation in a demesne struggling for balance—for its life." Again she stopped.

After a pause he said, "I am worse than you, because I have

spent useless days in the company of various members of my Circle, knowing that as Master I could send them away, but not able to believe in my Mastership enough to do so."

"That is only kindness," she said. "You will lose nothing in anyone's eyes for kindness, and something, I think, you will gain."

"That is a remark the Chalice would make," he said, "a Chalice wishing to affirm her Master's binding to his bloodright."

"You *are* bound," she said. "As am I."

"Yes," he said, "I am. But binding cannot necessarily quiet that which has been bound. My people fear me. They fear me and they fear my touch—with justice, as you know. They flinch away from me when I walk among them."

At the unfairness of this she cried out, "You have only burnt *one* person! And you were tired near death and only just returned from Fire!"

Gently he said, "I know this too. As does my Circle—as do my people. But they also know that there is always a hesitation—sometimes so slight that were they not looking for it they would not see it—before I touch anyone or anything. If I know the need is coming for me to lay my hand somewhere, I can prepare. A sudden grasp—I cannot do it. A stair banister, a dinner plate, even Ponty's mane—no harm. But if I touched bare human flesh suddenly, I would still burn it."

She did not know this. She could say nothing; think of nothing to say. No . . . she had guessed as much. Guessed that it was not only the Master's continuing physical awkwardness that caused all those brief pauses. She had sometimes thought that they came from his having to remember what he was doing, what gesture he needed, what action he had next to perform; a kind of physical translation, as from one language to another. But she had still known, though she had not wanted to know, that while that was a part of it, it was only a part. She must say something, but what reassurance could she offer? It had been over half a year since the Master had come home, and still Fire ran in him this strongly? Perhaps the priests of Fire had been right that he could not return.

"By the fourth level," he said sadly, "an Elemental priest can again go into the world, if he so chooses, because his metamorphosis is complete."

She knew of the temples in the cities where the priests' abbeys lay, where the Elemental priests occasionally came to hold rites for ordinary humans. The priests were described as superhumanly beautiful, miraculously graceful and utterly terrifying. "But they mostly choose not to come," she said. "And they cannot stay, because they can no longer live among humans. Among us. A fourth-level priest would never have been sent home to be Master of his demesne. And I have never heard of one stopping a forest fire."

Thoughtfully he went on, as if he had not heard her, "Occasionally I have seen one or another of my people creep up to Ponty—when I have been some safe little distance away—and pat him, quickly and as if surreptitiously, as if checking that he is real horseflesh—or as if he were a charm against his rider."

"Ponty," she said. "Ponty must do you good among the people of Willowlands; who could fear Ponty?"

"It is not Ponty they fear," he said patiently, as if she were a student who was refusing to learn her lesson.

She shook her head. She did not want to say yet more against his brother; but what she was thinking of were the increasingly wild, trampling horses her Master's brother had chosen to ride round his demesne, as if he were trying to frighten his own folk—as if he were trying to hammer the earthlines into passivity, into acceptance of his misuse of them. But he did not burn human flesh if he thoughtlessly touched it. Did it matter? Her Master touched the earthlines softly—she knew this; more and more she could read the influence he was gaining over the solid earth and invisible air of his demesne; those parts of his Mastership which he could not burn. Had a demesne ever had an inhuman Master before?

He said, "And they do not fear Horuld."

"There is still time," she said, hearing the emptiness of her own words: was there ever a more useless remark than "Give it time"? "The Chalice has no Heir—no apprentice. And I am not yet fit to take an apprentice—if I ever shall be."

"Did you ask Listening Hill for a Chalice's Heir? Or did you ask how to unbind mine, to reveal him as unworthy and incapable?"

It was no more than she deserved. She took a deep breath. "I do not know how to ask an oracle anything. The tale that was once told among us small people—among woodskeepers and bee-keepers and shepherds and dairy folk—is that Listening Hill, did you fall asleep on it, would tell a man if his wife were unfaithful, and a woman whom she was to marry."

He followed her thought, but not far enough. "A Chalice cannot be married against her will."

She thought of lying to him, but there were too many broken

laws and too much harm done to the demesne already by the lies of a Master who had dishonoured his bloodright and a Chalice who had not tried to stop him. Now she was Chalice, and she could not lie to her Master. She knew little enough, as the Grand Seneschal had reminded her, but even she knew that much. "I have been reading as hastily as I can about the treatment of an outblood Heir. It is not only the cups I must give him, it is—everything. It is all that *everything* that I do not know, that let me make the wrong decision the other day when he sought my company. I accept the responsibility of binding him as Heir as the Chalice must, but I—yes, I wish to bind you, the Master, more. You are Master, and so it is what I must do but I also do not—I do not feel—I do not feel *safe* with Horuld. The Chalice is not easy in me when he is walking in Willowlands. It may be that the Chalice bloodright only recognises that he is outblood. But it may be something more. I fear it, whatever it is.

"And I read, yesterday, that in the case of an outblood Heir coming to Mastership, the best way for the transition to be successfully made is that the Chalice marry him. It is a small dusty book—but all the books in the library are dusty—I believe it is not well known, that an outblood Heir may marry his Chalice; aside that it is against the usual law forbidding any such bond, there may be other reasons against it that I do not know. Those reasons may even be in that same small dusty book which I can no longer bear to pick up, let alone read. But I am sure the Overlord knows, and Horuld, of this exception, when an outblood Heir inherits. I saw—I wondered—I am sure, now, that this is in their minds—even perhaps that this is their *plan*. It was more, that day, when I spent that mistaken, irretrievable time with Horuld, than merely that he was currying favour with the Chalice. I knew it at the time; I only did not know what it was. I knew that it made my flesh creep.

"I—I cannot face this. I came to the Chalice too late; my apprenticeship should have begun when I was still a child, so that I could grow up within it—it within me—and it have the chance to shape me. I had inherited my father's woodright six years before the Circle came to me at my cottage, and my mother's bees four years before. They came and found a madwoman milking her goats three times a day while her cottage floor ran with mead and the bees were so thick they were like a canopy over the meadow. When I saw them coming I burst into tears. When they told me what they had come for, I could not believe it. I *could not.* Perhaps it is the Chalice's duty to marry an outblood Heir, but *I* cannot."

There was a long pause while Mirasol wished she could see his face.

At last, musingly, he said, "I had great difficulty when I was first sent away, because I had not wanted to be sent. But the priests are, I fear, accustomed to that, and care only that you are suited to enter Fire at last; the rest, they believe, will come in time. Indeed, when I finally did enter, I felt at home there, at home in a way that I had not been able to feel here, because of my brother. I had been too young to understand much of what the Master did when my father was still Master; the murmur of the earthlines seemed no more to me than the singing of the birds, and rather less than the nicker of my pony when he saw me coming with the bulges in my pockets that meant apples. But when our father died and my brother took the bloodright, I felt it, and felt it very strongly that he was not working in a way best for the demesne. . . . What I feel now is that Fire taught me what I should be looking to do now, but in some other land, language—dimension. Fire taught me a skill of care and guardianship that I feel I should be able to adapt but somehow I cannot.

"I do not miss Fire the way I missed Willowlands when I was sent away. And the way I seem still to miss Willowlands now.

"The priests would have an answer to that. Indeed I think they tried to tell me before I left. When I came, they said, I was too old; Fire too prefers its apprentices young. But Fire could still bring me to itself, if I let it, and having read me, they believed I would— could—let it. But it is hard to leave one's . . . humanity behind. Especially if one is already a man grown. How did you say it? That your apprenticeship should have begun when you were still a child, that you might grow up within it and it within you, and it have the chance to shape you. Yes." He held out a black hand. "I am blacker than most of the Fire priests, because there was more of me to burn. But perhaps that is also why, even from the third level, I was able to make the attempt to return to the mundane world. I almost did not make that journey, however; I believe I almost died, although the priests did not tell me so.

"And now . . . it is not Fire that is blocking my way back into Willowlands, but it is perhaps Fire that burned me too well, because I am hollow where I need to be full.

"I cannot promise to remain your Master, even to save you, although I would if I could. I—I cannot think how to say it. The *I* in Fire is not the same *I* as in the world, and *I* am neither the one nor the other. A Master must save his folk as he is able, and able he must be; it is what a Master is for. And a Master treats his Chalice as if she were the finest crystal."

"The Master's wedding cup is crystal so delicate that the rule is you may put only two mouthfuls of the drink in it, one each for the bride and groom," she said dully, as if reciting a memorised text.

There was another pause. "Mirasol," he said; she looked at him, puzzled. "Mirasol is your name. I . . . cannot remember mine. In Fire I was *Azungbai*."

"Liapnir," she whispered. "The last Master's younger brother's name was Liapnir, the younger brother he sent away to the priests of Fire."

"Liapnir," he said. "Liapnir would save Mirasol if he could."

The next few weeks were hectic. She was almost grateful, despite that it meant she did no more reading about outblood Heirs; at least it meant she also made no more horrifying discoveries. She was almost constantly in attendance at the House or the six and twenty-four fanes and outposts of the Circle; when she was not holding a cup she was pouring patterns of water and mead over the least quiet of the demesne's hills and dells, copses and meadows. She thought grimly, Now that it is possibly too late, folk are remembering what a Chalice is for. People asked her to lay the restless energies in this or that place that fell within their tending, or that they often walked near, or was where they drew their water. This tradition of the Chalice had fallen away during the last several years of the previous Chalice's governance. Mirasol did not know whether to be pleased that she was fitting into the role—or at least perceived as fitting into it—or worried that if the folk chose to come to an unsatisfactory Chalice, they must do so because they believed the Master to be more disappointing still.

She thought—she hoped—she could see the ripples spreading from Kenti telling the story of Tis' burnt arm. She'd had Kenti's neighbour Vel asking about his well first, where about once a sennight for about a day the water tasted strongly of roses—"It's nice, the wife likes it, and she'll be sorry if you take it away, but it's a little queer and queer is . . . queer." She forbore to ask how long this had been happening, and why he was only coming to ask her about it now. After Vel there was Frak, an old mate of Danel's, asking if she could do anything about a quiet, flat-seeming field where the furrows refused to cut straight; and after Frak was Droman, who worked on the same farm, who wanted something for the ground under a bit of fence that kept falling down and letting the sheep out.

She might, once or twice, have asked one of the others of the Circle to help her—Landsman or Oakstaff, perhaps, with a restless spinney or meadow—but she did not.

At this rate, she thought, I'll have to take an apprentice just because I need the help. At least I could teach her to take care of bees. She'd have to be able to read; but then maybe she could teach *me* something about the Chalice. . . . She surprised herself by considering this possibility seriously for a minute or two, and then thought, No. Not yet. Wait till . . . but she could not put it into words, even to herself.

But when Catu came to discuss with her the possibility of letting it be known that the Chalice could heal burns and wounds as well as Catu could, she said: "I'd be glad of it; and if you can cure a few stomach-aches too that would be even better; I have more work than Silla"—who was Catu's apprentice—"and I can do, and I'd rather be birthing babies." And Mirasol almost replied, "Only if you find me a good girl for apprentice. Silla doesn't have any younger sisters, does she?"

She said instead, "I'll help anyone I can."

Catu looked at her shrewdly. "You aren't getting enough sleep, are you? Is it work or worry?"

Mirasol shook her head. "Both. Everything."

"I should have come before—Mirasol, I'm sorry. You know how—confused—everything has been, since the old Master died. I know it's been a hard transition for you—I know that I can't imagine *how* hard a transition—but I've been run off my legs myself. The next time I'm going this way I'll bring you something to help you sleep. The quietening herbs I gave you helped, didn't they? Oh dear—if it's work that's keeping you up, I shouldn't be adding to it, should I? But—well, it would be good if . . ." She hesitated. "The Chalice before the last one—she was Chalice almost sixty years. And our Master's father—he was a good Master but not an easy man—and as is the way of things, most of his Circle was like him. That's some of the problem now, of course, there are a few of them left, and the others, they took as apprentices folk who were as near like to them as the rods would let them. And so the people went to their Chalice, who was not like the others. Everyone knew her."

"Yes. Nara is the commonest woman's name in Willowlands, because it was her name."

"Yes. In sixty years I hope the commonest woman's name is Mirasol."

Mirasol smiled, tiredly. And Nara's Master was as friendly and approachable as a puppy or your grandmother, compared to the one we have now, and most of his Circle is united only in their aversion to him. What would you think of Horuld as a Master? What would Silla think? What would the mothers of your babies think? "Send me your wounds and burns and stomach-aches then."

But it was Kenti who brought two little packets from Catu—"this one's for if you're lying awake thinking, and this one's if you're just too tired to sleep"—plus two loaves of bread and a big jar of potted meat. "I asked Catu—she didn't think it would be—she thought it would be—she told me these were to help you sleep, that you were working too hard, and I said I didn't think you were eating properly, I know it's easy not to when you're too busy, but even honey isn't enough by itself. . . ." Her voice trailed away and she looked at Mirasol anxiously.

Mirasol reached out and took the parcels. "It's very kind of you, thank you," she said.

Very little money changed hands among the small folk of a

demesne; some duty was paid in coin, but most of the economy was based on barter and exchange. The Chalice, like the other members of the Circle, received a stipend for the work she did (disbursed by the Grand Seneschal), and unless there was some very complex ritual involved, ordinary demesne folk were not expected to pay for help from a Circle member. (Given her book-and-paper habit, Mirasol was glad she had honey and beeswax to sell.) But popular Circle members tended to have very well-stocked larders and very well-maintained properties, or known and frequently augmented collections of things on display at the House. Nara had collected wood carvings; there was a dormouse in linden wood in the Yellow Room which had belonged to her that Mirasol was absurdly fond of. Occasionally she took her books and papers to the Yellow Room and when she did she always lifted the dormouse down from its shelf to sit on her work-table.

Mirasol's hands shook a little as she cradled the parcels. "How is Tis?"

Kenti laughed with an easiness that told Mirasol what she wanted to know. "She's absolutely fine. Except she gives the stove a wide berth—which is no bad thing. She's with her cousins today, so that I could get some things done." She hesitated. "I—I told Danel and my sister what you said about the Master—about him healing your hand. I—I hope you don't mind."

"On the contrary," Mirasol said sincerely, and her heart sang within her.

"It is hard to—to—to *like* him," Kenti said, obviously finding words with difficulty, "although I know it's not *liking* a Master needs from his people. Danel says his horses aren't always shying at ghosts any more—any more nor horses always shy at ghosts—especially the young 'uns, and that that'll be the Master taking hold like a proper Master, and the earthlines quietening under him, and never mind what he looks like. But those red eyes—I can't—what does he see with those red eyes?"

"He sees warmth," said Mirasol. "When he looks into a tree where a bird sits singing, where you and I could not see it hidden behind the leaves, he will see the outline of its warmth."

"But they— But he—"

"You get used to it," Mirasol said.

Kenti looked at her sidelong. "There's a story that you spent the day with the Heir. That you . . . favour him."

The *day*, thought Mirasol miserably. She took a deep breath and said, "I—I feel that the Heir's connection with the demesne is—is not as strong as it might be. If he is Heir, then he must be bound here—for the Master's sake. Binding is the Chalice's work. But we have a Master—a good Master. Whatever colour his eyes are. The Heir is only the Heir."

Kenti's face was wearing that hopeful, thoughtful look again when she left, the look she had worn when Mirasol had told her about the Master healing her hand. Mirasol hoped Kenti would tell the story of why the Chalice had spent time with the Heir too—and hoped that her sister was a chatterbox. She could not tell—or guess—how much or how little her mistake with the Heir might have contributed to any new restlessness among the demesne's folk. She heard other reverberations of both her behaviour and the Grand Seneschal's commentary on it. When she could—since few people asked her as directly as Kenti had, as if healing her daughter's arm had somehow made the Chalice accessible—she said she had mistaken the Heir's purpose in consulting her; that she had wished not to embarrass him by revealing his shortcomings. It was the nearest she could come to the Seneschal's suggestion that she insinuate the Heir was unworthy or unfit. She was afraid that her real revulsion would be exposed if she spoke too near it.

She had, by now, learnt enough to be Chalice when she wished not to be questioned further, and mostly she was as saddened as she was relieved when it worked. She told Selim the truth about that day: that she'd been stupid because she didn't know any better. She even managed to make Selim laugh by describing her consternation when she looked up and saw the Grand Seneschal standing in the library door. But the laugh stopped too soon and worry took its place. Selim was no fool, and she knew the danger the demesne was in; she was of another old family, and the land spoke in her blood too. Mirasol thought, if there were enough of the old families, perhaps we could drive the Heir away. Perhaps there is a better candidate for Heir right here in Willowlands, disguised as a houndsman or a small woodskeeper. . . . But what if it is not that Horuld is a poor tool in the hand of the Overlord which might snap from pressure; what if it is that this is the way it is, having an outblood Heir? That the true blood repels it, like iron filings from a magnet?

"Tell it around," said Mirasol. "Please. The Seneschal warned me what was happening—and Kenti asked me in so many words if I favoured the Heir."

"I will," Selim said grimly. "I may leave out the part about your being stupid."

Mirasol recognised the joke, and laughed.

"I worry about you, Mirasol," said Selim. "I am happy to trust you with my life—remember the night we saved Cag's barn from burning down?—but it seems to me that you've been thrown in quicksand and told to learn to swim. And the Master—"

"The Master is learning," said Mirasol quickly. "Remember Danel's horses."

"The land and the beasts may be learning to listen to him," said Selim. "I am not so sure about the people. Would the story of you favouring the Heir have flown so quickly if they weren't hoping it was true?"

* * *

Once Mirasol was so tired that she fell asleep sitting on one of the stone chairs outside her cottage, on an afternoon that was just warm enough to permit the chilly folly of sitting outdoors in the sunlight for a few moments. She had brought another book from the House library back with her to read, but her mind kept turning in spirals very like the ones she trickled from the lip of a Chalice cup. She only closed her eyes for a moment, her face turned up toward the sun, thinking that she could smell the mead and the herbs she had chosen that day for a field where the cattle would not stay . . . at least there had been no more cracks in the earth . . . Faine's wife had bought honey from her for the first time a few weeks ago, and said that Daisy's calf was a fine strong heifer . . . here by her cottage she could always smell mead and herbs . . . when she woke it was twilight, and her nose was cold, but she was warmly covered by a blanket of bees.

She did not see the Master alone again, although he looked into her face with a directness no other member of the Circle did when he accepted the cup she raised to his lips.

part
FOUR

When the Overlord came she hated him. It was a shock like a blow; much worse than when she had met the Heir. She hated him so much that she trembled with it, and clutched the welcome cup to her as if it were a crutch to hold her upright. If there had not been a tradition that the Chalice's hand should not touch the hand of whomever she offered a cup, she would have invented the tradition on the spot.

The Overlord touched the hands or the foreheads of the others of the Circle . . . all except the Master, who was tucked into his deep cloak and long sleeves again, although he wore the chain, collar and belt of the Mastership of Willowlands, as he must to greet his Overlord. The hierarchy between an Overlord and a Master acknowledged the superiority of the Overlord; but it would still have been a discourtesy—even an impertinence—for the Overlord to demonstrate his authority over a Master on the Master's own lands. Perhaps it was only Mirasol's attitude that made her feel that she could see the Overlord's hands twitch in a longing to do so.

Deager had accompanied the Overlord, which was standard conduct for an Overlord visiting a demesne; but he had also brought the Heir with him. Probably this was no more than the correct form also. But she took it as an indication of his desires in the matter of the immediate future of Willowlands; and she was sure she read it in the Grand Seneschal's face that he believed the same. But then the Grand Seneschal always looked bleak and disapproving. Mirasol tried to remember if he had looked so before the seven years of the previous Master's disastrous dominion; but she had been the daughter of a beekeeper and a small woodskeeper then, and had not noticed such things.

The cumbersomely elaborate ceremonial greeting took place in the Hall of Summoning. Then the Housefolk brought food and drink to the outer hall and flung open the double front doors, and the pattern relaxed into groups of people talking to each other; but it was a formal meeting still, with the Chalice present, holding her cup. Mirasol had wondered if the Chalice, when it chose its next bearer, took into account the effect of irregular meals on human beings. While the Chalice held her cup to a meeting, she could not touch food or drink. Mirasol's mother had been one of those who ate when she had time, and didn't think about it if she didn't; Mirasol's father had been one who had to have his meals generous and on time or he grew short-tempered and clumsy. Fortunately Mirasol took after her mother, but some days it was harder to miss meals than other days. Today she was hungry.

Sometimes there was a moment while a Chalice-held assembly regrouped that she could snatch a mouthful, and there was such a moment on this occasion. The Overlord was to be taken on a tour around the demesne, and the horses and carriages that would carry him and his entourage took a little while to bring together. Mirasol set the goblet down with a smack that made its contents slosh (of the Chalice vessels available she'd learnt very quickly to have a preference, when she could, for the ones with deeper bowls, against inadvertent splashes) and pounced on the nearest platter. She therefore didn't see what happened; she was only aware that something had when there was a shout followed by an angry clamour.

She didn't remember dropping the fishcake she was eating, nor snatching up her goblet on her way to the door; not that there was anything she could do. At that moment she thought agonizedly that if the Chalice had still been present it might not have happened . . . but she guessed, with a sickening lurch in her stomach, even before the shouting had died down and the disputers had moved to face one another like battle lines being drawn that what had happened was not an accident.

The Master stood inscrutably, nearly invisible in his cloak and hood; she looked for him first, and so saw the red of his eyes flicker as she ran through the door. Perhaps he had been looking for her, or perhaps he was only calmly waiting for the audience to gather. She was not even first out the door, though far from last, and the others made way for her, because she was Chalice. She paused with an effort at the top of the steps and came down slowly, her hands correctly on the base and stem of the goblet, trying to train her face to the frigid expressionlessness on the Grand Seneschal's face. The Grand Seneschal stood at the Master's elbow; the Overlord and his agent—and the Heir—stood opposed. The half dozen servitors who had come with them stood immediately behind them; the folk of the demesne, Mirasol was dismayed to see, including most of the other members of the Circle, were collecting at a little distance from their Master. The Prelate, Keepfast and Sunbrightener had disappeared.

She finished walking slowly down the steps and took her place at the Master's other elbow. She could not then see where—or who—anyone who might also take the Master's part stood; she heard feet behind them, but her pulse was thudding in her ears and she could not hear if the footsteps stopped or went on. She made a point, difficult as it was, to look directly at both Horuld and the Overlord. She thought Horuld looked at her worriedly, and the Overlord, briefly, narrowed his eyes when he looked back at her. A hot rush of fury stiffened her; even had she preferred the Heir, what Chalice would leave her Master's side? It was bad enough that the rest of the Circle stayed at a distance, but the first, crucial bond in any demesne was between Master and Chalice. For just a moment she thought of the Chalice before her, who had died in the pavilion fire, and wondered if she had been less willing than the tale of her made out to abet her Master's schemes and indulgences. If the Chalice is not strong enough to lead or redirect an ill-choosing Master into ways better for the demesne, what then can she do? To leave her Master would always be worse for the demesne she is sworn to cherish and protect than to stay with him.

Her mind paused, and grasped that thought, like a Chalice

grasping her goblet. And what if a Chalice can see disaster coming, and there is nothing, *nothing* she can do to stop it?

For an event that was to tear their world apart, it took astonishingly little time.

Horuld's voice was high and brittle when he spoke—dispassionately she observed that while he might have learnt his role he did not fill it. "I declare by this misdeed that you are no true Master, nor fit for the great and solemn responsibility of this demesne and its folk; and I challenge you to the single combat of *faenorn*, which will so demonstrate that I am not merely the rightful Heir but that it is my duty to seize rule now, ere some greater calamity come about."

The Overlord's voice, by contrast, was strong and sonorous. "I accept the terrible truth of what you say, and declare, as is my right and duty, that the combat of *faenorn* shall be held this day sennight, and may the demesne itself know what has befallen it, and drink the blood of the loser to its support and nourishment in this direful time."

Faenorn? Her memory scrambled for a meaning. There were ritual duels occasionally fought among members of a Circle but she remembered nothing about a challenge an Heir might give to a Master to take Mastership—*drink the blood of the loser*—a Master was Master. He could not be deposed, set aside. The only way the Mastership passed was by the death of the Master. The Overlord, she thought—even had the Master made the offer to cede that he had spoken of to her—would not have accepted it. It was blood that was binding—for good and ill.

Did the Master know the right form? Why should he know it? She wanted him not to know it, not to have been thinking about anything like it—about losing or ceding the demesne to the Heir. Did he respond, did he accept, because he had to?

What if a Master saw a disaster coming, and there was nothing he could do to stop it?

"I mourn the circumstances of this day to the full depth of the bloodright of Mastership I bear, and I mourn the turmoil and destruction that any resolution must have upon the demesne. I desire with all my strength that the meeting of *faenorn* in a sennight will produce a clear and swift completion of the business, and that no havoc be loosed upon this land and its people, which are innocent of the matter."

The Overlord bowed once, as magnificent as any emperor; the Heir bowed too—like an apprentice who had not done it often enough and was uncertain of his skill. The Overlord then turned on his heel—putting his back to the Master. Even in the midst of the first horror of the new situation, Mirasol was shocked at such deliberate discourtesy, and discovered that she was clutching her goblet so intensely that both her shoulders and her finger joints ached. The Overlord snapped out orders to his servants. Dazed as she was, it still seemed to Mirasol that the Overlord's carriages could not have come so quickly unless they had been held in readiness for this moment. It was the Master's carriages that should have been close at hand, to carry the party to the chosen points of the Circle.

Even the Overlord would not plot quite so cruelly, Mirasol told herself—tried to tell herself. It is only that I have not noticed how time is passing. But she raised her aching eyes to look at the Overlord as he was handed into his carriage, and far from appearing saddened or distressed by the catastrophe he had declared for a sennight hence for one of the demesnes under his vassalage, he looked elated. She thought he looked as if he was trying to be stern, but could not stop his mouth from smiling.

The demesne seemed to be heaving under Mirasol's feet—no, the earthlines were splintering, like walking on frost. With every stamp of the Overlord's feet, every crackle of the gravel under his horses' hooves, more of her land shattered into irretrievable fragments; Mirasol shifted her grip on her cup, which seemed to have grown very heavy, increasingly heavy, as if it contained every broken earthline, every earthline as it broke.

For the first time in months Mirasol heard the earthlines weeping.

The Overlord had turned away first, and the Chalice did not need to take note of the Heir—not yet; not while he was still only Heir—and while it would have been gracious of her to do so, she was beyond grace. She turned away too, and laboriously hauled herself back the last few steps to the bottom of the House stairs. She struggled to hold on to the goblet, the weight of which seemed to be dragging her shoulders out of their sockets. She could no longer hold it round the stem with her hands, but awkwardly shifted it till she clutched the bowl of it with her arms, the fingers of her clasped hands sweaty with effort. And how could the sound the earthlines were making seem to darken her eyes? The lamentations seemed sung, like part-songs, the half-comprehended melody like a draught, and her vision like a candle flame.

She could go no farther; this would have to do. She struggled to raise the goblet above her head, her arms trembling with the strain; she had to brace it against her shoulder before the last ragged heave. There were probably ritual words for this moment, but she did not know them, and she guessed she might not choose to say them even if she knew.

"I declare this demesne sound and whole, by all the strength that is in the long bloodright of Chalice, and by that strength I *bind* this demesne together." She shouted the words into the heavy dead air, and felt, or thought she felt, something—some unknown thing, some hidden and invisible thing—turn toward her. Then she tried to tip the goblet to pour its contents on the stairs to the front of the House . . . and as she tried, she fainted.

🐝　🐝　🐝

She came to herself again in the formal entrance hall. She opened her eyes a little and registered the great table that stood at its centre, still loaded with food; slowly she recognised the roughness against her cheek as probably brocade. Her mind began to fit the small immediate pieces together, so she could finish waking up without thinking about what she was waking up from, or into. She understood that she was lying on one of the ornamental settees; she recognised its shape, graceful to the eye but uncomfortable to the body. It had perhaps been pulled hastily away from the wall for this purpose, since she seemed to be too close to the table. Then she registered that there was a humming in her ears, but she heard someone say "drink this," which distracted her from both thinking and humming.

She opened her mouth, and tasted wine with honey. She might have laughed if she could; it was the wrong wine with the wrong honey. But it did steady her. She opened her eyes the rest of the way and saw, to her astonishment, the Grand Seneschal sitting beside her, holding a small ordinary cup. As she saw him she scrambled to sit up. The Seneschal's expression changed from grim to sardonic.

"Lie quietly," he said. "I am not sorry to sit quietly myself, and tend the Chalice." He looked up. "It is true that in other circumstances I might have asked someone else to do it but there is a slight problem about bees."

Then she understood the humming noise. She thought, How curious, that there should be bees in the front hall of the House; but it was undoubtedly a bee hum. Now that she thought about it, there was a bee creeping down from her hair and walking across her forehead. She brushed it gently away, and saw the Seneschal wince. She looked up.

The ceiling was black with bees. She could see nothing of the fresco of the founding of the demesnes, which was all golds and greens and pinks and blues; and the huge chandelier, taller than a man, was equally invisible: it hung seething like a monstrous swarm in the middle of the hall.

"Oh," she said inadequately. "Oh dear."

The Grand Seneschal said, "I am assuming—no, I am pretending to assume—that to stay near our Chalice, whose particular gift, as we know, is honey, which is unusual and we suspect unique in the long complex history of the Chalice—I am pretending to assume that to stay near her is the second-best protection against an invasion of bees. The first, of course, is to flee, which is what everyone else has done."

She did sit up then.

"They are your bees? The House bees—well, the House bees have never had a Master called to *faenorn* before, so perhaps strange behaviour might be expected of them too. But they are your bees?"

She couldn't see them clearly enough from where she was, but she felt still too weak and shaken to stand up and go closer. Even then the chandelier swarm would be far above her head if she stood directly under it, but a few bees were idly circling it, as if scouting the room for an appropriate nest site. Absurdly she put her hand out—and a bee came and landed on the back of it immediately. Perhaps the one that had been climbing over her hair had not gone far. A second one joined it, and then a third. She could sense the Seneschal stiffening. "Yes, these are mine," she said. She did not add, *They are more beautiful than any other bees on the demesne*, because she did not think he would find this information either interesting or reassuring. Especially, perhaps, because with their additional beauty they were unusually large.

Very, very gently she put a finger out and stroked the striped velvet back of one bee.

She took a deep breath. "Where is . . . where are . . ."

The Seneschal said, in a rather too level, too dry voice, "After you fainted there was a bit of a commotion. I do not think the Overlord anticipated any rebellion—or let us say, significant response—or perhaps he merely assumed that everyone would be too stunned to do anything at all. But for you, Chalice, he was right. And whatever he might privately believe, he can find no public fault in a Chalice trying to bind her demesne together against the cruellest of odds. But as he appears not to have planned for either your courage or your presence of mind, his leave-taking was perhaps not quite the dramatic triumph he had no doubt hoped for.

"The Master disappeared at this point, but Sama says she saw him enter his rooms, and the door to them is now locked. While he makes no reply to knocking, I believe that is where he is. Maury and Dar picked you up and brought you here, and I have risked curse and calumny by bringing your goblet, since I thought leaving it lying at the foot of the stairs was a worse blasphemy than touching a Chalice's chalice without permission. At this point the bees began arriving. I hope this had nothing to do with my transgression. I managed to extract some wine and honey from Maury before he too fled."

"If I leave, perhaps they will follow." She drew her legs up and turned to put her feet on the floor. The bees on her hand flew away. When she tried to stand, her head swam, and if the Seneschal had not stood up with her, and grabbed her as she swayed, she would have fallen again.

"Sit down," he said. "They are not doing anything but—hanging there," he said with a wary glance upward. "And the doors into the rest of the House are closed."

"No," she said, still standing, holding on to the Seneschal's other arm with both hands. "No. I must go home. There is—so much to do in the next seven days. Oh, I—" She stopped, overwhelmed.

"Much to do indeed, and all of it useless," said the Grand Seneschal. "It was a good thing you did just now, but it will be to no purpose, come the day."

She almost could not bring herself to ask: "This is not about . . . my blunder with the Heir, is it? That is not the straw that tipped the balance?"

"No. I would say the Overlord has had this in his eye since the first report of our new Master came back to him. I guess Horuld will have been discomposed by losing someone he believed an ally—I saw the look on his face as you shouted out your binding—and the Chalice is a very important ally indeed. But Horuld does what the Overlord tells him to."

"Planned," she said. *"Planned."* She heard the disbelief in her own voice as if someone else was speaking. She said what she had told herself just after the worst had happened. "Even this Overlord would not have *planned.* . . ." And then she remembered how she had hated him at first sight. That was not only me, Mirasol, she thought. That was also the Chalice in me. Would the Chalice waste such hatred if there were nothing she could do?

"If, as we approach our final extremity, you will permit me a great impertinence. . . . This is why I have found it so difficult to accept you as Chalice. You are a quick study in the rituals of the Chalice; I have admired your skill very much in this, and never more so than this afternoon. As a seer into the darkness in human hearts you are . . . a keeper of bees who has lived all her life in a small corner of woodland, who sees but few people, and they clear and straightforward as she is herself. Forgive me, if you can, for speaking to you so, but if the demesne is to survive Horuld. . . ." The Seneschal's voice stopped.

I will have to marry him, you know. She tried to make herself say the words. The "you know" would make it sound careless, not despairing. But she did despair, and she could not say the words.

"The *faenorn*—I don't think I know. . . ." Her voice trailed away. She'd been sure, when she'd heard Horuld and the Overlord speak Willowlands' doom, she knew nothing about a duel between Heir and Master called *faenorn*. But there was a memory trying to surface. It was another of those things she hadn't wanted to know existed, and when she'd read about it she'd turned the page or laid the book down and taken up another one—or possibly gone to answer the door to someone else wanting honey or help.

"It's another of the grisly lingering remnants of our demesne's early history," said the Grand Seneschal. "I don't know much either—little more than what most of Willowlands now knows. It happened often enough in the early days, I believe, but rarely since. I know . . ." He hesitated. "I know our Master's brother threatened his father with it, but the old Master just laughed." The look of hopeless weariness Mirasol had seen before on the Grand Seneschal's face reappeared. "That's how I heard of it. I knew one or two of the old fireside ballads about bloodletting between Master and Heir; I hadn't realised they might be true, that there was something called *faenorn* with a name and a heritage. My own master—he who was Grand Seneschal before me—was very worried about it, but the old Master just laughed again, said that it was boyish high spirits, that every son needed to rebel against his father. My master tried to warn me . . . at least he never knew how right he was." The Grand Seneschal rubbed a hand over his face, as if to wipe away the hopelessness and weariness. "There is some irony in our Master being called to the *faenorn*, but I do not feel we are in a position to appreciate it."

She released the Seneschal's arm. "I must go. I must go." The urgency was there; now all she needed was a plan to go with it. She stooped—slowly—to pick up her goblet, and noticed with regret that it was dented at the lip; that would have been when she dropped it, trying to pour. It amazed her how little, now, it weighed. It was perhaps appropriate that she had dropped it, though she would never have deliberately dropped a Chalice vessel. But the cup had been mixed for the meeting of the Master, Overlord and Heir, not for the treachery of the last two. To bind properly, the mixture must match the circumstances. Were there any records of a Chalice binding a demesne against her Overlord? But the new dent in the lip of a centuries-old goblet was a sorrow and a pity. It was, she thought, only the first small pebble, heralding the avalanche.

Beneath the humming of the bees she could still hear the lament of the earthlines. What did they grieve for? The coming of Horuld, the loss of the Master—or only the destruction of the change?

"At least let me send you with a pony," said the Grand Seneschal.

Her face was almost too stiff to smile, but the corners of her mouth did turn up at last. "And what pony will be happy trailing hundreds of thousands of bees?"

The Seneschal replied, "Ponty has carried the Master when he still smells of fire and char. I think Ponty might bear a few bees."

"What—what happened?" she said timidly. "What happened, that the Overlord . . . I did not see. I was indoors, I was *eating*," she said, as if this were a shameful thing, "and—"

The Seneschal interrupted. "They will have planned for it to have happened in the one moment the Chalice may rest herself in a long day of holding witness. That is not your fault either. In a way it should not have signified, because the Chalice was not there; the meeting was not whole nor held. But it was done to create this break, and no one, I think, could say that the Overlord was not within his entitlement to react as he did—indeed some would say he was required to do so.

"The Overlord stumbled. That is all. He stumbled while he was turning to ask—to say to the Master—I don't know what. His mouth was open; I saw that. Perhaps he was taking care not to say 'Watch carefully now, I am going to ruin you.' He stumbled—does he seem like a man who stumbles easily to you?—and the Master should have caught him. He was standing next to the Master, and no one else was near. The Master had to catch him. But the Master stepped back, and the Overlord fell."

The law was the law. The Master might as well have broken a blade under the Overlord's nose and dropped the pieces to the ground as what he did do. It did not matter to demesne law that this Master had been a priest of Fire less than a year ago.

There is always a hesitation before I touch anyone or anything. . . . If I know the need is coming for me to lay my hand somewhere, I can prepare. A sudden grasp—I cannot do it. A stair banister, a dinner plate, even Ponty's mane—no harm. But if I touched bare human flesh suddenly, I would still burn it. There were many reasons she did not like remembering the snowy night on the pavilion knoll. Frustrated she cried out, "But he is so much *better*! Think of when he first arrived—I don't only mean—" She stretched out her right hand and held it palm down. "When he arrived he could barely *walk*."

The Seneschal shook his head. "He can control it. But there is a pause before he touches anything, even now. The pause is shorter, but it's still there. He does not control it well, or for long, I think. If he had caught the Overlord instinctively—if he had let himself catch the Overlord instinctively—he would have burnt him. And in a sudden urgent moment like that, when you seize something harder, perhaps, than you mean to, simply to grasp it at all—how badly might he have injured him?"

She thought of what that momentary glancing touch had done on the day of the Master's arrival; and then she made herself think clearly of the night on the pavilion hill, when Fire had caught her away from cold death, and held her for some time. Last and unwillingly she remembered the conversation they had had that night, a conversation she had refused to think of, with its talk of ceding the Mastership. With the Master admitting he could not remember his own birth-name, but only his name in Fire.

She had never felt so cold.

"What I wonder," the Grand Seneschal went on desolately, "is why I did not guess something of what the Overlord had in his mind when I saw the coat he was wearing—those queer slashed sleeves and open shoulders. I only thought, What on earth is he playing at, dressed for a summer evening's ball? The Overlord has never been a favourite of mine. I decided the spectacle he was making of himself was only about intimidation and ostentation— the more fool I am. If I had glued myself to the Master's elbow for the day. . . . I have no excuse; I have not spent my life keeping a small lonely woodright and believing the best of people."

Mirasol shook her head. "If I may not blame myself for eating, then you may not blame yourself for being a Seneschal and not a soothsayer." She remembered a conversation she had had with the Master: *Let there be no further exchange of courtesies between us.* He had asked her to agree to a pact, that she supported him as he supported her—but it was at that moment a bee had stung him, and she had never answered him. Would it have made any difference now if she had? She had to tell herself—no. The real covenant between Master and Chalice existed as inherent in the bloodright of each. But she didn't quite believe it—as she didn't quite believe it wasn't her fault today for eating. As she was sure the Grand Seneschal didn't quite believe it wasn't his fault for failing to be prescient.

"I will accept the pony," she said. "I must get home—I do not know if there is nothing to be done, but there are still seven days in which to do it. And if my choice is to sit graciously in my best robes and accept the inevitable or to bail a sea with a bucket, give me the bucket. But you are right that I do not think I can walk very far just now. Let us see if Ponty is willing to be Overlord of bees."

Many years later her memory of the week before the *faenorn* was that—till the very last night—she had no sleep at all, except in those moments between blink and blink when you are so tired that you fall asleep standing up with your eyes open and wake again by finding yourself staring at the thing in your hands that you had been staring at just a moment ago. During that week, when she came back to herself, Mirasol was usually staring at a jar or a bottle or a flask containing honey or water or mead or a mixture of all three; she usually had those moments that almost felt like sleep—but couldn't be, because she was standing up and holding a jar or a bottle or a flask—when she was trying to decide what to mix next, and in what quantity and what proportions. Mostly she made the obvious choices—obvious choices drawn from a long tradition of beekeeping, like tree honey for strength and courage; obvious choices from this demesne, like Ladywell water for faithfulness; obvious choices from the Chalice tradition, like clay for stamina (although she didn't like working with clay: you had to stir and stir to convince it to suspend, and it still longed to revert to sticky lumps); and obvious choices from her brief experience of being Chalice, like starflower honey for rituals that took place after sunset. Plus herbs and a few small stones, most particularly a flint, for steadfastness.

Standing in her cottage with all the cupboard doors open, she had looked at the heap she had made of what must go with her with dismay. But the House grounds would need a different sort of serenity and connection with their surroundings than the deep woods would; the streams needed a different sort of loyalty than the ponds did; and the pavilion hill . . . she would leave the pavilion hill till last.

It could not be true that she had no sleep at all; but it might have been true that she never lay down for seven days. By the sixth day she would not have lain down because she didn't dare, for fear she would not get up again until it was too late.

She did remember the ride home, after the worst thing had happened, after the Overlord had declared a *faenorn* for a sennight hence—a thing so bad she hadn't even known to worry about it—while her mind was both paralysed with shock and scrambling frantically for any hint of a solution, a way out, of an alternative, of . . . anything. Anything but what was going to happen. What the Grand Seneschal had said could not be stopped from happening. No, she knew a solution was too much even to dream of. But she needed something, anything, she could *do*. She rather thought that if she decided there was nothing at all she could do, she would go mad.

She could not afford the luxury of going mad. Not now, and not . . . not after a sennight hence either. Not even then. She would have to marry him and . . . she would have to marry him, and teach him to hold the demesne together, when she knew so little of that great charge herself. And she would have to try to forget the stories of Meadowbrook and Fallowhill, demesnes that had not survived the transition to an outblood Master. When she could not stop remembering that while Silverleaf had survived, its name-trees had all died, and when the outblood Master's son took Mastership he renamed it Goldstone. Goldstone was almost a neighbour; Talltrees shared a border with both Willowlands and Goldstone; the previous Master had bought his carriage horses from the Goldstone stud.

The bees did indeed stream out of the hall and follow her, but they kept a little distance and Ponty, although his ears listened to the humming and not to his rider, otherwise bore their presence quietly. She couldn't remember the last time she had been on a horse; under almost any other circumstances she would have felt elated at the opportunity. Even so she found herself leaning forward to run her hand down Ponty's silky neck, not for her pleasure or his reassurance, however, but to help bring her back to herself by the touch of warm hair and horseflesh. And the gentle swing of Ponty's gait was soothing.

The fragments of her scattered wits began to drift together. Some time on that short journey she came up with her plan—with the thing she could do. She did not know when it happened; she did not remember the process of formulation and decision. But she knew what she had to do by the time she arrived at the cottage. She pulled Ponty's saddle off and rubbed his back, and his face where the bridle straps had sweated him, and then she hobbled him where there was good grass, in the middle of her meadow, where he had to share the wildflowers with her bees.

Most of their escort had dispersed by the time they arrived

back at the cottage; only a few dozen bees scattered away from them when she dismounted and looked around. But she listened to the hum—the sound holds my cottage like honey in a chalice, she thought—and felt it was louder than usual: as if the bees that had come to the House had preceded them home and were passing on the news—with emphasis. How many bees did she have living round her cottage and her clearing? As many as had been hanging from the ceiling and chandelier in the front hall of the House?

She had stopped trying to count swarms, hives and bee homes in the early days of her Chalicehood and had—half superstitiously, half because she did not have time, and superstition gave her the excuse not to make time—never tried again. She had been used since childhood to talking to her bees and had told them to stop pouring combless honey into her bowls, that winter was coming and they needed to be able to feed themselves. She was pleased to see that her bowls had begun to fill up much more slowly—although she doubted it was because of anything she had said. But this was the time of year that, any other year, she'd have been breaking cautiously into the hives and extracting what she thought they could spare of the final season's honey, which would also give her a rough count of their numbers, and also of their health. Not this year. She stared into the trees around her meadow—the trees drumming with bees—and then went indoors.

She began taking down jars of honey, and weighing them thoughtfully in her hands, and thinking, and making notes. She worked all night, and the next morning she saddled Ponty again (who sighed), and rode south. Her wood was near the southern boundary of Willowlands, and near also to the Tree of Memory and the Maidens' Arch. She returned to the cottage both jubilant and despairing; she could never do it in a sennight—in six days. She worked all through the second night, finishing her choosing and packing and list-making, and spending the last of the dark hours binding her own cottage and her own meadow and her own trees, and then, from the perfect centre of that binding, seeking what she could find out about the state of the demesne. She did not like what she found. At dawn she saddled Ponty again and went back to the House and asked the Grand Seneschal if she might borrow another pony for the next five days. She was already tired, and Ponty was old; but it had to be a pony who wouldn't mind bees.

They did not follow her this time in their thousands as they had come to the House two days ago; but a few had come to the southern border yesterday, and a few came with her today, back to the House. She kissed Ponty on the nose when she handed him over to a stableman, and walked the rest of the way to the House. She thought she had slipped indoors leaving her entourage outside, but the windows in the Grand Seneschal's office were open, and by the time she had greeted him and he had returned her greeting, several of her unusually large bees had flown through the window, despite its facing a small half-walled courtyard on the wrong side of the House. Half a dozen landed on her hair, and another half dozen on the Grand Seneschal's desk. He looked at them, and then back at her.

"I need a pony," she said. "One that can cover fifty leagues in

five days. And who won't mind a few bees—only a few, I think."
I hope, she added silently.

The Seneschal again looked at the bees. "You can have Iron-foot," he said. "He has never minded anything. He carried me through the floods four years ago, when the dam on the Wild-water broke, and the House was an island for a few days, and the Master's tall horses refused to leave their stables. I'm sure bees will be nothing to him, nor fifty leagues in five days." He looked at her again. "Is there anything else I can do for you?"

She hesitated, thinking of the size of the heap on the floor of her cottage. "I need to both ride and carry," she said. "Perhaps you could lend me a second pony."

"Who must also not mind a few bees," said the Seneschal, staring at his desk. Two of the bees had found something that interested them on the top of a pile of ledgers, and were inves-tigating it with their antennae. "You may have Gallant too. He is Ponty's full sister's son. Anything else?"

Again she hesitated. "Flasks," she said. "I need to carry honey and mead, and water from the Ladywell. Leather bottles that I can hang from a pony's saddle would be very useful."

"I will have them sent to the horseyards," he said. One of the bees was slowly creeping across the record book open on the Sen-eschal's desk; it had slid down the margin into the binding-valley and was now working its way toward the Seneschal. Another one had discovered his hand, which he had not removed quickly enough, and was ambling up his forearm. He looked at it, and away again.

"Make no sudden movements," she said. "She will fly away in a moment."

"It—she—they could sting me till I screamed with the burning of it, if it would save our demesne. I will not ask you what you are doing. I will say 'may the gods of the land and the earth-lines bless your journey.'"

"I thank you," she said. She turned to go. She paused at the door to look back. The bees had left the Seneschal's desk and followed her. She held her hand out, and two landed softly on her palm. "Pray for me—for the demesne. Light a candle. Do you have one of my honey candles?"

"Yes," he said.

"Light that one," she said, and left his office.

She took the bottles she had brought with her, and went round the House, sprinkling honey, mead and water at every corner of its long rambling walls and murmuring, *"Willowlands, be thou one and one-hearted; be thy House one and one-hearted; thy gardens and parks and fountains the same. Let nothing sunder the House from the lands, the lands from the waters, the beasts and people from all."* Sometimes she dipped her fingers in the sweet sticky water and drew signs on the stones; sometimes she scooped up a handful of pebbles and poured a little over them, and then dropped them, one or two at a time, in corners, in plant pots, in the shadows of thresholds, in gaps in the walls. Several of the Housefolk saw her, but none said anything, and when she inadvertently caught the eye of one, he or she looked away at once—and sometimes bobbed a bow or a curtsey, like a sanction, or a benediction.

She spent some time searching through the gravel of the drive at the foot of the stairs to the front door. She found it at last: the grey scitheree crystal that had been in the cup she had dropped two days before. She picked it up gently and held it to the light: three days ago it had been as clear as a glass of water. There was a spidery, feathery gossamer of cracks which filled it now, like sheep's wool mounded in a bowl, waiting for the hands of the spinner. The force of the fall would not have harmed it, but it had tried to contain the force of her binding, like a teacup trying to contain a flash flood. "Thank you," she murmured, and slipped it into her pocket.

Finally she went back indoors, and found the long twisty way toward the outlying wing where lay the rooms the Master had chosen to be his—far from the rooms his brother had lived in. She touched her wet fingers to the four corners of the door, and to a fifth spot directly above the centre of the frame. The doors in this wing were tall, and she had to fetch a chair to stand on to reach the last spot. There was a faint tremor under her fingers there, like humming. Then she went back outside again and picked up more pebbles, because she wanted twelve for each of the three fountains that stood outside the House to enhance the view of the park from its windows. Last of all she went round the gardens, sprinkling all the gates in and out, the in-between ways from one area to another, and the beginning and the centre of the maze.

As she was leaving, one of the gardeners came up to her shyly. After her experience with the Housefolk, Mirasol only glanced at her, trying to smile—being saluted was disconcerting—assuming it was merely an accident that this woman's path should seem to be crossing her own. But when the woman caught her eye—and dipped a tiny curtsey—she said, hopefully, "Me too, missus?"

Mirasol might have stared at her bewildered, but the woman looked at the flask in Mirasol's hands. Mirasol thought, I am carrying nothing for humans, and this woman is not brick nor stone nor yet tree or flower. And then she thought, But it is all about opening and binding, is it not? And this one is for the gardens, and she is a gardener. She touched her fingers to the contents of her flask once again, and pressed them over the woman's heart. She left a tiny damp tacky mark.

"Thank you, missus," the woman said, and dipped another curtsey. One of Mirasol's bees flew toward her, and landed briefly on the mark on the woman's blouse. The woman looked down at her and smiled. "And thank you too, little missus," said the woman.

When Mirasol arrived at the horseyards, one saddled pony was being led out. The stablemaster was standing by the courtyard gate with his hands knotted together as if he was stopping himself from wringing them. "Missus," he said.

"Thank you for your help," she said. "I've asked the Grand Seneschal if I might borrow two ponies who could go fifty leagues in five days, and he told me Ironfoot and Gallant."

"This is Ironfoot," said the stablemaster. "It is not every Grand Seneschal who would trouble to know the horses in the horseyard, but ours does. You will do no better than Ironfoot and Gallant. Ironfoot cannot be wearied, and Gallant will go till he drops. They will do fifty leagues in five days, if you do not expect them to gallop, and if you give them decent grazing at the halts, which you should be able to do if it does not snow again.

There is not much nourishment in the grass left at this time of year, but they are strong and tough, and they will do on hard rations for five days—even if their girths are going up an extra hole by the time you bring them home. There will be corn in a saddlebag for them. Gallant will be along as soon as the best flasks are chosen and hung." But his hands were still knotted together.

"What can the Chalice do for you?" she said gently.

"Save our demesne," he said immediately. "I don't care how you do it. But I know what the *faenorn* means. And I never heard that an outblood Master was anything but loss and ruin to any demesne. Whatever else our Master is, he's the right blood."

Despairingly she thought, Are his people are turning to the Master at last, now that it is too late? Or have I not noticed this happening because I have been too aware that his Circle still turns away from him? For a moment her mind went blank with grief and regret. But then she thought: It does not matter—even if all the people in a demesne stood together against him, an Overlord would still win out over them. There was never anything any of us could do to stop what this Overlord wills.

"I—I will do what I can," she said. "Before and after the *faenorn*."

A second pony was led up, its saddle creaking and clattering with flasks and bottles.

"Is there aught else I can do for you, missus?" said the stable-master.

"Pray for me," she said. "Light a candle. Do you have a honey or a beeswax candle?"

"Yes, missus," he said. "We all have one of yours, up here at the House."

"Do you?" she said, surprised.

"For luck," he said. "We know our Chalice is a honey Chalice—and that none has been such before. And we need all the luck we can find since the old Master, and the old Chalice, died. We, most of us, we can't afford beeswax candles, but we all have one of your candles, missus. We don't burn 'em. We keep 'em, for luck."

"Burn them now," she said. "Burn them over the next five days, between now and the *faenorn*."

"I will, missus," he said, and dropped his hands to his sides. "And I'll tell the others to do the same."

"Thank you," she said.

"May the gods of the land and the earthlines bless your journey," he replied.

She took the ponies straight back to the cottage and spent some time—too much time—arranging, rearranging and agonising. She needed rest so she might think more clearly; she did not have time for rest, and the ponies were fresh. But she would not come back here; what she took with her now would have to do.

They left at sunset, the ponies mildly puzzled at setting out again so late, but too polite to protest still wearing their harness when they wanted to graze and doze. They were lucky in the moon; she would be full in four days, and if they were lucky in the weather as well there would be light enough to see by for most of the dark hours. She pointed the ponies' noses southwest; they would go to the Great Tor, and the ponies could rest while she did a more elaborate ritual there. Then they would go to the Ladywell; she did not have much of her water left, and she must have enough for the next five days. They would stop long enough there for the ponies to rest again, but they would have to go on as soon as Mirasol was finished. They needed to begin the Circle points by tomorrow noon.

They did more than fifty leagues in the five days left to them. She had not looked at a map of the demesne since she had first been found as Chalice, though there were many maps at the House. She knew she could find her way around the edges, along the boundaries, because the earthlines would tell her where they lay; what she had not expected was how ragged and whimsical some of those boundaries were, or had become, over the centuries, as Willowlands learned to fit comfortably against its neighbours. It was like bodies in a bed, she thought, each trying not to put an elbow in another's eye. The old woodskeepers' map had showed the boundaries as being regular and straight, except when one followed a stream; at least the stream boundaries, she found, still ran through the streams, where the map showed them. The rest curled and curved, bent and dented. That made the way longer. And many of the places she wanted specifically to secure were not on the boundary itself, but a little way inside.

Also she thought of several places that as Chalice she should open and speak to, which she had not thought of when she made her plans, that the binding over all should be stronger, like extra fence posts in a fence. And then there were those small, anonymous dells and hollows or meadows and mounds which slipped into her mind like bees through a window as she passed them, and when this happened she turned off to go to them. When she slid off her pony and put her hands on the earth or the tree or the stone or in the water it seemed to her that something came to her, the something that had called her. *Be thou one-hearted*, she said. *Thou art Willowlands, each and all of you.* She thought they listened. She hoped they listened.

There were many of these. And they made the way longer yet.

Gallant, she found, was better at obeying her legs and heels while she scattered the sweet drops from her flasks as they walked, and so she rode him more often than Ironfoot; but remembering that Gallant might not let her know he was tiring till he was half foundered, and knowing that she wasn't paying enough attention to anything but what the earthlines were telling her, sometimes she got off and walked too. She only stopped at the places that needed more than a few drops from the tips of her fingers: the places whose attention she had to catch first—or those who had caught hers—or where she needed the opening or the binding to be particularly strong—the fence posts for her fence, the cornerstones for her House.

Other than these she only stopped when the ponies needed rest, and while they rested she mixed more mead and honey and Ladywell water from her flasks, and added herbs or didn't, and dropped in or took out stones; and topped the result up with whatever local water she could find. Occasionally the ponies had quite a long rest—or no rest at all—because she could not find a water source that suited her. Some ponds had lain in their beds and dreamed for too long; some streams rushed in spate for the love of the violence of it. Sometimes she could balance a sleepy or a riotous water with a particular honey, but sometimes she knew she did not want to try.

There were bees with them always.

Once, on the third day of their journey, the only water she could find—and Willowlands was very rich in springs—was a reedy pool so languid she was half afraid of letting the ponies drink from it, that it might give them a dislike for the long and weary work they were in the middle of; she stared at it, forlornly, with her empty flask in her hand, near where she had unloaded the saddlebags. A few of the accompanying bees circled past her face and then went and clustered on a particular bulge of one saddlebag. It contained a pot of honey she'd added at the last moment. Not all honey—she had concluded—had a specific use beyond what all honey is good for, sweetness and salves. But this honey, it was somehow so strong that it must be for something, though she had still not learnt what it was. The best she had come to was that this honey was for joy; it didn't seem suitable for such desperate work as this sennight was, but the seeming vigour of it heartened her, and she'd brought it so as not to have left any potential resource behind. It was the honey she had given the Master the day he had come to her cottage.

"Very well," she said to the bees. When she put her hand on that saddlebag, they all flew away. She filled her flask with the indolent water and added more honey than usual, from that particular pot, then tasted the result, which was also not something she usually did. And she felt a vast uplift of her sagging mood, as if her spirit had grown wings and soared into the sky. She didn't use that honey again to counter sleepy water, but she used it on herself when the road ahead seemed unbearably long, and she dropped it on the ponies' meagre nightly handfuls of corn.

She never remembered falling asleep. But on several of those occasions when she came back to herself standing up, she found a bee clinging to her mouth, pushing a tiny ball of pollen between her lips. It had a pleasant nutty flavour. My bees not only make combless honey and honeyless comb, she thought bemusedly, they also store pollen as squirrels store acorns.

After the first time this happened, she stopped trying to send her bees home, not that there was any way—as she had often told people who weren't beekeepers—that you could ever tell bees to do anything. But if bees were behaving in so un-bee-like a manner as to follow a human being anywhere at all, perhaps they would listen to that human being telling them to go home. They didn't. So in the evening, when she'd pulled the ponies' tack off, and rubbed them down, and given them their corn, she also opened a jar of honey and set it out for the bees, carefully wrapping it up again as soon as there were no bees left on it. She wondered if any of the woodland and meadow creatures who would be happy to eat honey any time they could, would follow the strange trail of sweet drips and drizzles she was leaving and investigate one of their campsites; but none ever did. But then they never stayed more than a few short hours anywhere either, and rarely even that long.

Occasionally their way took them along the margin of a field with cattle or sheep pastured in it. But farmhouses and barns were rarely built near the edge of a demesne, and with the harvest in, most beasts were brought as near home as possible to make winter feeding easier. Once they passed a field of heifers who had to gallop over and investigate; and Ironfoot, who didn't mind bees, was inclined to prance. The bees themselves tactfully disappeared and reappeared when the heifers had been left behind. Once they crossed a turnip field where sheep had just been loosed, and the sharp smell of freshly bitten turnips was a shock of reminder of why she was there and what she was doing: that the demesne could go on being a place where sheep and turnips grew and thrived.

She only saw other human beings twice. Once as she emerged from a wood she saw a woman, head bent, shawl wrapped closely round her, hurrying along a path on the far side of a leaf-fallen hedgerow parallel to the way Mirasol was going; she did not look up. And once, as Mirasol skirted along a freshly cut field, she saw the late stookers lifting and tossing their sheaves. They did see her, and paused. She raised a hand to them, and all their hands went up immediately in response. One of them shouted something. It sounded like *Good luck, Lady*.

During any night hours that she was sitting on a pony or by a campfire, the bees settled round her shoulders like a cape. If she was moving around too briskly, they would collect in little dark furry puddles on the heap of baggage. The ponies did not seem to heed the bees at all, or to have taken any time to adjust to their small companions' company; often she found a few bees buried in the ponies' warm manes in the mornings.

They were lucky with the moon; and they remained lucky with the weather. They were lucky too with the earthlines themselves, which often enough seemed to be expecting her, waiting for her—almost as if someone had been there before her and whispered to them, *Your Chalice is coming. Be ready.* By the third day she had realised that she would not have got round the entire demesne in time if the earthlines had been less unusually alert, unusually close to where human awareness can reach them, if she had had to spend more time calling them, asking them to listen to her. It was as if a ploughman found his horses already in harness, and all he had to do was lead them out and back them into their places. *Thank you,* she whispered; but she would have thanked the earthlines anyway. She was also thanking . . . she didn't know. But twice, when complex bindings had slid together like a belt buckling, and she had lit a little fire after, the fire had sprung to life almost before the flint touched the tinder. The first time she had been lighting a fire to eat hot food in celebration of the unexpectedly powerful and straightforward binding; the second time it was to see if the fire would leap into existence in the same eager way. It did.

If . . .

It was unusual for a Master to be able to speak to the earthlines all over his demesne from his House, but it was not unknown; and she thought she would have sensed his presence if he were walking the earthlines with her in the mundane world. Was it he? Was it his interference that was making her impossible task a thread more possible? Did that mean—she thought with a frantic little rush of hope—that he would fight on the day of the *faenorn*?

The hope drained away from her just as quickly. It would not matter if he did; he was still weak and clumsy—weaker and clumsier than the worthless Horuld.

She did not know how much the earthlines understood of human affairs; perhaps they were responding to the demesne's need for unity in the face of an outblood Master for their own sake. They had known something was wrong the day the *faenorn* had been declared. Whatever the cause of their ready cooperation she was grateful.

But on the morning of the day before the *faenorn* she had to take up the ponies' girths a second hole.

"It is almost over," she whispered to them. "Tomorrow you will be back in your own stalls, with as much hay as you can eat, and this journey will soon become only a harsh dream, and you will think to yourselves, Neither the Grand Seneschal nor our master of the stables would have sent us to be used so; it was only a dream." Let it only be a dream to them, she thought, and to all the ponies and sheep and heifers of the demesne. Let there still be a demesne, another sennight hence.

* * *

She had left the pavilion hill till last. It had meant a long awkward curve back on their own trail when, near the end of their journey, they were already very weary; but she had no idea how to address the hill, and merely by making it last there would be a strength to any binding she might be able to create. It was past midnight of the day of the *faenorn* when they arrived; from the pavilion they would have to go straight on to the House with only what rest the ponies had had while she tried to reach the earthlines of the old hill. She untacked the ponies and hobbled them while she thought about what she was going to do.

She had used candles sparingly, at the twenty-four points of the Circle, the Ladywell, and the First Tree. She put out all the candles she had left around the outside of the pavilion, setting them on the ruined walls so she would be able to see them from the inside. She had one fresh candle, and stood holding it, unlit, the winter wind hissing through her hair. As the wind moved through the dry leaves on the full-grown trees at the edge of what had been the parkland around the pavilion, it seemed to be muttering words she could not understand.

The earthlines here were confused and unhappy. She knew where they had to run because of where they came and left this place, and where the pavilion had been built, before it had been turned to bad purpose; but she could not see or hear them clearly. It was a little like listening to fretful voices in another room with the door closed. She could hear the distress and discomfort, but she did not know who spoke nor what they were saying. She knew it was part of her responsibility as Chalice to bring the pavilion hill back into alignment with the rest of the demesne, to smooth and quiet the earthlines—as you might untangle the fringe on a tapestry or soothe an agitated dog. But she knew that as yet neither her strength nor her experience was equal to the task—like a blind person untangling the fringe, or a stranger soothing the dog. But wouldn't the blind person have sensitive fingers for the knots, and mightn't the stranger make friends with the dog?

But if this place were a tapestry, it would be a tapestry to hang in the front hall of the king, where, legend had it, the ceiling was five stories high and the floor a hectare; if it were a dog, it was the Dog that guarded the entrance to the caves of the gods of the earthlines, where no mortal went. This hill had been a danger to the wholeness of the demesne since the death of the old Master. But the Chalice whose task it was to right and purify it needed to be able to call on her Master and the rest of the Circle for help. Mirasol feared her Master was no more up to the challenge than she was, and most of the rest of the Circle she did not trust; and there was always so much other work to do. And so the pavilion had been allowed to smoulder on, like a cave fire that might find a dangerous new portal to the surface at any time, and rage out over the land. . . . And now, if the *faenorn* went as everyone believed it was going to. . . . She had to keep shutting off thoughts about her own future to concentrate her sore and weary skill on the future of her demesne.

Hesitatingly she went and stood where she had lain and slept the night the Master had found and saved her. If there were anywhere in this haunted spot that she might be able to make her presence—and therefore her message—felt, then this was probably it; despite that she had failed in her aim, on that previous visit. If she was very lucky, the Master's own power had been felt here too, and the earthlines might respond to that memory, if she was able to reach it, to touch it. . . . If she was able to name him as different from his brother, who as Master had done so much hurt to this place. Different, and yet Master. Master, human and no priest of Fire.

Or if he had been here before her, as she suspected he had been elsewhere. But she knew almost at once that the earthlines here had spoken to no one recently. If he had tried here, he too had failed.

She left her candle where she had been standing while she lit all the rest. She had never felt so feeble and ineffectual as she mixed a driblet of every kind of honey she had brought with the last of her Ladywell water and went round the base of the hill, scattering the drops with her fingers, murmuring, *Be thou one and one-hearted.* She climbed the hill and scattered the last of her sweet water around the ruined walls. The flicker of her candle flames seemed to fall on her like drops of honey.

Last she knelt and lit her one remaining fresh candle, and put herself into the mind frame where she became a part of the earthline system herself. After the last six days this was much easier than it had ever been, while at the same time she was bruised and chafed and aching with the effort of repetition, as bruised and chafed and aching as her legs and back were from too many hours in a saddle. As a bloodright bearer she had always been able to listen to the earthlines, but when she had become Chalice she had had to invent her entrance among them, where they might listen to her, because there had been no one to teach her how. And she suspected she hadn't done it very well. The soreness was probably the result of her awkwardness; shouldn't the Chalice find the earthlines as familiar as the shape of her own hands on a goblet, the contact as sleek as flowing water? She was still much more familiar with the shape of a honeycomb, of knowing worker brood from queen cells, of recognising when the drones' idle flying on a warm summer day suddenly takes on purpose because they have sensed a young queen on her maiden flight.

She was trying to hold that sense of peace and comfort and the hopeful future of a vigorous young bee queen on a warm summer day, trying to take it with her, into the troubled murk of the earthlines beneath the old knoll. She was gripping warmth of summer and daylight so hard that she lost her sense of cold and winter and darkness. She didn't feel the snow starting again, drifting down against her face. The soft touch of the flakes felt a little like bees' feet. And she was so tired. . . .

Sitting up, she fell asleep.

And dreamed.

She dreamed she was walking down a long dark corridor with many branching passages, and the sound of mournful voices all around her, so she could not tell from which direction they came. She seemed to walk in the dark for a very long time; the sense of a circulation of air told her which way to walk, and kept her from bumping into the walls. She was glad not to turn down any of the other ways, both for the eerie sound of the sad voices, and because the darkness in all but the corridor she followed seemed absolute. The corridor began to climb, and the darkness lessened till it was no more than twilight, and at last a bright spot slowly cohered out of the twilight, and became the end of a tunnel.

When she emerged, blinking, into the daylight, there were many people around her, and a gallery or summer-house made of tall poles with flowers woven into ropes hung between them. A wedding party. She didn't want to know who was getting married. She turned around, but the tunnel had disappeared; there was only grass and sunlight, and poles and flowers and people. She saw the little group of priests, waiting to perform the various rites necessary for a grand wedding: by the number of poles and flowers as well as the number of priests, this had to be a very grand wedding. The priests were too far away for her to see any of their faces clearly. She also saw the back of the man waiting for his bride. She recognised him as the bridegroom, as she recognised the priests, by the clothes he was wearing. She saw several members of a Circle; these too she recognised only by the badges they wore.

She hoped she did not know who the bridegroom was. She stared at him with dread as he began to turn around.

But he wasn't turning to look toward her at all. Everyone was looking up, and some people were backing away, and there were a few exclamations of dismay. And she registered what she had not yet noticed in the bewilderment of where she found herself: the birdsong of a bright summer day with poles and flowers for birds to perch on was being drowned out by an increasingly loud humming noise.

And then her bees dropped down on her like a dark cloak, and wrapped her round, lifted her up and bore her away.

She woke on the pavilion hill. All the candles had burnt themselves out, it was nearly dawn, and the hill was white with snow. She was covered with a thick blanket of bees, and the snow lay upon them in bright broken spangles. She sat up in distress—bees cannot survive hard cold outside their hives—but they seemed to shake themselves, twisting their bodies back and forth almost like tiny dogs, only with six legs, wings and striped fur; and then they all flew up together in a huge thrumming swirl, and she found out how warm they had been keeping her, because she shivered violently in the shock of the sudden cold. There were many more bees than there had been for the five days of their journey.

Five days.

It was the eighth day; the sennight was passed, and it was the day of the *faenorn*. She could not pause to think about the bees, nor about whether she had done any good on the old hill or anywhere at all during the last exhausting seven days, nor about anything else. Just for a moment longer she sat where she was, and pressed her hands against the cold earth, and listened. Were the earthlines more tranquil than they had been, or was it only her foreboding about the day ahead that made them seem so?

She gave them a quick rite of blessing and peace, and then ran down the slope and began saddling the ponies in haste. They were standing nose to tail in a little windbreak made by half a dozen saplings, and seemed perfectly content; they looked like hairballs, but their ears were warm, and they sighed as they felt the girths tighten. She gave them the last handfuls of corn, and set out. She allowed time for them to finish waking up, and to digest their paltry breakfast, and then—since it was the last day, and they could have a real rest soon—she asked them to trot.

Perhaps they knew they were going home at last; and they did not fear the *faenorn*. Their heads came up and they went forward with a will, Ironfoot even leaning on the bit and asking to go faster. Her saddle sores burned, but she barely noticed; and she let the ponies canter, Gallant with his ears pricked, keeping pace beside Ironfoot when the way was wide enough, and clinging to his heels when they had to go single file. The flasks and bottles and panniers that had jingled and clanked with emptiness when she rode back to her cottage from the House's horseyard six days before jingled and clanked with emptiness again.

The ponies had nonetheless had a long journey, and when she asked them to slow down before they came to the edge of the parkland around the House, they fell back to a walk almost with a thump, dropped their heads and blew. She patted them absently; she would not have been able to do what she had done without them, but that was over now; what she could do was either done or not done. The final catastrophe was on them, if it was a catastrophe, if she had done nothing to avert it—if she had not done enough.

But she knew she had not done enough. There was no magic in the Chalice that could make the Master fit to stand against Horuld—that could make this Master capable of standing against any able-bodied adult human. She had not saved the Master—nor herself. She had to tell herself again and again (repeating it with the thud of the ponies' hooves, as if sturdy drumming could drive it into her) that she was Chalice, that it was the demesne that was her concern. If the demesne was to bear an outblood Master without tearing itself apart, she must do everything in her power to hold it together—that was what she had spent the last sennight doing. If the Master had been helping her, as she was half sure he had and half sure he hadn't, then that would have been his objective too: to do everything he could to make his demesne strong and whole, before he . . .

Everything in her power. Including going on living. Including bearing a son to Horuld.

Everything in her power. . . .

She did not notice that the sky behind her was darkening with bees.

The *faenorn* would be held on the open drive in front of the House. It was where the original insult had occurred which caused the *faenorn* to be called; it was also where the new Master had first stepped down from his carriage as Master of Willowlands, and climbed the stair to the front door to be greeted by his Chalice. The place would in itself support the better claim of the two combatants; she realised in despair that she was not even sure who that might be—she was only sure of whom she had chosen, for whom she would do anything, even live on after . . .

Surely it was the Master who had the better claim? But it was here that the calamity had occurred; should not the land itself have leaped up, to prevent the Overlord falling?

She had not had time to find out the rules or traditions of the *faenorn*; she had had—she had chosen—other work to do. Now she could only come back to the House to see the end. She had to see it; she was Chalice. She would bear witness to this momentous thing as she was obliged to bear witness to all meetings and events that concerned the unity and accord of her demesne. Her tired mind stumbled, and found itself walking down another path, the path that had become the most familiar of all to her in the last year: What would she mix for this cup? . . . Her stomach lurched, and for a moment she could neither breathe nor see.

She had no Chalice cup for the *faenorn*.

When she had packed for the last sennight she had thought only of what she would be doing before the *faenorn*; it had been cruelly clear in her mind that she would not be able to come back to the cottage before it was all over, and yet she had thought only of what she would need for her clearing and binding, for her journey around the boundaries of Willowlands. The *faenorn* seemed an absolute, like a vast monolith at the end of her road—like a headsman standing with his axe. She knew that was where she was going, but she could not think about it, she could only try to bear it. And yet—this was the most important, the most urgent and critical meeting that she was likely ever to attend as Chalice. How could she *not* bear a cup?

The only cup she had with her was the small brass silver-bound and -chased cup she had used for some of the work of her journey; it was a pretty thing, finer than anything a minor woodskeeper would possess, though small and tough for travelling; but it could in no way bear the immensity of the scene to come. She remembered the weight of the goblet she had carried through the aftermath of the Overlord's fall, her sense that it was filling up with broken earthlines. . . . It had happened occasionally, in the long history of Chalicehood, that some frightened or incompetent Chalice had misjudged her witnessing so badly that the cup she had chosen shattered under the pressure brought to bear upon it. This had never produced a less than ruinous result; and the *faenorn* was disaster enough.

How could she have forgotten—how could she not have thought of this?

It was too late now. She had to be there, with the rest of the Circle.

She could see the beginnings of the crowd as soon as she rode past the final hedgerow. What she was not expecting was that most of them turned toward her as the news of her arrival spread. She was also not expecting to see that most of them were carrying candles. Many of the candles were nearly stubs; there were very few fresh ones. As the people noticed her and turned toward her, a few knelt, and their flints came out, and sparks were struck; and once the first candles were lit, they lit their neighbours', who then lit their neighbours', and long spreading winding lines of candle flames moved through the crowd till finally a low, twinkling, wavering forest of candlelight was raised to her. "Chalice," the murmur came; and with the murmur a faint aroma of warm honey. Some of them said "missus." Some said "Lady."

She thought the thrumming in her ears was her own blood; she thought that she did not hear the voices clearly because she did not want to. There were bees around her, but there were always bees around her recently; she still had not looked behind her. She had no reason to look behind her; she only looked ahead.

What could she do about the cup she did not have? The people—*her* people—were looking to her.

The Overlord's coach and a second, smaller one behind it, were drawn up opposite the front stair of the House, and at least twenty horses and riders in the Overlord's livery lined the drive, and more on foot; but the Grand Seneschal stood at the top of the stairs alone. She looked around for the other members of the Circle; most of them were standing in an awkward and irresolute-looking group near the foot of the stairs: not quite treacherously close to the Overlord's company but too far to be counted as loyal to the Master either. And yet what good was loyalty now? Let them save themselves. The Prelate seemed again to have disappeared. *All* the Circle must be present; even if he stood at the Overlord's elbow it were better than that he was missing. Could he be so selfish as not to care that the survival of Willowlands might depend on an unbroken Circle, today of all days?

A Circle whose Chalice, today of all days, had no cup to bear.

Chalice, she heard again. *Lady.* These were her people now, as much as they were the Master's. She saw into the crowd without meaning to, looked into their faces—realising how many of them she now knew as individuals—how many she could put names to, and say what they did, how many children they had, where they lived. And—especially today, the day of the *faenorn*—they were expecting her, relying on her, to hold the demesne together. Only the Chalice had the strength of connection to the Mastership to bridge the difference between a blood Master and an outblood one.

I've only been Chalice such a little while! she thought despairingly. You cannot ask this of me!

But they had to. There was no one else.

And she had brought no cup to bear for them.

She turned Ironfoot's head toward the horseyard. The horseman who took the bridles from her had an unlit candle end tucked in the breast of his shirt. "Thank you," she said, and briefly touched the candle, as if reminding herself of the presence of a friend. She did not think what it would look like to the man. Nor did she think of what she was doing when she unslung the one pannier that held what was left of her honey, water, herbs and mead, stones and the little travelling cup, and hung it over her shoulder. It was too late for her to do anything further with these; she did not dare mix a last-minute, haphazard, unplanned cup for such as the *faenorn* with the odds and ends left after her journey. But she had carried them a long way, and if there was any reason for her doing it, it was to have a friend with her. The pannier was made to hang from a saddle, against a horse's side, but it settled easily against her back.

She went to join the Grand Seneschal at the front door. She was trembling now, trembling as she had not done for almost a year, when they were waiting for their new Master, their new Master who had been a priest of Fire. The people parted before her, holding up their little candle flames as she passed them. She paused at the bottom of the steps.

She saw neither the Overlord nor the Heir.

She climbed the steps slowly, heavily. The pannier thumped against her leg, and it occurred to her that there was even less sense than none that she had brought it with her. Not only did she have no goblet to carry for the *faenorn*, she had no goblet to welcome the Master with afterward. However this meeting ended—and she knew how everyone present believed it would end—she would have a Master to welcome. And nothing to welcome him with.

She half imagined she could feel the stairs she walked on crumbling, the broken earthlines sinking farther into the earth, leaving the House nothing to stand on. She could almost feel the first tiny lurch, as the House's foundations began to slip into the abyss; could almost hear the stirring, the pattering of sand and soil and plaster dust into sudden crevices, a sound almost like humming.

The earthlines were silent; silent as no live thing should be silent.

The Seneschal put a hand out toward her, as if she looked so tired she might not be able to climb the last step. Perhaps she was that tired. Perhaps it was something the crowd should see, the Grand Seneschal putting a hand out to the Chalice, and her taking it. She took the offered hand, and leaned on it.

He glanced at the sky behind her, disinterestedly, and back to her again. "The *faenorn* will be swords," he said without preamble.

She was not so tired that she didn't jerk forward and grunt *What?* as if his words were blows. His voice had been low, and she struggled to make hers low too to answer him. "Swords. That is no *faenorn*; that is slaughter."

The Grand Seneschal shrugged. "The Master did not protest. And, indeed, what weapon could he have suggested that would suit him any better?"

"Fire," she said.

"He would not," said the Seneschal. "You know he would not."

She shook her head. She had not considered this aspect of the *faenorn*; she had tried not to consider it at all, but she had involuntarily remembered what she had read about it, before she had closed the book or gone to answer the door, these last few days, while she was scattering drops and murmuring *Be thou one-hearted.* It was as if the *faenorn* itself were a part of what she had been trying to do; as if it were a member of her Circle, and she could not bind round it without knowing its shape. She did not want to know and remember, but she did: that while this battle for the Mastership of the demesne was symbolic, and only the two rivals themselves were involved, it was still a meeting with real weapons. That it was not required that either die of it, but failure was such a disgrace that the loser generally preferred to die, and the victor was considered to have behaved with honour if he yielded to such a request. In the old, barbaric days, when *faenorn* was almost a commonplace, you wanted your enemy dead; it was the only way you could be sure he would not regroup and attack you again.

Their Master would not have to ask; Horuld would kill him with the first stroke.

By the fourth level an Elemental priest can again go into the world, if he so chooses, because his metamorphosis is complete, the Master had said to her. *But they mostly choose not to come,* she had replied. *And they cannot stay, because they can no longer live among humans. Among us. A fourth-level priest would never have been sent home to be Master of his demesne. And I have never heard of one stopping a forest fire.* A fourth-level priest could not be killed by a blow with a sword. But a third-level priest could be killed as easily as a human could.

Before the Master had been sent to Fire by his brother, he would have been trained to use a sword, an eligary and a bow; Mirasol had a faint memory of a rumour that he had been better than his brother at all three. But even if it was true, it was of no use to him now: not after seven years of Fire. While he was no longer as weak or as clumsy as he had been, he still found walking strange and laborious, and anyone watching him climb or descend stairs must look away in distress. There was still too much Fire in him—so much that he still had to remember not to burn what he touched with his hand, even if that meant letting the Overlord fall, and losing his demesne for it.

She saw the people looking up the stair toward herself and the Grand Seneschal; she did not notice that they were looking over their heads, to the sky above the House, where her bees hummed and hovered and where, with every moment that passed, more and more bees joined them. It was a heavy, cloud-oppressed day, and she did not notice the increasing shadow they cast. She thought of her Master, who had too much Fire in him, and wondered why the Seneschal did not ask her why she was not carrying a cup, a crucial, critical cup, to bring the demesne through the *faenorn*.

She did notice that the great front doors of the House were open, but that there were no Housefolk standing on either side, as there should always be. She did not know if that was by the Seneschal's order, but she guessed it was. If there was to be a new Master the Seneschal would not want any of his folk to be in danger of accusations of preference for the old Master. As Grand Seneschal, he had to be there. As Chalice, so did she. If they were to be harried later for their suspected preferences, that would be as fate—and the Overlord—ordained. And he probably would ordain, for the Prelate at least should stand with them, and the rest of the Circle should not be skulking with the ordinary folk of the demesne.

The Seneschal was almost an old man; he could be pensioned off; of the Circle, only the Master and Chalice could not retire, and pass their burden on with their own hands. She did not think even this Overlord would see any purpose in harassing an old, retired Seneschal.

Her they needed—they needed a Chalice even above all the rest of the Circle combined; a Chalice to grasp and hold a new Master till he could grasp and hold his Mastership. And they needed a Chalice with an established link to the demesne; they could not afford to—to kill her, she thought almost dispassionately, and let the rods find her replacement. She was sure that news of her activities these last seven days would have been taken to the Overlord and his choice for Willowlands' Heir; but surely what she had done was wise, whichever way the *faenorn* fell, for she had been tying the demesne together as well and tightly as she knew—as she could guess—how, perhaps tightly enough to withstand a change to an outblood Master.

Perhaps tightly enough to hold on to the Master it had. . . .

No. The *faenorn* was swords. There was no help for that.

She hoped the Overlord would choose to see her activities as merely the Chalice's best effort for her demesne. She guessed that officially he would have to, so that she could marry the Heir—the new Master. Marry him, and bear his child—bear him a son to be Master after him. Even then there would be no escape; a demesne can only contain one living Chalice; she could not retire, nor could she run away, for a Chalice could not leave her demesne; to try would kill her. There is always that last recourse, she thought bleakly. But she had been Chalice long enough to know that, however desperate that hope, her demesne's only real hope was in her.

She felt rather than heard when the Master came out of the open door behind them. She turned to look at him; he too was alone. He too would risk none of his folk—and that told her, as if she needed to be told, that he too knew how this meeting would end. She felt that his shambling, limping walk was more conspicuous than it had been in months. She looked into his face, into his red eyes, and knew, despite the expressionlessness of his black face and the strangeness of his eyes, that he would not merely fail to raise his own sword but step—stumble—forward into Horuld's blow. Let it be over quickly, his eyes said. Let my blood tell the land it has a new Master, and that it must obey him now.

And she had to stand, and watch, and witness, with no cup to steady her or her demesne, and hope that the land would listen.

The Master went slowly down the steps; he could not go quickly, or he would fall. She could not watch; she could never watch. She stared out over the crowd; they, too, were looking away—most of them looking up, into the sky, as if hoping for a sign or a saviour. She gazed slowly around. The Circle were contemplating their feet.

When the Master was halfway down the stairs, the door of the Overlord's carriage opened, and the Overlord appeared. He stood at the foot of the carriage steps and stared steadily at the Master till he reached the ground in front of the House.

Then the Heir emerged from the same carriage, and behind him another man carrying a long thin box. Two more men in the Overlord's livery came forward to open it with all ceremony; it contained, of course, two swords.

She didn't hear what the Overlord said; he said it in a powerful voice he wished to make sound sad and regretful, but all she could hear was the barely contained delight in his successful stratagem behind the false regret, and she remembered the Grand Seneschal saying to her, long ago in another life, that her understanding of the human love of power was the understanding of a small solitary woodskeeper.

There were only the motions of this token battle to be gone through now, and then the Overlord would have won. She was perhaps some shadow over his pleasure, but he would assume that her spirit would be broken—if it was not already, then soon. She thought of the Master gently holding the bee that had stung him and telling her not to struggle, and she thought she could feel her spirit breaking now. She thought, I need no cup. *I* am Chalice. *I* am filling with the grief and hurt and fear of my demesne; the shattered earthlines weigh *me* down; I am brimming with the needs of my people. After the *faenorn* I will be stuffed too full to move; I will be too heavy to lift a foot.

Without noticing she was doing so, she raised her hands in the first ritual gesture of the Chalice holding a goblet.

The candles were still twinkling in the hands of the crowd, and at the top of the House steps the smell of warm honey and beeswax was sweet and strong. She thought she saw the Overlord register what he was seeing and—perhaps—some brief narrow look of annoyance. What were the little people getting up to? This demesne was *his* now—or would be in but a few minutes more—to do with what he wished. He wanted no foolish clinging to the old; no rebellion, however small. But his face cleared immediately, if it had ever clouded. She might have imagined it. Candle flames were fire: but perhaps he smelled the honey and beeswax too, and decided the people were wisely putting their trust in their Chalice. The ordinary folk did not care for the politics of Overlords, and knew their Chalice, still young herself in that role, would have to hold the demesne together through the next difficult years.

And she would be married to Horuld.

She would have to marry him. Marry the new Master, and bear his child.

The Overlord looked up at her, at the Chalice, standing at the top of the House steps, and made her the least possible bow: just enough of an acknowledgement that he should be seen to be acknowledging her.

She prevented herself from closing her eyes, met the Overlord's gaze steadily, and made the tiniest of bows in return. Whatever he had in mind for her later, he needed her now. And would a short life be bad, if she were Horuld's wife?

The Master was offered the choice of the swords. He still wore his billow of cloak, and the sleeves tangled with the filigree around the case's edge. He needed both hands to lift his sword—his choice was merely the one that lay nearer. She thought she saw him hesitating before touching the hilt, perhaps so that he would not burn the fine lining of the case.

Horuld, stripped to his shirt, stepped forward and seized the other sword with a flourish. Holding it aloft in a gesture she disliked intensely, he too looked up to the head of the House stairs, and his bow was as flourishing as his grasp on the sword. But when he straightened out of his bow his gaze too seemed to go above the heads of the Chalice and the Grand Seneschal, and the sword wavered slightly. She thought, He knows he is not fit to govern this or any demesne. She gave him the same tiny acknowledgement she had given the Overlord. She would have preferred to give him no acknowledgement at all. But if he won . . . when he won, when this grotesque charade was over with. . . .

Two of Horuld's—or the Overlord's—folk paced out and stood at two of the corners of the area where the *faenorn* would take place. There was a brief pause, and the Master seemed to shake himself. He began to say something—and then two of the demesne folk came forward and bowed awkwardly; she could see the gestures—equally awkward—of asking leave to speak to the matter at hand. At first she recognised neither of the men, and strained to see, because they were finely dressed, like members of the Circle, but with none of the individual marks and badges that identified each Circle member; that and their strange gracelessness with the ritual gestures. . . . One of them was Lody the shepherd, and the other, the butcher for the House kitchens; Gess? No, Gresh. Although he was still a young man, he bought honey from her for his aching knee—a hunting accident, he had told her.

She glanced at the Seneschal, who gave a tiny nod. "They volunteered," he said. "They have no families."

Little to lose, she translated silently. Little to lose, and courageous with it, and briefly her eyes blurred with tears.

The Overlord's men carried tokens for north and south, tree and fruit; the shepherd and butcher held those for east and west, the sun and the earth. Mirasol suddenly became aware of her hands in their empty cradling; and almost without thinking, she pulled the bag over her shoulder forward, and opened it. Still watching the people on the ground, she groped for the shape of a particular jar and lifted it out. It wasn't till she looked at it that she realised what she was doing—or rather that she didn't know what she was doing—but her hands seemed to know, her Chalice hands. The jar her hand had chosen—and it was an odd old wooden jar, a recognisable crooked shape under her fingers, a reject because it would not sit straight on a shelf, the only empty jar she could find when at the last minute she'd decided to take a little more honey on her journey, a little of the mysterious honey, the honey that seemed to suggest laughter and joy and a long bright horizon, the strong-tasting honey whose distinguishing source she could not identify.

She'd almost laughed when she decanted it because the bigger crock it lived in was also very crooked, not merely a reject but so lopsided that her mother had kept trying to throw it out, and her father kept rescuing it; and when her father died her mother kept it after all, for those memories of him. Mirasol had thought, as she carefully poured, that perhaps this honey had an affinity for those who do not sit securely, who do not rest peacefully, who limp instead of walk. She hadn't quite been able to laugh, but she'd been smiling when she tucked it into its corner of a saddlebag, and the smile had been as refreshing as cold water on a hot day. This was the honey that had given her energy in the sennight past when she had none, the honey she had put last into the cup for her last-of-all stop on the pavilion hill. It was the honey she had given the Master, the day he had come to her cottage, and a bee had stung him.

She opened it because why else would she have taken the jar out? The smell of it made her think of the last dream she had had, on the pavilion hill.

It was not easy to arrange her hands in any Chalice grasp on a small round crooked wooden pot, but she managed. She held the little fat shapeless thing against her breast, beneath her chin, and the smell of the honey, even in these circumstances, still tried to make her smile. She was not thinking of her bees, but as she fitted herself into the Chalice stance, composing herself to stand true and straight and still, like a statue on its plinth, several bees landed on the backs of her hands, and several more on her hair—and one on the end of her nose. Again she tried to smile—as if there is a smile here, as real as a bee, trying to make me wear it, she thought, as I am trying to hold—to wear—being Chalice. Even with no chalice to hold as evidence. "Welcome, my little friends," she whispered. "Do you remember your Master, who saved your sister?"

If the Grand Seneschal heard her, he gave no sign. Probably he was watching the scene below too closely to notice her or her bees.

Awkwardly the Master raised his sword in the ritual gesture. Gracefully Horuld did the same.

One of Mirasol's Chalice hands loosed itself from holding the little jar, and with the same formality as if the gesture were a ritual as old as Chalices, as old as demesnes and Masters, extended its forefinger, drew it through the jar, and put the finger in Mirasol's mouth.

The flavour bloomed on her tongue.

Thousands of years of Chalices, following the practises and services, the ceremonies and conventions, binding the demesnes, listening and speaking to the earthlines, sustaining and strengthening their Masters, witnessing the work of the Circle, doing as they must, and as every Chalice had done before and would do after them. Even when a Chalice died suddenly with no apprentice, the force of the tradition would lift and carry—no, *sweep,* flood, overcome—her inheritor into what she had inherited; into the Chalice way. It had always been like this; it had been this way since the demesnes were drawn. Chalices did not create; they cultivated.

There had never been a honey Chalice before.

The flavour of the honey filled her mouth; it felt as if it were seeping through the skin of her mouth and tongue, into her blood, running through her body with every beat of her heart.

The Master and Heir each took the ritual step forward, lowering the blades of their swords, and then stepped back again, again raising the blades to the beginning position. The Master stumbled as he stepped back, and again needed two hands to steady his sword.

Any decent man would refuse to raise a sword against a Fire-priest whose strength is in Fire, not swordplay, she thought. *Any Heir fit to be Master of a demesne would refuse to go through with this.*

The *faenorn* began. Horuld danced forward, one step, two steps. And the Master—as she had known he would—dropped his sword, spread his arms and stepped forward.

And at the top of the grand front stair of the House, the Chalice stepped forward too and screamed *No* through the taste of the honey in her mouth.

And the bees—hundreds of thousands, millions of bees, the Chalice's own bees, the House bees, the wild bees of the forests, the bees of hundreds of hives in hundreds of meadows and gardens and glades all over the demesne—the bees plunged down from where they had hovered above the roof of the House, making a noise more like thunder than like the humming of bees, and covered the *faenorn* field in a black cloud.

The Overlord seemed frozen where he stood; the four men at the four corners of the field stepped uncertainly back, seemingly more bewildered than frightened.

The *faenorn* field seethed with bees, peaking like sea waves lashed by storm winds. There was one shriek above their thunder, a man's voice: *"I'm on fire! Burning—I'm burning!"*

And then . . . nothing.

Perhaps half the bees flew away, dispersing like ordinary bees, making a humming noise as they went no different from any ordinary bees. The rest remained, lying in dark motionless heaps and hummocks over the space at the foot of the stair that ran up to the front doors of the House from the edge of the parkland

and the end of the drive. The squared-off *faenorn* arena, as well as the crescent of gravelled drive, had disappeared under the dunes of dead bees.

My bees, Mirasol thought. My bees! What have I done! But she was the first to move. Still clutching her jar of honey, with the leather saddlebag still banging on her hip, she ran down the steps and waded into the rough sea of dead bees. There was one hummock, bigger and blacker than the rest, where the bees were all her own. My bees, she thought, weeping. She fell on her knees beside the hummock, and for a moment hesitated, not in fear but in sorrow; and then she leaned forward, her free hand disappearing to the shoulder as she brushed away the bodies of her bees, golden glints appearing and disappearing as the yellow stripes on their bellies appeared and disappeared.

What was under the hummock moved.

The Master sat up. His cloak was gone; he was bare-headed and bare-chested. His skin was the colour of Mirasol's, and his eyes were brown. He looked up, first at her, then at the sky; then at his own hands. He touched the back of one with the other. It was an ordinary, easy, smooth, human gesture. Mirasol stood up and offered him her hand, and he grasped it—grasped it with no hesitation—to stand up too, although he moved lithely and gracefully. His hand was no warmer than Mirasol's own. He was wearing but a few tattered rags; she let go of his hand to take off her own cloak and drape it round him. He smiled at her. She held out her jar of honey. He took it doubtfully, and stood looking at it.

"It's only honey," she said. "It's the honey you ate with me, the afternoon you and Ponty came to my cottage."

"Only honey," he said musingly, and his voice too was human, deep and resonant, with none of the crackly disturbing echoes of Fire. "I am not sure I can think of 'only honey' ever again. I saw you, just now, at the top of the stair, holding this little pot of honey as your chalice, straight and proud as any jewelled queen, with your saddlebag over your shoulder and the dust of your journey still on you. I knew I had no hope left—I had even convinced myself that I was relieved that the struggle was about to be over, because I knew I had already lost. And when I looked up and saw you as you were, in no gaudy robes and bearing no solemn goblet—suddenly I had hope."

"I did not see you looking," said Mirasol.

"I did not want you to see," said the Master. "And I looked away quickly, because I knew the hope was false. I knew—I think I knew—that it was not really about hope, it was about looking at you. And so I looked at Horuld, and at his sword, and reminded myself that they were about to kill me."

"But you have been helping me, this sennight past," said Mirasol, and as she spoke she was sure she was speaking the truth. "The earthlines were waiting for me. I did not have to reach for them; they were already looking for me, turning toward me. You cannot have been doing it only for the demesne. That is too bleak, too bitter, and the earthlines would have felt this, and shied away from me."

"I did it for you," he said. "You and our demesne. I might have gone mad, these last days, waiting for my death, staring endlessly at my failure, prisoned in my rooms, in my body, because I did not wish to go out among my people and force them to choose how to react to me—in these last few days, before my weakness forced an outblood Master on them. I had to do something. The Ladywell and the First Tree told me what you were doing, and so I went on before you where I could. Most of the earthlines were already roused; even the air over our demesne, this sennight, has been restless and fretful; the earthlines were feeling the apprehension in every foot, hoof and paw pressed against the ground. It was a matter only of helping them to look for you, to tell them you were coming. But at the pavilion hill I could do nothing."

"No," Mirasol said slowly, thinking of the dream she had had there only the night before, of the wedding, and the bees. "No. I think it did hear you. I think it is trying to come back to us, as you did, from Fire. It is having a difficult journey. We will go there—tomorrow—and try to reach it. Try to lead it home."

"Tomorrow," he said, and smiled.

Mirasol saw that he had a beautiful smile. She dropped her eyes to the pot of honey he was still holding. "I am still Chalice," she said, "and I bear witness to this meeting. I have offered you a cup, and you must drink."

"I believe in the luck of the Chalice—of this Chalice. Of my Chalice," he said, and he took one of her hands and gently placed the honey jar in it, folded both his hands around it, and, that way, raised the jar to his mouth; together they tipped it, and she saw a flash of gold, brighter even than her bees' bellies, as the honey poured onto his tongue.

They dropped their linked hands, but Mirasol's free hand found one of the Master's, and when they turned to look round them, they did so with their hands clasped.

Other folk had begun to move uncertainly through the swirls of bees flung over the *faenorn* ground. There was a muted exclamation when they found Horuld's body. Mirasol looked over at it, almost indifferently, but with a touch of fear like a bad memory. It was, at first glance, difficult to differentiate from the dead bees that had covered it. He was black and shrivelled, as if burnt in a fire to temper sword steel, his legs drawn up and his hands curled into claws. He wasn't recognisable as Horuld; he was barely recognisable as human.

The Overlord made an inarticulate sound, of grief or of rage. He did not move from where he stood—from where he had stood since the sword box had been opened, and the Heir had danced lightly forward to kill the Master—but he made a sharp gesture, and two of his folk ran to the carriage and, after a moment's confusion, brought a blanket to where the pathetic remains of Horuld lay, and wrapped them up in it. Mirasol thought, watching, that what was left weighed nothing at all, as if it were barely more than ash, and would have fallen to dust by the time it was carried to . . . she thought, I don't even know Horuld's home demesne. Deager told us—that among many other things—but I don't remember. Or perhaps the Overlord will take it to his own great estate outside the capital city, and bury it there.

But Horuld—what was left of Horuld—was being taken away. Away from Willowlands. That was all that mattered.

She was still watching as the two men carried their light burden back to the carriage, when her gaze crossed the Overlord's. He was staring at her, his face blazing with . . . something she could not read, and did not want to. When he had looked at her long enough, his scorching stare shifted to the Master, standing handfast beside her.

The Grand Seneschal had followed her more slowly to the foot of the stairs and stood now on the shore of the bee-ocean, its outer limits barely brushing his toes. He too had been looking at the Overlord, but he felt Mirasol's gaze, and he turned to look at her, smiled faintly and began to wade toward them. When he came close enough to speak privately, he murmured, "I had taught myself to like the prospect of retirement; of enough sleep every night, and meals taken at table, not at my desk. But you will need me, I think. Your Chalice, Master, sees all things clearly, which is both her strength and her weakness."

Mirasol could feel her cheeks go hot; it was true, she could, at this moment, only think that they had won, after all, won when there was no possibility of their winning. In a moment she would remember that she had made a bad enemy, and that the game was not over, and perhaps would never be over in her lifetime. Her mind shifted immediately to its second-most familiar track: after the question of what cup to mix next was always the question of what knowledge to seek next. Had any *faenorn* before now been won or lost by external agency? And had there been thereby any attempt to set its result aside, to declare it void?

No. It would not happen in this case, whatever tradition there might be—and she would find out if there were any such tradition. No Master who could guide and direct the earthlines all over his demesne from self-exile in his rooms at the House would have his demesne taken away from him. No such Master who was also human.

The Overlord was still staring at the Master, and he seemed utterly absorbed in what he was thinking, but at the sound of his carriage door closing on what had been the Heir he turned on his heel and strode back to his carriage himself. Someone leaped forward to open the door again for him.

He climbed the carriage steps as if treading on the bodies of his enemies, and the squeal of the springs sounded like a protest or a lament. He turned and sat down, now staring straight ahead, facing the padded seat where—presumably—Horuld had sat on his journey here, the journey both had confidently expected to result in his assumption of the Mastership of Willowlands. Briefly Mirasol imagined a pathetic lump, blanket-shrouded, on that seat now.

The Overlord's folk dithered a little, and then moved to their places in the smaller carriage or mounted their horses. Mirasol suddenly recognised Deager: he looked twenty years older and . . . frightened. She wouldn't have known it was he to look at his face; it was his walk that she recognised, and was shocked, then, at the face he turned toward her, toward her and her Master and the Grand Seneschal, standing only a little distance from him, in the dark, eerie, temporary new landscape created by the bees who had died to keep the demesne for its real Master, and out of the hands of the Overlord and his false Heir. Deager turned toward them only long enough for her to identify him, then turned away quickly, and almost ran to his carriage, the second, smaller, plainer one behind the Overlord's own.

Coachmen were clambering up to their perches and taking up reins; postilions let go horses' heads and climbed to their places.

The Overlord's party left without saying a single word since Horuld had cried *"I'm burning!"* although a few of them glanced back, as Deager had, at the House, its Master, Chalice and Grand Seneschal, as they turned down the drive. The Overlord's coachman was one of those who looked; but of them all only three of the riders following the carriages, out of the Overlord's sight even had he stopped staring at the seat in front of him and chosen to look round him, gave the proper salutation to the *faenorn* victor.

Mirasol, holding her Master's hand in hers, remembered thinking that as Chalice, witness and cup bearer, she would be spared having to make that sign to Horuld.

"I am grateful to have a Chalice who sees clearly, and will gladly bear her weakness for her strength," said the Master. "I fear that she will have to teach me to see anything at all—everything. You will have to say to me 'House,' 'tree,' 'stair,' 'horse' . . ." and as he spoke, while she could hear that he spoke in jest, she could also hear that he spoke the truth: he had to make an effort, each time, as he identified House, tree, stair and horse.

"'Bee,'" said the Grand Seneschal. "'Circle,' for we will need a new one. I'm not sure I wish to depend on any apprentices the current lot have bred up to their ways of thinking either. We will have to hope the finding rods agree with us. I am not looking forward to prying them off Prelate, however. I suspect he will resist. I haven't seen Prelate today at all, have you? If he's run away I hope he left the rods behind. Is there a cup of augury, Mirasol?"

"Yes," said Mirasol, "but I haven't learnt to use it. There's always been so much else . . . we may not have to look for every-one. Perhaps we can start with a shepherd and a butcher." She thought of the woman she had met the day she came to the House to borrow ponies and panniers, who had called the bee that had landed on her shirt front "little missus." "And perhaps I know a gardener to make a third. And perhaps they will find something comfortably in common with the philosophy of a woodskeeper. And with learning by doing, when you don't know what you're doing."

"It has worked well enough for you," said the Grand Seneschal. "For my first task I shall see to it that no one in all the demesnes under the king does not know the story of how Willowlands won back its Master from the priesthood of Elemental Fire—for that is how the tale shall go."

"Perhaps," said the Master slowly, "some of the present Circle may think better of their Master now."

"Perhaps," said the Grand Seneschal grimly, "but do we think better of them?"

"We are all only mortal," said the Master, even more slowly. "We do only what we can do. All the Elemental priests have certain teachings in common: one of them is that everyone, every human, every bird, badger and salamander, every blade of grass and every acorn, is doing the best it can. This is the priests' defi-nition of mortality: the circumstance of doing what one can is that of doing one's best. Only the immortals have the luxury of furlough. Doing one's best is hard work; we rely on our sur-roundings because we must; when our surroundings change, we

stumble. If you are running as fast as you can, only a tiny roughness of the ground may make you fall."

There was a silence, and then the Grand Seneschal said:
"Master, I fear that during the seven years preceding your return,
we all fell."

"Yes," said the Master. "I remember my brother. And I have not
been able to smooth the way again as a Master should."

"You will be able to now," said Mirasol.

"I hope so," said the Master. "And I think the Circle will have
some new members, but perhaps not all."

The Grand Seneschal sighed. "Weatheraugur and I were friends
once, when we were young in our posts, under your father's Mastership. And Talisman . . . Talisman was a very beautiful young
woman, and your brother . . . made it difficult to be a woman, and
beautiful."

"I think my Circle has perhaps found it difficult to forget that
I am—was—not only a priest of Fire, but brother to their previous Master."

The Grand Seneschal murmured, "When we were younger—
when you and Chalice and Clearseer were still children, and your
father was Master—we used to say that his sons were born in the
wrong order."

"Fate does as fate wills," said the Master. "That is a common
saying to both demesne folk and Elemental priests."

"I think poor Clearseer has only not been allowed to learn his
job," said Mirasol. "There are advantages to being high in the
hierarchy; I have had to find my own way because no one dared
interfere—much."

"Yes," said the Grand Seneschal. "I'm afraid that was one of the occasions when I stubbed my foot on the rough ground and fell."

"Oh—gods," said Mirasol, half laughing; she had put her hand on the Seneschal's arm and then drew it back again. "I do not even know your name. I cannot always be calling you Grand Seneschal."

"Nicandimon," said the Grand Seneschal. "My parents—and the Grand Seneschal who apprenticed me—called me Nicci."

"Nicandimon," said Mirasol, "for I shall *not* call you Nicci without exact and specific permission, you held the demesne together for almost eight years—through the time of the previous Master till the time this Master came home to us. You of all of us have earned a few falls."

"And you will offer me honey for my bruises, will you not?"

"I will," she said, smiling.

Mirasol looked after the Overlord's procession, disappearing down the drive at a smart trot—too smart, as if they were fleeing. And she looked down at the black waves of dead bees—her poor, heroic bees, and silently promised them that no one would take any honey from any hive anywhere on the demesne this season, that those that remained might rest and recover. And, she thought suddenly, I will teach all the beekeepers in Willowlands to bring their bees through the winter alive. There shall be no more killing of bees in this demesne, ever again.

As she thought that, there was a faint buzzing behind her left ear, and she raised her free hand to part the tangle of her hair for the bee to escape. Before it flew away it did a little dance in front of her, as if drawing a symbol in the air, a symbol she should recognise. She thought, Left to right (do you read a bee-message from your perspective or hers?), bottom to top, and a spiral squiggle off to the side. She would go home and write it down.

"Look," said the Grand Seneschal.

The little group of eight Circle members was breaking up. Five of them had, or were in the process of, removing their badges and signs of office, and laying them at the foot of the stairs. Each of the five looked toward the smaller group of the three highest-ranking of their company, still standing among the drifts of bees, and each bowed, gravely and solemnly, before squaring their shoulders and walking away. The remaining three were removing their insignia more slowly, but they did not lay them down, but carried them in their hands, and looked toward the Master. These three were Talisman, Weatheraugur and Clearseer.

Mirasol found that she was still holding the Master's hand when he squeezed hers. She looked up. Thoughtfully she said, "I think I had better marry you anyway. It is against all tradition, but *we* are against tradition. And we will need to protect each other."

"Well done," said Nicandimon. "You are coming out of your woodright."

"I must," she said. "We will have most of a new Circle to train."

The Master still had a sticky gleam of honey on his chin. He rubbed at it with his free hand, and licked his fingers. "What might a priest of Fire and a honey Chalice do together? We shall begin a new era."

Mirasol held out her pot of honey to the Grand Seneschal and said, "And with this cup I bind us three together with all the strength that the Chalice can find in me."

The Grand Seneschal smiled—and for the first time since Mirasol had known him, the smile reached his eyes. They were caramel-brown, almost the colour of dark honey. "If the Chalice would do me the honour." And he opened his mouth, that Mirasol might tip the honey in.

All around them their folk were blowing out their candle stubs, and there was a faint, pleasant aroma of charred wick and beeswax. As Mirasol lowered the honey pot again, the first of their people came up to them, to lay the candle ends at their feet among the bodies of the victorious bees; and three of those first were the butcher, the shepherd and the gardener.

Turn the page for a sneak peek at
Robin McKinley's newest novel

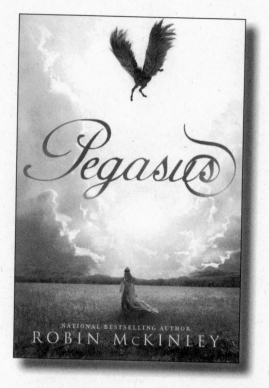

CHAPTER 1

BECAUSE SHE WAS A PRINCESS SHE HAD A PEGASUS.

This had been a part of the treaty between the pegasi and the human invaders nearly a thousand years ago, shortly after humans had first struggled through the mountain passes beyond the wild lands and discovered a beautiful green country they knew immediately they wanted to live in.

The beautiful green country was at that time badly overrun by ladons and wyverns, taralians and norindours, which ate almost everything (including each other) but liked pegasi best. The pegasi were a peaceful people and no match, despite their greater intelligence, for the single-minded ferocity of their enemies, and over the years their numbers had declined. But they were tied to these mountains and valleys by particular qualities in the soil and the grasses that grew in the soil, which allowed their wings to grow strong enough to bear them in the air. They had ignored the situation as without remedy for some generations, but the current pegasus king knew he was looking at a very bleak future for his people when the first human soldiers straggled, gasping, through the Dravalu Pass and collapsed on the greensward under the Singing Yew, which was old even then.

They sat up quickly when seven pegasi circled the meadow above the pass and flew down to investigate. The journal of that company's second commander still exists in the palace library: a small, worn, round-cornered, hand-bound book, slightly bowed to the shape of the pocket it was carried in. He reported the historic meeting:

We had but just come through thee final rocky gate, and had sett ourselves down in thee shade of a strange great tree, which had short soft spikes or needles all along its branches, and no leaves; when swift-moving shadows fled briefly between us and thee sunne, but against thee wind. We looked up in haste, for rocs are not unheard of, and I had raised my hand to give thee signal for thee archers to string their bows. We saw at once that these were no rocs, but still I held up my hand, for they were nothing else we knew either; and they clearly had seen us, and did approach.

But these creatures are nothing like rocs except they do also possess wings; they are like nothing I have ever seen, except perhaps by some great artist's creative power. They are a little like horses, but yet far more fine than any horse, even a queen's palfrey; they are a little like deer, except that deer are rough and clumsy beside them; and their wings are huge, huger than eagles', and when thee lowering sunne struck through their primaries, for as they cantered toward us they left their wings unfurled, thee light was broken as if by prisms, and they were haloed in all thee colours of thee rainbow. Several of my folk came to their knees, as if we were in thee presence of *gods*; and while I told them to stand and be steadfast, I did tell them gently, for I understood their awe.

The pegasi were happy to make a treaty with the humans, who were the first possibility of rescue the pegasi had had, and the humans, dazzled by the pegasi's beauty and serenity, were happy to make a treaty with them, for the right to share their mountainous land; the wide plateaus, which ran like lakes around the mountaintop islands, were lush and fertile, and many of the island crests were full of gems and ores.

The discussions as to the terms of the treaty had had to be held almost exclusively through the human magicians and the pegasi shamans, however, who were the only ones able to learn enough of the other's language to understand and make themselves understood, and that was a check to enthusiasm on both sides. "Is it not, then, a language, as we understand language?" wrote the second commander, whose name was Viktur. "Does it encompass some invisible touch unavailable to humans, as a meeting of *our* hands in greeting, or a kiss between dear friends? What can we not grasp of it, and why cannot our magicians explain this lack to us?"

Sylvi's tutor, Ahathin, had brought Sylvi to the library while they were studying this portion of the annals. Ordinary people needed a sheaf of special permissions to look at anything half so old, frail and precious as the second commander's journal; Ahathin, as the princess' tutor, had merely made the request, and when the two of them appeared at the library door, the head librarian himself bowed, saying, "Princess, Worthy Magician," and led them to the table where the journal already lay waiting for them—with an honour guard of the Queen's Own Lightbearers standing on either side of the table. The queen was the library's governor. Sylvi looked at them thoughtfully. They were wearing their swords, but they were also wearing hai, to indicate that they could not hear anything she and Ahathin said to each other. There were two kinds of hai: the ceremonial and the invested. The ceremonial ones just hung over your ears and looked silly; invested hai had been dedicated by a magician and really stopped the wearer's hearing. You couldn't tell by looking at them which kind they were. Sylvi had often wondered how hai-wearing guards were going to protect anything if they couldn't hear anyone coming. Was there a protocol for when an honour guard wearing ceremonial hai could stop pretending they couldn't hear?

Sylvi tried to concentrate on what she was reading. She liked reading better since Ahathin had become her tutor; she would still rather be outdoors with her hawk and her pony, but it was thrilling, in a creepy, echo-of-centuries way, to be looking at Viktur's own journal. She was allowed to touch it only while wearing the gloves the librarian had given her, and there were furthermore these odd little wooden paddles for turning the pages. But she had—carefully, carefully— turned all the pages over, back to the very beginning, to look at Viktur's signature on the flyleaf: *Viktur, Gara of Stormdown, Captain of the White Fellowship, who do follow Balsin, Gara of Mereland, All Commander of His Companies.* Most of the curly handwriting was still surprisingly black and sharp against the pale brown flyleaf. A tiny faded arrow, almost invisible, had been drawn just before *Balsin*, and the word *King* written in above, and the *Gara of Mereland* following had been struck out. "Gara?" said Sylvi.

"Lord," said Ahathin. "A gara is below a prince and above a baron. It is a rank no longer much in use."

"Then Viktur was pretty important," said Sylvi. "Balsin was only a gara to begin with."

"Viktur was important. Some commentators say that Balsin would not have made king if Viktur had not supported him—that perhaps Balsin would not have been able to put a strong enough company together to come this far through the wild lands, nor to drive our foes

4

out of it once they arrived. That perhaps our country would not have been created, were it not for Viktur."

"Stormdown and Mereland—they're *here*."

"The original Stormdown and Mereland are in Tinadin, which is Winwarren now, where Balsin and Viktur originally were from. They'd won a famous victory for their king—who now wanted to be rid of them before Balsin started having fancies about being king of Tinadin. Everyone is very clear that Balsin was very ambitious; and, of course, he had the Sword. It was apparently worth it to their king—whose name was Argen or possibly Argun—to lose half his army to be rid of Balsin. Argen married the daughter of the king Balsin defeated, so presumably he thought he could afford it."

Sylvi cautiously turned the pages back to Viktur's first sight of the pegasi, and then on to the second marker. There was something that looked like the remains of a grubby fingerprint on one corner of the page she was looking at, and what might be a bloodstain on the bottom edge of the little book.

. . . and why cannot our magicians explain this lack to us?

She stopped, startled, and reread the entire sentence, and then looked up at Ahathin. "That's not—I haven't seen that before, that last," and gingerly she touched the brittle old page. Even through the thin glove she could feel the roughness of the paper: modern paper was smooth—paper-making was one of the things the pegasi had taught their allies, and for special occasions or particularly important records, pegasus-made paper was still preferred.

Mostly she did her studying in the room off her bedroom in the main part of the palace, where she now spent several (long) hours every day with Ahathin. The copy of the First Annals she was reading was the copy several generations of royal children had read, and included several games of tic-tac-toe on the end papers, imperfectly erased, played by her next-elder and next-next elder brothers, who were only eleven months apart in age, and a poem her father had written about an owl when he had been a few years younger than she was now. (It began: The Owl flies at night. To give the mice a fright. It soars and swoops. The mice go oops.) Her eldest brother, and heir to the throne, had never written in his school-books.

She looked up at Ahathin, who stood beside her. There was only one chair at the table. She wanted to stand up herself, or drag another chair from another table so that Ahathin could sit down, but she knew she mustn't. The single chair and the presence of the honour guard with their hai meant that this was a formal occasion. Princesses sat down. Lesser mortals did not. This included tutors—even tutors who were also magicians, and members of the Guild of Magicians. She didn't like formal occasions. They made her feel even smaller and mousier than she usually felt.

She also didn't like it that the familiar, beat-up—almost friendly, if a school-book was ever friendly—copy of the annals that she knew had a missing phrase; she didn't like it that Ahathin was making such a fuss about her reading the missing phrase. She especially didn't like it when her own binding was so near—her binding to her pegasus.

Ahathin was small and round and almost bald and wore spectacles and a harmless expression, but he was still a magician. He looked no less small, round and harmless than he ever had right now as she stared at him, but for the first time she thought. Looking harmless is his disguise.

She had known Ahathin all her life. She could remember him sitting on the floor to play with her when she was tiny—she could remember looking dubiously at her first set of speaking tiles, with human letters and words on one side and the gestures you were supposed to use with the pegasi on the other, and Ahathin patiently explaining them to her. She'd learnt to sign "hello, friend" from Ahathin.

She'd known him all her life, and suddenly she didn't know him at all. She tried to swallow the lump in her throat, but it stayed where it was.

Ahathin nodded. "It's not in any of the copies of the annals I've looked in—there are quite a few."

"Why?"

At his most harmless, he said mildly, "I don't know."

She looked back at the journal. "Does my father know? Does Danacor?"

Ahathin nodded again. "Certainly the king knows. And the heir. I asked your father if I might show this to you."

"Why?"

Ahathin said nothing. This meant he wanted her to answer her own question. But sometimes, if she said something unexpected, she got an unexpected response. "Why *can't* magicians explain what it is about the pegasi language that the rest of us can't learn it?"

Ahathin nodded as if this were an acceptable question. "It is a curious skill, speaking to pegasi, and not even all magicians can do it—do you know this?"

Fascinated, Sylvi shook her head.

"We are well into our apprenticeship before it is taught at all, and many of us will already have been sent home to be carpenters or shepherds, for we will not make magicians. And indeed there is little enough of teaching about it, to begin with. Imagine learning to swim by being thrown into a lake in perfect darkness, never having seen water before. Those who do not drown are then taught; the best of them may then go on to become Speakers. But that is the moment when as many as half of us are sent away, although by that time an apprentice has learnt enough that if he—or she—wishes he can set up as a village spell-caster somewhere."

Imagine learning to swim by being thrown into a lake in perfect darkness, never having seen water before. "But the pegasi—they—they are so *light.* They—they *fly.* Drowning in a dark sea—I—it doesn't sound like anything to do with pegasi."

"No, it doesn't," said Ahathin. "It does not at all."

Sylvi knew the rest of the official story of the making of the treaty. She was obliged to be able to parrot a brief accurate version of it as part of her training as daughter of the king. She was obliged to be able to parrot a number of historical titbits on command (although *why* this was considered a necessary attribute in a princess she had no idea, her father sprang questions at her occasionally so that she did need to was not in doubt) but this was one of the few of her history lessons that were live pictures in her head instead of dry words in her memory.

The first beginnings of the treaty had been almost insurmountably difficult; not only was there the obstacle of their spoken languages, of which neither side could learn the other's, but the pegasi did not have an alphabet as humans understood it. Instead they had a complex and demanding art form of which various kinds of marks on paper were only a part. . . . The human magicians translated its name into human sounds as *ssshasssha* and said it meant "recollection," and that it appeared to include or address all the senses—sight, hearing, touch, taste, feeling—although how this was accomplished the magicians were uncertain. There were pegasus bards and story-tellers in some manner, presumably, as there were human bards and story-tellers; there were also pegasi . . . they didn't know. This was the first time the humans heard about the Caves, and the sculptors; but none of this assisted the drawing up of a document that humans understood as legal and binding.

"Did we not both want this union very badly," wrote the second commander, "such impedimenta as there manifestly are would have stopped us utterly and our company would be homeless again; and I am grateful hourly that thee pegasi want us, for already I love this sweet green land, and would not willingly leave it."

This sweet green land was probably the most famous phrase of the second commander's journal; it was one of those phrases everyone used, like *sick as a denwirl owl* or *mad as a mudge*. One of the first songs Sylvi had ever learnt to sing herself, when she was still so small she couldn't say her *rrr*'s yet, was an old folk ballad about a wandering tinker whose refrain was: *On the road to nowhere through this sweet green land*. The second commander seemed almost to be standing at her elbow as she read the old phrase as he had put it down the first time.

Both sides at last declared themselves satisfied with the final draft of the treaty. "The pegasi ask for little," wrote the second commander.

They wish their lives—and their Caves, which appear to bee thee chief manifestation of their *recollection*. But thee Caves lie many days' journey farther into thee mountains that steeply rise from these lush and fruitful plateaus we humans desire; Gandam says he is middling sure human feet could not take us there besides, and we have not wings. Balsin laughs and says, Good: that he wants all human forces to bend themselves to thee palace he already has in his mind's eye to build upon thee greatest of these plateaus. It is his own consort, Badilla, who has begun to measure thee landscape for this building; she was trained for such work in thee old countrie, although Balsin says he married her for her beauty. My own Sinsi says she wishes only to finish thee job of securing our new land from its enemies; that what she most wants is to see her belly growing too large for its battle leathers, and a safe place where our babies may play.

The first song Sylvi could ever remember hearing was about the pegasi. Her nurse used to sing it to her when she was a baby, and would then "fly" her around the room. The tradition was that Viktur's wife, Sinsi, had written it for their children, although no one knew for sure.

Oh hush your crying
Your friends come flying
In the plumes of their wings
The south wind sings

The treaty was written by human scribes and depicted or portrayed by some makers and devisers among the pegasi upon thick supple paper made by the pegasi:

"Balsin would have it bee parchment, but thee pegasi demurred, that they did not use thee skins of beasts for such or any purpose, and proffered their finest made paper instead, which is very beautiful, with a gloss to it not unlike thee flank of a pegasus, and faint glints of colour from thee petals of flowers. Dorogin did not like this however, and said there was magic pressed into its fibres, but Gandam held his hands over it and said thee only magic was that of craftsmanship, and as Gandam was thee senior, Dorogin must needs give way; and Balsin looked at Gandam and nodded, and Dorogin looked as if he had swallowed a toad.

Sylvi gave a little hiccup of laughter; the toad wasn't in the school-room copy of the annals either. But reading of Gandam in the beginning always made her sad, because of what happened to him after. She'd never liked Dorogin; he was one of those people who always wanted everything his way.

The signing of the treaty was interrupted by an incursion of their enemies, taralians tearing at them from the ground, ladons, wyverns and norindours soaring overhead to dive and slash from above: "It is a new sort of fighting we must learn," wrote the second commander, "for we have but rarely known aerial enemies ere now." But learn it they did; and drove off the attackers with arrows and spears, and any of the winged company who fell to the ground were dispatched with sword and brand.

"Balsin is the worthiest commander of this and perhaps any age, so I do believe," wrote Viktur. "And it is my honour to serve him. But it has seemed to me in this battle that he is something almost more than human, and that none and nothing can stand against thee Sword he carries, which he won from its dark guardian many years ago, when he was but a young man, as if for this day."

Balsin called for the treaty to be signed during a lull in the battle: "It will hearten us," he said, which was another of those phrases the citizens of the country he founded were still saying almost a thousand years later. There was a seal that had been struck by Balsin's great-grandson which the sovereign still used, which said *It will hearten us* around the edge, coiled around a heart with a sword through it, which Sylvi thought looked more *dis*heartening, but it was used for things like trade agreements and mutual defence accords, so presumably it looked friendly to delegates and ambassadors.

And so a table was set up, and Balsin and Viktur and two more of the most senior company commanders, and Gandam and Dorogin and another magician named Kond stood on one side, and the pegasus king, Fralialal, and several pegasi with him, stood on the other side, and the gleaming paper with the treaty written upon it lay between them.